PENGUIN BOOKS

THE TWO DEATHS OF SEÑORA PUCCINI

Stephen Dobyns is an acclaimed poet and author. He is a professor of English at Syracuse University, New York, and also teaches in the MFA programme at Warren Wilson College in North Carolina. His other novels include *Dancer with One Leg*, *Cold Dog Soup*, *The House of Alexandrine*, *Body Traffic* and the 'Saratoga' books: *Saratoga Swimmer*, *Saratoga Headhunter*, *Saratoga Snapper*, *Saratoga Longshot*, *Saratoga Bestiary* and *Saratoga Hexameter*. He lives in Syracuse with his Chilean wife.

STEPHEN DOBYNS

The Two Deaths of Señora Puccini

PENGUIN BOOKS

PENGUIN BOOKS

Published by the Penguin Group
Penguin Books Ltd, 27 Wrights Lane, London W8 5TZ, England
Penguin Books USA Inc., 375 Hudson Street, New York, New York 10014, USA
Penguin Books Australia Ltd, Ringwood, Victoria, Australia
Penguin Books Canada Ltd, 10 Alcorn Avenue, Toronto, Ontario, Canada M4V 3B2
Penguin Books (NZ) Ltd, 182–190 Wairau Road, Auckland 10, New Zealand

Penguin Books Ltd, Registered Offices: Harmondsworth, Middlesex, England

First published in the USA by Viking Penguin Inc. 1988
Published simultaneously in Canada
Published in Penguin Books 1989
1 3 5 7 9 10 8 6 4 2

Film and TV tie-in published 1989

Printed in England by Clays Ltd, St Ives plc
Set in Bodoni Book

For Isabel Bize

CHEAP VASE

Pursued by threat of war and violence in the streets,
we came to a friend's house for dinner.
In the middle of the table was a dead body,
a naked man, not too young, not too old.
We did not know him. We ate and
passed the wine, trying not to look at the man,
trying to pretend he was not really there,
lying flat on his back on the white cloth.
We will make him disappear, we said,
that is not a man, those are flowers
in the middle of the table, yes, a large vase
of white flowers and on the vase itself
are pictures of people dancing and drinking wine.
You know, said one of the guests, when
old age wipes out our generation
that vase will remain behind surrounded
by other troubles than our own. You fool,
said another, what makes you think
any one of us will reach old age? And again
the dead man took his place among us.

The Two Deaths of
Señora Puccini

Chapter One

Pursued by threat of war and violence in the streets, we came to a friend's house for dinner. Nine of us were expected; I was first to arrive. Even though I live only a mile away, my cab was stopped twice by the police. On both occasions, as officers inspected my papers, young smooth-cheeked soldiers kept their weapons trained on the driver. They looked like country boys, suspicious of tall buildings and city-dwellers alike. In the distance, we heard the staccato clatter of automatic weapons punctuated by small arms fire. I asked what was happening but my questions were ignored. The late afternoon light was hazy with smoke and several times we had passed the burning remnants of automobiles. After seeing that my papers were in order, the officers waved us on without comment. Being a journalist helped, and certainly my name is not unknown in the city.

The dinner at Dr. Pacheco's had been on my calendar for six months. In a way, it had been on my calendar for nine years, ever since the doctor moved back from the south and joined our group. After waiting nine years for this evening, was I to be stopped by military shenanigans? We are a number of men who were once in school together, and every six months one of us gives a dinner for the rest. For all I knew, the dinner was canceled since the phones at the newspaper had stopped working around four. Nor did the radio tell me much. At times of trouble the stations invariably play classical music. A general strike was scheduled for the day after tomorrow and word came up from the city room that several labor leaders had been arrested, but whether that was connected to the shooting and roadblocks, I could only guess.

The cab let me off in front of Dr. Pacheco's house, which was the largest on an old cobblestone street—a few tall trees, plane trees mostly, but also some palms. The adjoining white-washed fronts were pushed right up to the sidewalk. Many of the houses had small second-floor balconies, windows covered with black iron grates, and flower boxes with bright red and yellow flowers. It was the middle of the summer and the city was broiling. Even though I had gone home to shower and change my clothes, I could feel my shirt clinging damply to my back. I climbed the steps. The air smelt of burning tires. No one else was in sight and on many houses the shutters were closed.

The door was painted black and on the highly polished brass name plate I read the words: DR. DANIEL PACHECO. Beneath the name was a large brass knocker in the shape of a hand holding an apple. As I reached out to lift it, some object at my feet caught my attention. It appeared to be an untidy heap of gray feathers. I knelt down. It was a dead dove—no, a pigeon—which had presumably flown into the wall. A spot of blood stained the edge of its beak. I was struck by how calmly it returned my gaze. Standing up again, I touched the pigeon with the tip of my shoe. Then I nudged it off the step and it fell to the sidewalk with a soft plop. From somewhere down the block someone was practicing the scales on a badly tuned piano. Turning back to the door, I lifted the brass knocker and let it fall. I lifted it again. It was just six-thirty.

My name is Nicolas Batterby, age forty-nine, a widower with no children. I am the associate book review editor of the city's largest paper. I like to think of myself as an observer of life. Why else would I court danger by going to Dr. Pacheco's for dinner? Surely I had every reason to cancel. But I had known Pacheco for forty years. At the same time, I didn't know him at all, nor had I ever set foot inside his house, even though he was famous for his little dinners. Indeed, the food editor at the paper claimed he had the best cook and the finest wine cellar in the city. In addition to being a distinguished surgeon, Pacheco was said to have made love to a thousand women. Perhaps he raped them. Possibly they begged him for it.

The door was opened by a woman in a black dress who I assumed was a servant. What was my first impression? I'm not sure I had one. The gunshots seemed closer and my main wish was to get off the street. I was aware of a woman about forty-five, tall, thin with large breasts, thick black hair streaked with gray. Her face looked worn; not just middle-aged but worn, as if it had been used too much, too much emotion, too much crying. Am I telling the truth? I think I am a truthful man. From moment to moment I believe myself sincere, but sometimes looking back I can see I've been mistaken, even that I've lied. On this occasion I'm sure I did no more than glance at her. My mind registered a tall, dark, middle-aged shape. Certainly, had I thought her beautiful I would have looked more closely.

It was the hall that took my attention, not the woman. Once the heavy front door was closed, the only sound came from the splashing of water in the fountain in front of the great marble staircase. It was, in fact, two staircases—both covered with red runners—since one could ascend either side. They came together at the top at a small balcony with a marble balustrade. The double staircase was like a pair of symmetrical brackets and what it bracketed was the balcony and fountain.

Everything was marble: the walls, the floors—white marble with black veins. In the middle of the fountain was a life-sized marble statue of a girl balancing on one foot and holding a small pitcher out of which trickled a stream of water. She was naked, with small, emergent breasts. The water splashed into a pool with green lily pads and goldfish. It was very soothing and, after the heat of the city, almost cold.

The hall was a large, high-ceilinged room. Beneath each stairway was a door leading to the rear of the house, while several more doors stood to my left and right. Set into the walls were four small niches with classical busts: bald men in togas with damaged noses. I approached one and had the impression the statue was weeping. There appeared to be a splash of tears under one eye. Looking closer, I saw that what I thought were tears was in fact a little gray lizard, one of those tiny creatures that seek out cool places during the summer and fall. It was completely motionless, a small gray curve under the left eye. Staring at the lizard, I felt it bore no similarity to tears or weeping, and briefly I was embarrassed that my imagination had run away with me.

Perhaps as striking as the hall was a great tapestry that hung on the wall on my right. Although faded to browns and yellows, it clearly showed several centaurs pursuing a group of rather heavy-set women through the trees. The women were laughing and holding up their arms. There was a sense of carnal hysteria, too much to drink, and the sort of party that one regrets in the morning. Presumably it was valuable but even so, it seemed a strange thing to find in a surgeon's entrance hall, and I imagined Pacheco bringing home young women and showing it to them before leading them into the den for drinks. Around

4

the walls were arrangements of red flowers in silver contraptions that looked like champagne buckets with legs. The air was thick with their scent, a heavy smell reminding me of funerals more than dinner parties.

During this time the housekeeper continued to stand a few feet behind me. When I thought about it, I realized she was used to letting people in, then giving them a moment to be impressed. I glanced back and she walked toward one of the doors on the left, beckoning me to follow. She had not asked my name and I could only assume she knew who I was.

The room which we entered was a library. Books lined the dark shelves from floor to ceiling, while along one wall was a great stone fireplace. It was the sort of room I would have liked for myself: dark red leather chairs and sofa, a Persian carpet, three Piranesi prints of Roman ruins over the mantel. As in many of the city's oldest houses, the room had a ceiling of white wooden slats, a concession to the earthquakes, which crumble anything made of plaster. Two leaded windows looked out on the street, but the street, from a room as peaceful as this, seemed very distant. I walked to the nearest. There was a window seat with a red cushion. It was hard to imagine that nearby men were shooting at each other. Listening carefully, I tried to make out the pop-pop of gunfire, but all I could hear was the soft whir of the overhead fan.

The housekeeper walked to a black lacquer cabinet with oriental pictures of fat naked gods on small pink clouds. She opened it to expose a row of bottles. "The doctor would like you to make yourself a drink," she said. "He will be here shortly." Her voice was low for a woman and entirely without warmth. Then she left the room, shutting the door quietly behind her.

I don't know if others do this, but when I look into a man's liquor cabinet a small cash register gets busy inside my brain.

Is the Scotch Johnnie Walker Red or the more expensive Johnnie Walker Black? Is the brandy Regal or Remi, V.S. or
V.S.O.P.? Here the Scotch, brandy, sherry, various whiskeys
were the best available—I would have been disappointed
otherwise. Unfortunately, I am diabetic, and having eaten little
during the day, I was concerned about my blood sugar. Usually
I have to carry with me small containers of peanut butter. That
is how it is as one gets older; the little pleasures are replaced
by the little pains: bad back, sore feet, dry skin. What is it
Diogenes said? "One must learn the pleasure of despising
pleasure."

I poured out a tumbler of mineral water, promising myself
a glass of wine with our meal. Then I began to investigate the
books. I used to think you could know a man just by looking
at his library. Now I no longer believe that, primarily because
I myself have a few books which I keep in a back room away
from the eyes of prying guests. Not sex books or anything
questionable. Rather they are diet books, exercise books, a
couple of excessively romantic novels, a few volumes of sentimental poetry—the sort of books one doesn't care to defend
oneself about.

So the question was whether the library represented Dr.
Pacheco as he wanted to appear or as he was. But as I glanced
over the shelves, I found myself experiencing the complicated
envy I had experienced as an adolescent. In Pacheco's library
were the classics of literature as well as contemporary novels,
ancient and modern history, all sorts of biography, scientific
books, even poetry, even philosophy. I wandered around the
room with my drink, stopping every so often to pull out one
book or another. All appeared to have been read. They showed
Pacheco to be intelligent, well-rounded, an obvious humani-
tarian, perhaps even a liberal, perhaps even a little mysterious.
After all, wasn't it out of the ordinary for a surgeon to read
the letters of Madame de Staël, Baudelaire's *Petits poèmes en*

6

prose, essays by Simone Weil, and the latest novel by Vargas Llosa?

In our class of thirty boys, Daniel Pacheco had been the smartest. Some teachers said he was the smartest to come through the school in recent memory. He was also handsome, witty, popular, a superb athlete. If Pacheco had allowed it, we would have followed him anywhere. But he didn't allow it. Quite early, he had reminded me of Kipling's cat that walked by himself. Sometimes he went with us and sometimes he didn't, but always it was by his own choice. Even at that age he was mysterious. At fourteen he had the reputation for wandering the city at all hours of the day and night. No one knew what he did but sometimes one of our fathers would spot him in a café near the docks or some house of questionable repute, and so the rumors would grow.

Much later I decided that Pacheco enjoyed being seen as mysterious and that he occasionally engaged in small deceptions which made us think him larger than life. He actually wanted us not to know him. But even when I believed this, I was still enchanted by the mystery. Nor could I determine how much was illusion and how much fact. Despite the love and admiration I felt for Pacheco, my envy, which I thought to be slight, kept me from being able to determine the truth of my friend's life.

His mother had died in childbirth and as a boy Pacheco lived alone with his father and his father's mistress: a detail that put his house out of bounds for those of us with solid middle-class parents. Still, on several occasions, I visited his attic room with its dormers and sloping ceilings. As an adolescent, Pacheco was dark and elvish, no more than five feet tall. It was only in the last year of high school that he gained his full height of six feet. He would balance precariously atop the back of a chair with his shoes on the cushion, watching me with a half smile as I prowled around the room, picking

7

up one object after another—a seashell, an ivory-handled pocketknife, a single white carnation turning brown at the edges. Leaning against the night table was a wonderful black ebony sword cane which Pacheco swore he carried when he went out at night. One afternoon, he led me to the window, then drew the sword and pointed to a spot on the blade where some reddish substance had darkened and grown hard. "I suppose I don't have to tell you what that is," Pacheco said. I felt a thrill of excitement and tried to look wise. Later, I thought the stain might easily have been tomato sauce.

Because of Pacheco's sense of privacy, I was surprised when he agreed to join our group. By then we had been meeting for eleven years and must have seemed quite established. The idea of the dinners had come up when we were all in our late twenties and drifting apart. There were twenty-two of us, not including Pacheco, and the plan was that each would be responsible for·hosting a dinner either at his home or at a restaurant. Some of us had been close friends but even when we started I thought it was mostly in our imagination that we had ever formed a group. More likely we were afraid of letting our youth slip away without protest or remark.

Not that these evenings have made us more intimate. Even after twenty years of dinners, I hardly see my ex-classmates except on these biannual occasions. Sometimes I run into one of the group on the street or have a quick drink with someone after work. Perhaps there are close friendships among the others. In the beginning we met to celebrate our past, but as we stand on the brink of fifty, it seems these dinners are mostly reminders of how we have aged, what our successes have been and, more often, our failures. Already there have been deaths among us and sometimes I see us continuing into old age, increasingly weighed down by our sense of failed promise, decay, and inevitable demise.

Dr. Pacheco came back to the city having been gone for seventeen years. Several of us had attended his graduation from medical school, but then Pacheco had done his residency in a city far to the south. Afterward he elected to stay there. Two or three times he had made trips north and, more frequently, one of the group would have occasion to travel to the south and would return with stories about Pacheco's success as a surgeon and his affairs with women. In one story a jealous husband had attacked him with a shovel. In another he had made love to the mayor's wife in the men's room of the City Hall. Obviously it was impossible to tell what was true and what was the gossip of a provincial town. About his success as a surgeon, however, there seemed no doubt, since when he returned to the capital it was to take up a position at the best hospital.

When Pacheco joined our group, there was some discussion as to where he should go on the list. I had argued that Pacheco should give the next dinner—after all, each of us had already had a turn—but the majority decided that Pacheco should be added to the end, which put his turn some years in the future. But, of course, time has passed and what with deaths and various departures, Pacheco's dinner has arrived earlier than anticipated. Now we are sixteen, but some are in Europe and others are scattered around the country. Even though tonight nine are expected, because of the troubles it seems doubtful that all will attend. This is a pity. Considering Pacheco's wealth and success, the reputation of his cook and wine cellar, this should have been a dinner for all of us—all us boys grown old.

I had taken down a volume of Rilke's poetry and was sitting in the red leather armchair in front of the fireplace. Despite the hot weather, several eucalyptus logs and kindling were piled on the andirons.

> *Alle Blicke, die sie jemals trafen,*
> *scheint sie also an sich zu verhehlen,*
> *um daruber drohend und verdrossen*
> *zuzuschauern und damit zu schlafen.*

The poem was "*Schwarze Katze*" or "The Black Cat," and the lines seemed to be about all glances being hidden in the cat's eyes. Unfortunately, I have forgotten most of the German I once worked so hard to learn in the university, but the gist suggested concealment, a person whose face revealed nothing. The poem had attracted my attention because of the words "like her!" written in the margin with blue pencil. Just then the door opened and the housekeeper reappeared, followed by Carl Dalakis. I got to my feet as Dalakis hurried over to embrace me.

"So you made it," cried Dalakis, clapping me on the back and engulfing me in a hug that smelled of garlic and sweat. "What a day! My taxi was actually fired upon. Believe me, this dinner is the only thing that could have made me leave the house. What we won't do for our friends!"

The housekeeper had left the room so I made my way to the liquor cabinet to fix Dalakis a drink. "There's a story at the paper," I said, "that the air force wants to take control." Pouring several ounces of Johnnie Walker Black into a glass, I added ice and handed it to my companion.

"The army would never allow it. In any case, there's no reason, the government's sound." Dalakis spoke almost aggressively, defying me to disagree.

"Well, I expect we'll know more in the morning," I said, not wanting to argue. To tell the truth, I am not a political person and really I had very little sense of what was happening. Resuming my seat, I looked to see how Dalakis had fared during the last six months. He was a great bearlike man with long brown hair that was perpetually mussed and thick glasses which gave him an inquiring look, as if he were always on the point of asking a question. He wore a wrinkled brown suit and I could see food spots on the lapels.

Dalakis has spent nearly thirty years working with the Park Service within the Ministry of the Interior. Now he's in charge of the picnic areas at all the National Parks. It is he who replaces old swings and slides with new ones, who is in charge of picnic tables and grills and trash containers, who determines how the toilets are functioning and how much sand is needed for the sandboxes. Because he works for the government, he often imagines himself to be its spokesman, and although he was strongly against the military when it took power ten years ago, these days he tends to defend their actions.

Dalakis stood a few feet in front of me sipping his drink and slowly shifting his weight from one foot to the other. He has great hairy hands with long blunt fingers and his glass was nearly hidden within his grip.

"I must say the soldiers made me nervous. We even passed a corpse, a young fellow. I suppose you're used to seeing corpses, what with working for the newspaper."

"We don't see many at the book review."

"But years ago, when you were a regular reporter?"

"Yes, of course, but that was different." I wished Dalakis would sit down. I've never liked people standing directly over me. "So what do you think of the doctor's house?"

Dalakis looked around as if noticing it for the first time. His movements are slow, as is his speech. When we were adolescents someone was always shouting, "Hurry up, Carl!"

"It seems large for one person," said Dalakis.

"Perhaps he entertains a lot."

"But how wonderful to have all these flowers. Do you think he grows them himself?"

In the library too were vases of red flowers. I had hardly noticed them even though their smell filled the room.

"I have no idea," I answered.

"Do you think he reads all these books?"

"Probably. He was always a great reader."

"I don't see where he finds the time." Dalakis glanced at the books as if he found their presence burdensome.

We were silent a moment. Sometimes it seems that we talk not to communicate but just so the other person won't think any worse of us, so we at least stay the same in his eyes, that what we are really doing is waiting for his attention to be lifted from us.

"So how have you been since I last saw you?" I asked. "Did your daughter get married?"

"I'm afraid so. It's been a great trial. Not the marriage, of course, but their move. Now she lives five hundred miles away and I haven't known what to do with myself. I guess that partly explains my being here tonight. I would have crossed the entire city, I'm that bored."

Dalakis's wife deserted him about seventeen years ago and he has had sole responsibility for the raising of their daughter, who lived with him into her late twenties.

"Haven't you been to visit her?" I asked.

"Yes, twice. She's pregnant, as a matter of fact. But I can't just sit around their apartment and watch television. They think I should retire early and move up there, but I don't know. I would feel a burden to them."

"You should get married again. Find a young wife to entertain you."

Dalakis laughed and sat down on the sofa. The leather made

12

a squeaking noise. "I haven't noticed you getting married, and you've been a widower for twenty years."

"Yes, but there are women I see."

"To tell the truth, I still miss my wife."

"Good grief, Carl, you're supposed to get over that."

"Believe me, I've had all sorts of advice, but it doesn't seem to work."

"Do you know anything about her?" I asked.

"Not much. She's living in another city. I went there years ago. I knew she was living with a man and I was going to confront him. I don't know what I intended to say, just 'Hey you' or something like that. I saw her on the street wheeling a baby carriage."

"Was it her child?"

Dalakis sat with his arms crossed and his hands tucked under the lapels of his brown suitcoat as he stared at the fireplace. "I assume so. That hardly mattered. What struck me was how happy she looked. You remember she had that bright blond hair? Her whole face shone. She didn't see me and I did nothing to attract her attention. I watched for a while, then went away. I haven't seen her since, although I believe my daughter has written her. Perhaps they'll get to be friends."

Dalakis has always been a sentimental fellow and I was afraid he might shed a tear or two. It is hard to reconcile his strong feelings with his unprepossessing appearance. His ears, for instance, resemble large pieces of grapefruit rind fastened to the side of his head. Only the handsome or beautiful can afford feelings which are inherently foolish. But he is a good man, a good man, and I was sorry for his loneliness. Getting to my feet, I walked to the window. From somewhere came the high whine of a siren. I wondered about the others. They were supposed to arrive at six-thirty and it was nearly seven. In my imagination I saw Dalakis watching his wife wheeling a baby

13

carriage. She'd been a pretty girl; perhaps that was part of the problem. I pictured Dalakis ducking down behind a parking meter and looking silly. It's terrible how people we care about can cause us to lose our autonomy.

"And how has your life been?" asked Dalakis. "Are you still working at the orphanage?"

"Well, not working, exactly. I go there on Sundays." For years I have visited an orphanage each Sunday where I try to make myself useful. Originally, I was supposed to play games with the children, but I'm not very good at games so now I read to them, or at least to those few who have any interest in hearing a middle-aged man read Grimm's fairy tales or from an expurgated version of Cervantes. I also bring them books from the book review, although only the suitable ones, of course. But I don't mean to speak disparagingly. I quite look forward to these Sunday visits.

"And what about your novel," asked Dalakis, "have you started that?"

"I hope to start it sometime this fall," I said, walking back to the sofa.

"It's been a long time. Can't you get a leave of absence for a year?" Dalakis has a low bass voice that resonates sympathy no matter the subject.

"I doubt it. Unfortunately, the book has required more preparation than I anticipated." I couldn't help but feel the irony of these remarks as I stood surrounded by the greatest works of Western literature. The best reason I had for not beginning my novel was that I didn't know how to begin it; the worst was a fear of the blank page.

"And the novel's about a married couple? A divorce or something like that?"

"Actually, I had hoped it to be an analysis of betrayal and the psychological effects of betrayal." It seemed I had said

14

this before, yet there was Dalakis's interested face looking like a mound of bread dough rising out of a bowl. But then, because of his history, he had a special interest in betrayal.

The door opened again and the housekeeper entered followed by Luis Malgiolio, looking eager and energetic. It amused me to see how Luis focused on the objects of the room before noticing the occupants. Then he saw us and gave a mock salute.

"This is a great place, Nicky. I see why you wanted dinner here before. Nearly got killed on the way over but no matter. And Carl, how're you doing? I feel like a drink. D'you know the taxi driver got a bullet hole in the trunk of his cab?" Malgiolio continued to talk as he inspected several different bottles of brandy. "They have tanks stationed downtown. The roads were blocked but I could see them in the distance, just sitting there like great metal toads."

Malgiolio laughed, a squawking noise that rang without humor. He had half-filled a brandy snifter and began inspecting the room, lifting one object after another—silver cigar lighter, a ship in a bottle, a small bronze statue of a naked woman—as if he intended to buy something but didn't have much time. He was a short balding man, no more than five feet six, and overweight, so that when he moved quickly he appeared to roll rather than walk. He had a thick neck and wide face, and the combination has always reminded me of a thumb. It was a white, puffy face, as if he rarely went outside, and his nose looked haphazard, like a chunk of clay rolled into a ball and stuck into place. His blue eyes never seem to look straight ahead but always to the sides. Malgiolio was dressed in a well brushed blue suit that had seen better days. Despite his looks, he carried himself with great authority. I remember him as an adolescent, given to writing bad poetry and having crushes on inappropriate women.

Malgiolio was a fantastical figure for me. For more than

twenty years he had worked for a big hotel, at last becoming assistant manager. Then, five years ago, he won a huge state lottery, over $300,000, and quit his job. He and his wife bought a large house, new cars, clothes, and lavishly entertained members of the upper middle class with whom they hoped to become intimate. But after thirteen months the money was gone. Malgiolio tried to find work but was unable to. The hotel refused to rehire him and no place else was interested. For a while he supported his wife and two teenage daughters by selling everything they had bought during that one rich year: cars, clothes and jewelry, the furniture, the house. When that was gone, they had moved in with his mother. Now his wife supported the family with various odd jobs: selling dishes and housewares, making and selling candles, cleaning houses, taking care of neighborhood children.

Astonishingly, Malgiolio galloped through his $300,000 with nothing to show for it but a sort of conceit, as if he had sipped from the golden dish of life and still kept the taste in his mouth. Even though a pauper, he put himself forward as a man who knew the best wines, the best tailors, who had grown accustomed to driving Mercedes. Sad to say, Malgiolio's turn to give a dinner came after he had lost his money. It had been a sorry affair at a Chinese restaurant. At the close of the evening, I had to lend him fifty dollars, although "give" would be the better word since I didn't expect to see it again.

I tended to view Malgiolio with scorn tempered by amazement. It didn't surprise me that he'd squandered a fortune. I had known him for forty years as a man given to foolish gestures, who acted on impulse only to have the action turn out badly. What amazed me was Malgiolio's lack of regret, that he never complained or seemed guilty, but rather thought it something to be proud of. He behaved as if squandering the money was a telling social criticism, even a form of protest.

Malgiolio bore himself with absolute assurance, not as someone who had lost, but as someone who had triumphed. On the other hand, Carl Dalakis, who came from a wealthy family and held a good position in the civil service, looked, with his shambling manner and clothes stained with ashes and food, to be the economic disaster that Malgiolio in fact was.

Malgiolio was still prowling the room, picking up one object after another, sometimes inspecting them or looking underneath as if for the price tag. Dalakis followed his movements with mild disapproval. "You sound happy about the fighting," he said. "Doesn't it matter that people are being killed?"

Malgiolio stopped by the window. The lowering sun was behind him, putting his face in shadow. "It's stirring up the pot," he said. "If everything gets turned upside down, then there'll be more chances for me. Who knows, Carl, if we get a new government, maybe you'll be thrown out and I'll have your job ordering toilet seats for a thousand bathrooms."

"Six hundred and twenty-two," said Dalakis.

"That will make the job all the easier. Or maybe I'll get Batterby's job scribbling book reviews or be hired as a surgeon at the hospital." He waved one hand in the air as if he were writing or making an incision or even sewing up a patient.

"I don't find it a joking matter," said Dalakis, smiling despite himself.

"That's because you already have a comfortable position, but for me whatever happens is a source of optimism. No offense, Batterby, but I think I'll be a surgeon. Perhaps tomorrow this house will be mine. I can't tell you how much I'd like to take over Pacheco's life. Think of the women! How could one choose between them? But maybe I'll pick that one," said Malgiolio, pointing to a photograph on the mantel, "maybe that's the one I'll start with."

I walked over to the photograph which earlier I had hardly

noticed, a large photograph in a plain silver frame. It showed the head and shoulders of a young woman in a white blouse leaning up against the trunk of a tree. Her fingers were linked behind her head so that her elbows stretched out on either side in a way that reminded me of Pacheco's double staircase, that same bracket shape. She was about eighteen years old and very beautiful, with long black wavy hair and large, full lips, thick with a dark lipstick. Her eyes were somewhat feline and stared from the picture flirtatiously, even brazenly, yet also with innocence and fear. Dalakis had come over to look as well. I found the mixture of innocence and flirtatiousness extremely appealing. The tilt of her chin suggested confidence, as if she felt there was nothing she couldn't do or control, while her large breasts were almost aggressive in the way they pushed themselves forward. Beneath the fabric of her blouse, I could see the outline of her brassiere.

"What do you think," asked Malgiolio, peering around my shoulder at the photograph, "do I have a chance?"

Dalakis wrinkled his brow and looked disapproving. "Maybe she's Pacheco's niece, even his daughter."

"No," said Malgiolio, growing serious, "I think I know who she is and it's not a pretty story."

"Who is it?" I asked. I believed I could identify the girl, but I wanted to hear what Malgiolio would say.

"She's the daughter of Jorge Mendez. Do you know him? He taught in a suburban high school but also did a little writing for the paper, mostly on school affairs—what plays would be performed in the spring and who made the honor roll."

I looked again at the photograph, then sat down on the leather couch. The overhead fan was directly above me and I felt its breeze mussing my hair. "I met him years ago. Didn't he die recently? A car accident or something like that?" I vaguely remembered a tall wispy man whose ambition was to become a professor at the Catholic university.

Malgiolio leaned against the bookshelves, slowly swirling his brandy in a snifter. "His car went off a bridge into a river, but it's only out of kindness that people called it an accident."

"I can't believe she's Mendez's daughter," said Dalakis. "Why should Pacheco keep her picture on his mantel?" He had returned to the armchair. Even when sitting, he appeared to slouch, as if his spine were fixed in a permanent quarter-circle. He had hardly touched his drink.

"Because he loved her," said Malgiolio. "Even though he killed her, he was still in love with her."

For a moment we were too surprised to respond. I found myself thinking that the very room was listening, as if all those thousands of books with their leather and paper and cardboard covers were ears bent to discover our purpose.

"Really, Luis, how impossible you are!" cried Dalakis.

I tried to show no surprise, if only because Malgiolio had wanted to shock us. "What happened?" I asked.

Malgiolio walked back slowly toward the fireplace. What hair he had was arranged in thin black strands across his bald head and he had the habit of combing them with the fingernails of his thumb and middle finger, as if searching for lice. He did that now as he lifted the photograph and looked at it more closely. "She was still in high school, then in her last year she became sick. It turned out she had to have her spleen removed. Mendez called me. Pacheco had been recommended to him and he'd heard I knew him. What could I say but that Pacheco was known as a wonderful surgeon? The next thing I learned she'd had the operation. But Pacheco wasn't satisfied with removing her spleen. I suppose he was struck by her beauty, just as we were.

"Think of it, an innocent girl, still in high school. Pacheco saw her every day, ostensibly to follow up on her recovery. But actually he was drawing her to him, fascinating her with his presence—"

"How can you possibly know this?" interrupted Dalakis. Normally his wide face appears impassive, but when he asks a question he begins to blink rapidly.

"Pacheco has an office in the medical center next to the hospital. The receptionist and my wife are close friends. It was Pacheco's nurse who told this story to the receptionist. You can imagine how little time Pacheco has with his patients. It takes weeks to get to see him, then you have to wait hours in his office. The nurse said that Pacheco would see the Mendez girl almost every afternoon. One day there was an emergency and she had to interrupt them. She went in and found Pacheco with his pants off. You'd think he'd be ashamed, but he just laughed. Of course he's had her too, as well as the receptionist."

"How can you tell these stories?" cried Dalakis. He was standing now and acted as if Malgiolio's words caused him physical pain. "Don't you realize you're a guest in his house?"

"It's true," said Malgiolio calmly. "Do you want the name of the receptionist? She can tell you all sorts of dirt."

"What happened after that?" I asked. "Surely there's more." What amused me was the hushed tone Malgiolio had adopted for his tale, like the radio dramatizations of our youth.

Malgiolio put the photograph back on the mantel, then took out a cigarette, lit it, and tossed the match into the fireplace. It was a colored cigarette, dark blue, and looked expensive. "Well," he continued, "they kept meeting like that. She'd go to his office and he'd have his way with her. Maybe he even saw her outside the office, I don't know. The nurse, of course, saw her all the time and so did the receptionist. Soon they knew something was wrong. She was pale and tired looking. It was the nurse who first realized the girl was pregnant. Her breasts got larger; she began wearing baggy clothes. It was almost summer. Shortly she would graduate from school. The nurse said she could hear the girl crying when she went in to see Pacheco. And he too seemed upset; you at least have to give him credit for that. Anyway, the next thing they knew the girl was dead." Malgiolio paused to tap cigarette ash into the fireplace, then he glanced at Dalakis, who was staring furiously down at the carpet.

I knew that Malgiolio was expecting us to ask the obvious question, but I kept silent. The story struck me as preposterous. I wondered where Pacheco was. It was nearly 7:15. I disliked talking scandal about a man in his own house.

"Not only was she dead," said Malgiolio, continuing despite our silence, "but she died under strange circumstances. She was the last patient to see Pacheco and when the nurse went home the girl was still there. The next day the nurse heard she had been rushed to the emergency room late that night with internal hemorrhaging. Pacheco was with her. Officially, the cause of death was tied to her operation. Can you believe it? Five months after the removal of her spleen and she has a relapse. But perhaps the explanation was more complicated. In any case, the facts are that she began hemorrhaging and died. To the nurse it seemed perfectly clear that the doctor had performed an illegal abortion that had gone wrong."

"Why didn't she report him?" I asked.

"What, and never work again? No, she knew better than to open her mouth. The doctor too was extremely upset. After all, it was his child and, as I say, he probably loved her. The father, Jorge Mendez, never recovered. You should see her tomb, an elaborate mountain of granite topped by an angel. A few days after it was in place, Mendez had his accident."

"I still don't believe it," said Dalakis, "and even if the story's true, what makes you think the girl in the picture is Jorge Mendez's daughter? Did you ever see her?"

"Just once. She was with her father at the opera. But of

course she's also been described to me—those eyes, those high cheekbones, one wouldn't forget them easily. Yes, that's the girl all right: Cecilia Mendez."

Dalakis seemed torn between refuting Malgiolio and telling some story of his own which might betray a confidence. He took a sip of Scotch, then walked to the mantel and reached out for the picture. His hands were so big that I was afraid he might accidentally break the glass. As he looked at the picture, his anger disappeared and he began to look sad. He was easily eight inches taller than Malgiolio and standing together they appeared to be preparing a comic turn. It is odd the relationship you have with people you've known since childhood—not love, not hate. It's more like they are of your own skin. Looking at Malgiolio and Dalakis, while musing on their comic potential, was like looking at myself.

"You see," said Dalakis after some moments, "I recognize the girl and her name isn't Cecilia Mendez and Pacheco never made love to her. That's his daughter, his illegitimate daughter, and the reason I know is because she was a close friend of my own daughter. Her name is Sarah something, I can't remember her last name. She's in school in Paris now."

"And I suppose you knew her personally," said Malgiolio, his voice skirting the edge of mockery. Despite the mistakes in his life, he was not a man who felt much doubt.

"She came to my house a few times several years ago. Pacheco had just brought her up from the south and enrolled her in the university. My daughter, you know, is an art teacher in a high school. This woman, Sarah, was also an art student, and she and my daughter were in three or four classes together."

Malgiolio raised his eyebrows and glanced at me as if seeking my agreement that Dalakis was mistaken. To tell the truth, I felt a little skeptical. I had my own idea who the woman was. "You mean he put her through the university?" I asked. "Did she live in this house as well?"

Dalakis stood facing us with his back to the mantel. "No, she lived in the women's dormitory. Actually, only a few people knew she was Pacheco's daughter. It's quite an odd story. He didn't even know the girl existed until about seven years ago. Her mother was the wife of another doctor in the south, the doctor who took Pacheco into partnership after he finished his residency. He was an older man with a young wife. Well, you know Pacheco's reputation with women. They had a brief affair. But when the child was born she swore it was her husband's.

"Anyway, they broke off and their lives drifted apart. Pacheco started his own practice. The old doctor and his wife were later divorced. She taught school for a while, then opened a tea shop. The old doctor saw the girl regularly. Then, about eight years ago, he died. The woman expected he'd leave the girl something in his will. She was seventeen and it was probably around then that the picture was taken. Well, the old doctor didn't leave her a cent. Perhaps he knew the girl wasn't his. The mother had little money but she wanted the girl to go to the university. She was a very talented artist and it seemed a pity for her to spend her life in some small town.

"The upshot was that the woman contacted Pacheco and confessed that the girl was his daughter after all. Many men wouldn't have believed her, but Pacheco believed her and, what's more, he offered to support the girl and pay for her education while also promising not to divulge the secret of her parenthood."

Dalakis walked back to his chair and slowly lowered himself onto the leather cushion until his legs stretched straight out in front of him on the carpet. I noticed holes in the soles of his unpolished black shoes. Malgiolio stood by the bookshelves leafing through a book of photographs for no more reason, I'm sure, than to irritate Dalakis.

"The girl came up here. Of course she had no idea that Pacheco was her father. They saw quite a lot of each other.

He took her to dinner and the theater or they would meet and talk over a cup of coffee. She was a lively and attractive girl and Pacheco must have liked her. As you might imagine, the girl soon developed a crush on him. She saw him as a handsome man, a friend of her parents, who was going out of his way to help her get settled in a new city. She began to flirt with him, show him that she was available, but he ignored her. She began to doubt herself, to think, perhaps, she was even ugly. Truly, we only have to look at that photograph to see how foolish that was.

"Pacheco realized there were going to be problems. He began to see less of her, which made matters worse. She became desperate. Then one night, very late, she came to his house. Pacheco was already in bed. She waited for him to come down, waited in this very room. When Pacheco entered she was standing by the fireplace. She was wearing a black coat. He approached to kiss her cheek. When he had nearly reached her, she opened the coat. Underneath, she was naked. She didn't say anything; she was too frightened."

Dalakis lifted his hands and pressed them together in front of his mouth. Then he blew through them, making a rushing noise. Malgiolio had stopped leafing through the book and was waiting to hear what Dalakis would say next.

"Can you imagine that moment? Of course Pacheco looked at her. Who can blame him? Think of her immaculate, untouched body. But at last he turned away. 'Do you find me so ugly?' she called after him. He stood with his back to her. 'Ugly?' he asked. 'You are extremely beautiful. Unluckily, you are also my daughter.' Of course, she was astonished and at first she didn't believe him. Pacheco told her the entire story. Then she felt humiliated but Pacheco said there was nothing to feel guilty about, that only a simple mistake had been made.

"But, in fact, it wasn't so simple. Even though she knew

24

Pacheco was her father, her feelings were unchanged. She told my daughter about it. She said she still desired him, that she hungered for him. It was not long after that she went to study in Paris. She couldn't stay in the same city with Pacheco, couldn't stay in the same country.

"My daughter hears from her occasionally. She knows no men, won't go out. Here she is, one of the most beautiful women in the city of Paris, yet she refuses to give herself to another man because the man she loves, whom she passionately desires, happens to be her father. Amazing, isn't it? If you look at the picture closely, you can even see a resemblance—those almond-shaped eyes, for instance, and that wide chin. . . ."

There was an abrupt squawking noise as Malgiolio tilted back his head and laughed up at the ceiling. "That's the most ridiculous story I've ever heard. Really, Carl, you should have been an actor. I'm not saying Pacheco didn't have a daughter under such circumstances, but I'll swear that the woman in the photograph is not she."

I stood up and walked over to Dalakis. The story struck me as both charming and foolish. I put my hand on his shoulder. "You really are an incurable romantic, Carl. How could you bring yourself to believe such a thing?"

"It's true," said Dalakis, half angry and half laughing. "The girl really is his daughter and it was my own daughter who told me the story. Why should I lie to you?"

He asked the question so forcefully that I retreated a little. "I don't mean to say you're lying, but even if your story is true, why are you so certain the girl in the picture is Pacheco's daughter? You said you saw her a number of years ago. Perhaps it's someone else, some third woman."

"And I suppose you know who it is," said Malgiolio.

His tone irritated me. "Perhaps I do," I said. Walking to the liquor cabinet, I poured myself more mineral water. Then

I looked again at the photograph. There was a yielding quality to the face, as if she were willing to let herself be taken but only by the right man. Truly, she was offering herself, offering and refusing at the same time. Returning the picture to the mantel, I walked toward the window. I had no wish for Malgiolio to laugh at me as he had laughed at Dalakis. Why should I tell my story when there was no hope of communication?

"Don't let Malgiolio upset you," said Dalakis, standing up, "you know how he is."

Yes, I thought, he's the man who squandered a third of a million in thirteen months. I looked out at the street. There was no one in sight. Over the buildings to my left a huge column of smoke rose up in the shape of a dog's head. The windows were the sort that had to be cranked open. I opened one, then sat down on the red cushion. Again there were gunshots and sirens, but they seemed far away. Behind me Dalakis and Malgiolio were quarreling about their respective stories.

The story I knew about the woman in the picture was quite different. I'd heard it from a reporter at the paper who had pointed her out to me in a restaurant several years before. Her name was Andrea Morales and her husband was an engineer for a highway construction company. Her beauty was well known and before her marriage she had been an actress and appeared in a couple of television plays.

She had met Pacheco at a dinner party. She and her husband had no children and my friend suggested she was bored and had no idea what to do with herself. Of course Pacheco wanted her. He called her, he wrote to her, and eventually they had an affair that went on for some months. Then her husband learned about it. He was deeply in love with his wife. Distraught and miserable, he took a bottle of sleeping pills. She found him on the kitchen floor after she came back from being with

Pacheco. He was barely alive. She got him to the hospital and for a week he remained in a coma.

The husband recovered, but not completely. Physically he seemed perfect, but he had some nervous disorder. His wife took care of him. Even so, he no longer trusted her or found pleasure in her company. He was constantly making scenes in public, even bursting into tears. The woman decided to remain with him no matter what, feeling she was responsible for his condition and that perhaps he would improve. But, according to my friend, he showed no signs of improving and the two of them, man and wife, remained locked in this suspicious and guilt-ridden relationship without pleasure or love.

Malgiolio and Dalakis continued to argue. It occurred to me that even if we were wrong about the photograph, the stories themselves were probably true. And of course there were other stories about Pacheco and women, there were hundreds of stories. As I walked back across the library, I was struck by the idea that the stories probably said more about the men who had told them than about the photograph or even Pacheco—Dalakis's story was romantic and basically kind, Malgiolio's showed envy and lasciviousness. And my own, what did my story tell? And who, if anyone, was right?

But then at last Pacheco arrived. There was a noise on the other side of the door. Then it opened and he hurried into the room, pulling on a dark gray suitcoat. Pacheco's expression was apologetic yet good-natured, as if he were sincerely happy to see us.

"I'm terribly sorry. A man on the next street was injured and I had to see to him. Clearly, this is an awful night for our dinner. Carl, it's good to see you. And Batterby. You too, Malgiolio. How brave of you all to come."

Pacheco hurried to each of us and embraced us. He was a

tall, thin man, seemingly very muscular, with long silver hair combed back over his head. His face too was long and thin. It was an angular face with bright blue eyes and it reminded me of someone in an El Greco painting. All he needed was one of those pointy little beards. As on other occasions, I was struck by the care of his movements. Even as he hurried to us, his every motion seemed studied and precise, as if it would be impossible for him to do anything by accident or to act on impulse. He had thick, full lips and his teeth were somewhat crooked and stained with nicotine from his constant Gauloises. The first two fingers of his right hand were also stained yellow because of the way he smoked a cigarette down to its last half inch. He always dressed conservatively but with a bright tie or brightly colored handkerchief. Tonight the tip of a garishly orange handkerchief protruded from the breast pocket of his gray coat. With me, he took my hand and asked about my health, especially about my blood sugar level. It had been low recently, but I didn't care to mention that. To tell the truth, I have always been slightly offended by the degree of intimacy doctors assume. He put his hand on my shoulder and turned back to the others.

"I'm afraid they've called a curfew," he said. "But there's plenty of room here and I'll see that you're made as comfortable as possible. We may make quite a small group. There've been cancellations. Cardone called before the phones went out and said he had to work."

Although I had no wish to sleep at Pacheco's, neither did I want to go out on the street if there was still trouble. "He's covering the demonstrations?" I asked. Cardone was a reporter for my paper's main rival and I often envied him his job.

"Yes, that's what he said, although I gather there's been a total news blackout. Several reporters, including some from the foreign press, have been detained."

"Who else isn't coming?" asked Dalakis.

Pacheco had made himself a drink, French dry vermouth with a little ice, and was refilling Malgiolio's glass with brandy. He moved quickly, lighting a cigarette, holding up a glass to see if it was perfectly clean, assuring himself that neither I nor Dalakis was in need of a drink, glancing at his watch, slipping a small wedge of lime into his glass, and all the while he would turn to us and nod or give a slight smile. He had a way of drawing people into intimacy, of almost, by his manner, suggesting you shared a secret that set you off from all the others. He made you want to trust him, which was partly responsible for his success as a surgeon. I thought again how I knew nothing about him.

"I very much doubt that Hernandez or Serrano will come," said Pacheco, handing Malgiolio his brandy. "Hernandez will be kept quite busy at his church, and Serrano, what with his government clients, will stay quiet until he senses the turn of the political tide. As for the others, Kress is in the military and Schwab is with the police, so I don't expect them either."

"I expect we can cross off Sarno as well," said Dalakis. "His market is in a poor area and he'll be afraid of looting."

"So there'll only be four of us," said Malgiolio. He seemed pleased that the rest weren't coming. "It will be our duty to eat for ten. It's too bad that Batterby only picks at his food."

"Then he'll have to pick carefully," said Pacheco, giving me a wink, then smiling at Malgiolio. These seemed automatic gestures, facial responses that had little to do with what was said or going on around him, existing only to soothe and re-assure. "As a matter of fact, you can eat for twenty if you like. I told my cook that a large number of hungry men were expected. Unfortunately, I may have to go out again. There have been many injuries."

"Do you have any idea what's going on?" Dalakis asked.

Pacheco and I had sat down on the couch, while Dalakis and Malgiolio stood by the mantel. Dalakis was leaning forward as if to hear better. His face when listening reminded me of two hands preparing to catch a ball.

"There seems to be trouble within the military itself," said Pacheco. "Not surprising, considering what we've heard about disagreements between the army and air force. But there's also trouble at the university. The students took over the main campus last night and this morning the military tried to take it back."

"You mean they're killing the students?" asked Dalakis.

"I gather it's a stalemate. The students seem to have destroyed a tank. You find it amusing, Luis?"

Malgiolio's small eyes were almost twinkling with pleasure.

"Malgiolio is still looking for a job," I said. "He feels there'll be a lot of vacancies after today."

Pacheco gave Malgiolio a scientific sort of look, as if he were looking at a machine about which he had no feelings. "If Luis is not careful, he will become a vacancy himself. There's been a great deal of random shooting."

There was a knock at the door. Pacheco got up, then stood aside as the housekeeper pushed a large cart with a tray of canapés into the library. Although I was expecting a feast, both the variety and physical beauty of the food almost made me forget Pacheco's warning to Malgiolio. There must have been twenty varieties of canapé, some with caviar, some with smoked salmon, some with pâté. I studied them all to see what my diet would allow me to eat. Not much, I was afraid. The prettiest were the tips of four asparagus decorated with a small red X made with strips of pimiento. My favorite was made up of alternating slices of lobster and grapefruit, garnished with black olives.

"I had no idea what you might like," said Pacheco, "so I

ordered a little of everything. Put the cart by the fireplace, Sēnora."

I watched the woman push the cart past Malgiolio, who reached out to take a square of toast topped with a small circle of shrimp. She didn't look at us. Although not unattractive, she seemed so removed from the room that it was hard to think of her as more than a piece of furniture. Once the cart was in place, she began arranging the white napkins and straightening a row of little silver forks. As she bent over, a wisp of black hair fell across one eye and she paused to tuck it back.

Malgiolio finished his shrimp and reached for something with black caviar. "By the way, Pacheco," he said, "we've been having a discussion while waiting for you. Perhaps you can help us."

Pacheco stubbed out his cigarette in a green ashtray. "I'd be happy to do what I can."

He was famous for that sort of phrase, or offers of assistance, or inquiries after your health, and I've never had the slightest idea if they were sincere. Of course, he does help and give advice, but his civilized manner is so flawlessly constructed that one almost wishes to see him fall apart, to tumble into hysteria or grief, just to learn what kind of animal lies behind the mask.

"It's about that photograph on the mantel," said Malgiolio with his mouth full. "I think it's a picture of Cecilia Mendez. Dalakis says it's a picture of someone named Sarah, and Batterby has some third idea which he is being coy about."

"I thought it might be Andrea Morales," I said. Was Malgiolio being offensive? Perhaps that's not quite possible with someone one has known since childhood. Certainly we have changed in forty years, but, in our dealings with one another, instead of being nearly fifty, we are all those different years at the same time; we are ten and fifteen and twenty-one and thirty-five—and we each see the others in this same way, so that Pacheco was both the successful surgeon and the solitary adolescent who prowled the city at night carrying a sword cane.

"So tell us," said Malgiolio. "Who is correct?"

Pacheco resumed his place on the couch. In the curve of his lips there was just the slightest suggestion of disdain. "I am afraid you all are mistaken," he said. "The picture is of my housekeeper, Señora Puccini, the woman who at this moment is offering you another cracker, Malgiolio."

We turned and stared at the housekeeper with one movement. She stood holding out the tray to Malgiolio, who was too surprised to take anything. Her face seemed cut from stone, and I couldn't match it to the beautiful face of the girl in the picture.

"Surely you're not serious," I said, unable to stop myself.

Señora Puccini looked up from the tray of food and the corners of her lips lifted into a smile that was so devoid of warmth that it was more a kind of grimace. Then she turned to us, revealing or pointing the smile at each. She seemed to be calling us fools, while also indicating that she didn't care, that she had no interest in us whatsoever. But with her smile, I could at last see a similarity to the girl in the picture. Yet where the girl appeared soft, this woman was unrelenting. Nor was there any sign of fear or uncertainty. Like Dr. Pacheco, she seemed perfectly controlled. As for her eyes, they were like the eyes of a dead person.

As we stood staring at the housekeeper, there came a pounding on the outside door. Señora Puccini put down the tray and left the room. We watched her go, then looked back at the doctor.

It was Dalakis who spoke first. "I don't mean to be offensive," he said, blinking several times, "but why do you keep a photograph of your housekeeper on the mantel?"

32

Pacheco lit another cigarette. There were loud voices in the hall. I assumed with some surprise that more guests had arrived, but hardly paid attention as I waited for Pacheco's answer.

He shook out the match and tossed it into the fireplace. "To remind me of the woman I chose to destroy," he said. Then he lifted his head and looked at us in turn. There was grief in his face and I was so startled to see it that I thought I must be mistaken.

Suddenly the door of the library was thrown open and two soldiers with automatic rifles pushed into the room. More soldiers could be seen behind them. In the hall a man began screaming.

Chapter Two

When I was a boy I had a passion for electric trains, to which I was introduced by my father on the Christmas of my seventh or eighth year. Additional Christmases and birthdays brought more steam, diesel, electric, and turbine locomotives; stockcars, hoppers, tank cars, boxcars, cabooses, passenger and lounge cars; plus railway yards, cattle crossings, water towers, stations, tunnels, bridges, small villages, artificial grass, dozens of little trees, and yards and yards of track, until by the time I was in my early teens, I had two rooms in the attic with a train system that any great nation would be proud of. I also had a wind-up Victrola and a stack of 78 RPM records with the sounds of different locomotives, conductors calling "All Aboard!," the clack and rattle of speeding wheels, and a variety of bells, whistles, sirens, and horns, so that every day the attic rang with the noise of commerce and transportation.

It was there I spent most of my time away from school and even while reading or studying I would don my engineer's cap, then set the trains in motion. Often, while I did my homework, half a dozen engines would be pulling as many as seventy-five passenger or freight cars along my quarter mile of track. Stuck away in a far corner of the house, surrounded by a miniature country, I had a strong, although certainly childish, sense of my own power, even divinity, as I pursued my railway strategies, taking on loads of coal, unloading shipments of lumber, lowering highway barriers, and setting the warning signals ringing. This was my world and I even had several hundred little figures to populate it and jump to my commands. My favorites were given the most prestigious positions—mayor, engineer, yard boss, police chief—the unpopular or merely ugly were the drones who swabbed out the lavatories and did other unpleasant tasks. Being an only child whose parents were often away, I found the hustle-bustle of this activity immensely comforting.

Consequently, it was to the attic that my parents or the servant would send any friends or visitors who came seeking me. And it was in the attic that the man employed by Daniel Pacheco's father probably found me one Saturday afternoon in early summer when I was just fourteen. I say "probably" because my memory is not entirely clear, the later events of the day having wiped out whatever happened in the few hours following my return from school around noon.

But I recall for certain that this man had a written message from Pacheco asking that I join him immediately. The servant would guide me. His name was Boris and he did the chores and garden work around Pacheco's house. He had a cadaverous face and his head was completely bald—I think he shaved it—and in one ear he wore a large gold earring. Apparently he had once been a sailor, because in the middle of his left cheek he had a tattoo of a small blue skull the size of a thumbnail. My mother found him a repulsive creature and had ordered me to tell Daniel not to send him to our house, since Boris carried all of Daniel's messages and was more his servant than his father's. Of course I did as my mother said, but Daniel paid no attention.

That day I went off with Boris without a thought. It wouldn't have occurred to me not to, such was Daniel's influence over the rest of us. Also, though I was a solitary child with elaborate and expensive diversions, I was not solitary by choice and so was eager for the chance to be with other boys. Years later I sometimes wondered why we followed Daniel so readily, and I came to the conclusion that it wasn't so much his intelligence or courage but that he was the first among us to develop a sense of irony. It kept us from being able to trap and confine him within our boyish definitions.

We took a bus down to the docks, which was an area my parents had told me to avoid. I expect they thought I might be shanghaied by a Chinese ship. If possible, I would have asked Boris the nature of our destination, but he was unable to speak; whether he was born dumb or had never learned the language, I don't know. Some of the boys claimed that his tongue had been cut out or his vocal cords severed by torturers, which seemed clearly fanciful. But he was friendly enough and when he saw my nervousness about being near the docks, he smiled and patted my shoulder.

We left the bus near the customs building, then set off through the narrow streets with warehouses on one side and cafés and cheap hotels on the other. My companion walked quickly and I had to trot in order to keep up. It was mid-afternoon on a hot summer Saturday and the streets were nearly empty. After half a dozen blocks, we turned up the hill into a maze of even narrower streets shaded by four- and five-story tenements from which were strung masses of laundry, sheets mostly, hanging from clotheslines that crisscrossed above our heads. These houses have always intrigued me, since each appears to have been designed as an argument against the styles of its neighbors, so different are they in color—those blue and yellow and pink pastels—so different in the degree of filigree and decoration, complicated balconies, stonework and clapboards and stucco and brick.

We turned at last up a very narrow street, too narrow for cars, and I remember garbage and the ubiquitous smell of urine. Several scrawny dogs lay scratching in doorways, too bored and sleepy even to look up. Steeply ascending the hill, the alley made several turns, twisting to the left and right as the tenements rose high above us, making the alley almost dark in the midst of the sunny day. After a few minutes Boris stopped at a door and motioned me to enter.

"Aren't you coming?" I asked.

He shook his head, then opened the door for me. Inside was a dirty landing and a flight of narrow stairs. I had little inclination to go in by myself, but I trusted Pacheco, as well as his servant, and it wouldn't have occurred to me that I might be in danger. I looked back at Boris. The tattoo of the human skull on his cheek had a perpetual grin, almost a leer, and I found myself focusing on it. Then Boris again patted my shoulder and hurried off down the hill.

It was only as I shut the door behind me and climbed the stairs that I began to feel some anxiety. They were dark, very steep, and had a sour smell, a mixture of old food and stale bodies. At the top was another door and I knocked. There was no answer. I tried the handle and the door opened into a long narrow room with about twenty straight chairs lining the walls. It too was empty. I remember it had a floral wallpaper of huge yellow blossoms unknown in the real world. The paper was peeling and great sheets dangled toward the floor as if the flowers were intent on escape. Beneath it, the dank gray plaster appeared to be sweating. I called Daniel's name, then crossed the room to another door. There was no sound except that of my own feet on the linoleum. The second door opened onto a long hall with doors on either side. Again I called Daniel's name and this time he appeared, sticking his head from one of the doorways.

"There you are," he said impatiently. "What kept you?"

He was dressed all in black, even his boots were black, and his dark hair was greased and slicked back like a tango dancer's. Despite his clothes, his face had the smoothness of a girl's, and he looked younger than the rest of us, maybe eleven or twelve. "I came as fast as I could," I said. "What is this place? What are you doing here?"

"I have a gift for you," he answered. "Come with me."

I entered the room. The window was covered with brown paper, which made the room not so much dark as murky. On the far side was a white metal bedstead and with a shock I saw that a woman was lying on the sheets and that she was naked. I started to back out of the door, thinking that Pacheco had made a mistake. He saw my embarrassment and put his arm around my shoulder.

"That's for you, Nicky. Maria is very nice. Go to her. She'll show you what to do."

I felt confused and hardly understood. After all, I was only fourteen, and even though I spent much of my time thinking about sex, the actual deed was a mystery. My parents had never discussed with me what were called the facts of life and all I knew of the subject came from hushed conversations with my schoolmates, who knew as little as I.

Pacheco took hold of my elbow and slowly walked me toward the bed. "You have nothing to be anxious about, Nicky."

Despite my reluctance, I moved forward. "Why are you doing this?" I asked.

"It's a gift. Calm yourself."

I had never seen a naked woman except in art books and

here was one lying a few feet away. What's more, I was supposed to make love to her. Obviously, love wouldn't enter into it, but at fourteen that was how it seemed. I felt on the verge of panic.

"But who is she?" I whispered, hoping she wouldn't hear.

"A friend. Go to her. I'm telling you to do it."

How do I describe the woman? First of all, there was nothing romantic or beautiful about her, but neither was she entirely repulsive. At the time I thought her old, but she was probably about thirty. She must have been part Indian, because she had those high cheekbones and slanted eyes and her skin was a light tawny color. She lay on her back, propped up on her elbows. She was a very large woman, not so much fat as swollen, with a great round belly. Her breasts were huge but also rather flabby so they lay on her chest and stomach like two pigskin purses. The room was hot and her skin was shiny with sweat. Even now I recall the tiny rivulets of perspiration that ran off her belly. Around her neck was a thin silver chain from which was suspended a small letter M. Her nipples in the dim light looked black. Her pubic hair had been shaved.

She looked at me with a sleepy grin and motioned me over with one finger. Pacheco gave me a little push and I approached the bed, so terrified that I could barely stand. Slowly, the woman reached out and took hold of my belt; then, with her eyes still on mine, she unfastened the buckle and the snap. She had short black hair that surrounded her head like a bowl and very round cheeks, like a chipmunk with its mouth full of seeds.

Giving my pants a yank, she pulled them down so they fell about my ankles. Then she took my cock in her hand. I was in such a daze that I didn't seem to be doing something so much as watching from outside my body. Slowly, she pulled me to her, forcing me gently onto the bed as if my cock were a little leash. Had I been older and more experienced, I'm sure my anxiety would have kept me from having an erection, but at that age I knew no better. I was too confused to think and my body did the only thinking necessary.

As I lay on top of her, she slipped my cock inside her, then wrapped her legs around mine, pinning me to her. I've said she was big but she was also very tall, because my head barely reached her shoulder. She smelled of oil, the warm olive oil that my mother sometimes used to clean the wax out of my ears when I was a child. I lay with my head pressed against her breast. She felt very soft and her skin was wet and rubbery. It was like lying on top of a warm and greasy inflatable mattress. I tried not to touch her flesh with my hands, partly for fear of offending her nakedness; but, given my anxiety about falling to the floor, I was afraid not to hold on and my fingers fluttered nervously about her ribs. But then she wrapped her arms around me and I lay pinned to her breast like a little brooch as she manipulated her hips. I came right away, a small explosion of light. Afterward she let me lie a little longer so I could catch my breath and get over my surprise. Then she gave me a slight shove and I slid off her body and onto the floor.

"You boys," she said in a rather masculine voice, "it's like eating too much white cake." She patted my hand, then turned over on her side and appeared to go to sleep. Although the sheet was white, she was lying with her hips on a bright red towel. I stood for a moment, not knowing what to do. Pacheco put his hand on my shoulder.

"Well done, Nicky. There's a bathroom over there if you want. Then go down through the door on the other side and you'll find the others."

I washed myself carefully, not that I felt she was dirty but to wash from my skin the strong smell of her oil, which I was afraid my mother would notice and even recognize. Then I went through the second door and down a flight of stairs. Certainly I was too astonished to think much about what was happening. At the bottom, through another door, I found ten of my schoolmates in a long room like the dining room at school. There were even tables. They sat and studied me seriously as I walked slowly across the bare wooden floor.

"Did you do it?" asked Eric Schwab.

I felt immediately guilty, as if I was the only one who had given in to the woman, while they had abstained. I nodded my head.

With that they all leapt up, clapped, hammered on my back, and filled the room with their laughter. Some were still in their school uniforms from that morning—white shirt, blue pants and jacket with the school shield over the heart. "We too," said Schwab. "We all had a turn. Pacheco's letting the whole class fuck her. Of course, I've had women before."

He said this and the other boys laughed or groaned or called him a liar. One boy had found a broken chair leg and let it dangle from the button fly of his pants in mockery of Schwab's sexual prowess. We were all extremely excited, even hysterical. The hugeness of Pacheco's prank made our hearts race.

"I could have another go at her," said Schwab. "I like those big ones."

Of all of us, Schwab probably looked the most mature. Even then, he must have been six feet tall and had hair on his upper lip. He was muscular and blue-eyed and something of a bully. He pretended to be afraid of nothing but once we had seen him taunt Pacheco and be so badly beaten that he had missed several days of school. Now, if Pacheco had told him to jump through a flaming hoop, Schwab would have jumped.

I doubt that any of us had been with a woman before, not even Schwab, and our talk, which in memory strikes me as silly, was full of nervous hilarity as we compared our different

41

yet similar experiences. Schwab swore he had made her moan with pleasure and that he had held himself back for thirty minutes. Some said it was great, some weren't sure. Two boys wept. Another was angry, another full of guilt. Throughout the afternoon, more boys came down the stairs and were astonished to find us. Some laughed, some felt embarrassed, most did both. Of the twenty-five Boris had found out of a class of thirty, only two had refused to climb into the whore's bed. One was Carl Dalakis. Another two admitted they hadn't been able to have erections. I expect there were others who had been unable to perform, but they kept their mouths shut. Those who admitted failure were badly teased. Schwab said that he would bring them back and show them how to do it.

Malgiolio was one of the ones who wept. In those days he was quiet and wrote Symbolist poetry in the manner of Verlaine and Rubén Darío. That's not to say he didn't enjoy the woman. He was one of the ones who tried to locate her again, Indeed, a little field trip of eight boys came down to the area a few days later. But either they couldn't find the right door or, if it was the right one, the door was locked or the room empty. I don't remember the exact details, only that they couldn't find the woman and ended up going to a regular whorehouse, where they were made fun of and it cost them a lot of money and where one boy—was it Malgiolio or Schwab—got the clap and for weeks he cried every time he had to pee.

But that Saturday afternoon, which began with my trains and ended with the Indian whore, was a wonderful time of good-fellowship. After the last of us had descended the stairs, Pacheco's servant Boris entered with several hampers of food: cold chicken sandwiches, potato salad, apples, buckets of lemonade and a large chocolate cake. Looking back, that menu seems absurd, but at the time it felt exactly right. After all, we were having a party, and that was what fourteen-year-old

42

boys ate at parties. We stuffed ourselves and then had a fight with the apple cores in which I was hit in the eye.

About half an hour after the last boy had joined us and we were done eating, the door opened to reveal Pacheco with the whore standing beside him. She was truly mammoth, well over six feet tall and at least three hundred pounds. She wore a black beaded slip that reached her ankles and her great breasts ballooned forth out of the skimpy black lace. We stared at her with fear and astonishment. Schwab, who had sworn he was eager to have another go, hung back behind us all.

She returned our stare, looking at each of us, staring right into each boy's eyes and holding them for a moment. None of us knew what to do. Her face was wide and flat, almost like the blade of a shovel, and her eyes were slits.

"Were there really so many?" she said at last. "White cake, white cake, you were very sweet." She said this without sarcasm, but neither did she seem particularly warm-hearted. She was like someone after a large meal and I almost expected her to belch and rub her stomach. Then Pacheco took out some money and gave it to her. She counted it once, then once again, licking her finger as she turned over the bills. When she was satisfied, she took a few steps farther into the room with her hands on her hips and leaning back so her breasts and belly stuck out like great black pillows. The money was in both hands, the bills protruding from between her fingers. She began to hum slightly and as she hummed she began to sway from side to side. Slowly she began to dance. She was barefoot and her feet made a scraping sound on the floor. Her humming grew louder and Pacheco started to clap to the rhythm of her movements. Several others also began to clap, although to tell the truth, I found something frightening about this. She was so huge. It was like being in a cage with a female bear. The song was very simple: five ascending notes in the first phrase, then three ascending and two descending in the second. She repeated this over and over.

As she danced, she reached down and plucked at the fabric of her black slip where it covered her knees. Then she began to pull it up while sliding it from side to side across her legs. Her humming grew louder, both violent and nasal, and between the phrases she would snort through her nose to catch her breath. I don't believe it was a regular song, or at least I didn't recognize it. She continued to lift her slip until her genitals were exposed. As I say, she had no pubic hair and her bronze-colored pudendum glistened as if oiled. Then she spread her legs and toed-out her feet, and we saw that on the inside of her left thigh was tattooed a cock—a great fat red cock with bright red balls and a black bush of pubic hair hanging downward and nearly reaching her knee. As she tensed and relaxed the muscles of her leg, the cock itself appeared to dance, twisting and heaving, while the rest of her body grew still and her humming grew louder. I really expected a vagina to be tattooed on the other leg, but there was nothing, just this cock by itself which quivered and undulated to the husky sound of those five notes repeated over and over.

I don't know how long it lasted. At first some of the boys cheered and laughed, but after a while all grew quiet as we watched her performance. Most of us stood still, but about five or six, including Malgiolio, went to her, forming a ring around her; and as she danced, they circled her first to the left, then to the right, with their heads bowed and seemingly staring at the floor or perhaps her great bare feet. As I say, several were in their school uniforms and one still wore the little blue beanie with the tiny black brim. For that matter, I still wore the engineer's cap that went with my model railroad. But I had the sense that the dancing boys were her creatures, that she had hypnotized them, and I remember tensing myself and even pinching the skin on the inside of my wrist to keep from falling under a similar spell while I watched that tattoo of a great red cock heave itself about her leg, as the boys continued their circle and the woman continued her song. Really, her thigh was so thick that its circumference was probably greater than my waist.

At last she stopped. Her song had no conclusion, just an end. She brought her thighs together with a clap and let the black slip fall back over her knees. Then she began to yawn, great open-mouthed yawns, like big cats in zoos. Still yawning she turned and patted Pacheco's cheek and, without another glance at us, she slowly climbed the stairs with the money sticking like thistles from her fists.

Pacheco stood facing us. "I have given you a little something. Are you grateful?" he asked. No one answered. We were still too caught up by her dance. "Now you will always remember each other. I suppose you think this has made you men. It hasn't, but perhaps you will whine a little less."

All of a sudden we felt released, and we laughed and whistled and clapped our hands. Pacheco was always saying serious things to which we paid little attention. Every boy has a constant game in which he plays the hero, and this Saturday afternoon it seemed we had taken part in Pacheco's game, for which we were grateful. All of us? Well, I was grateful, or at least I thought I was. And years later, when we formed our group and committed ourselves to biannual dinners, I felt that the root of our decision was not that we had been in school together or had similar interests and backgrounds or were even particularly close to one another, but rather the beginning, the event that tied us together, was that afternoon when Pacheco had hired the whore. Even at forty-nine, I still vividly remember being pressed to her immense greasy chest while she gyrated her hips very slowly and methodically. It was almost like chewing. Others thought the same, and much later Malgiolio said how the whore had eaten our childhood. But I didn't think anything so grand. I was a fourteen-year-old boy in a black and white striped railway cap. I was simply amazed.

Such were our sexual beginnings. At fourteen we boys were so similar as to be like a series of ditto marks. It was only later that we grew more defined and individual: one entered the church, another the military—doctor, lawyer, used car salesman. As for me, I am someone who has spent his adult life on the periphery of literature in the way that a small animal will remain just beyond the glow of a campfire, observing the strange doings of the human creatures settling in for the night. I am not an artist but a journalist, and even though my essays and interviews with Borges, Mailer, Günter Grass, and others may someday be collected and published in book form, I am not a critic but a reviewer. It is my job to compare a new book to what has already been written, not to speculate on the paths literature may take in the future. But the hardest task in any writing is to present the truth so it can be seen as true. One cannot just give the history of an event in a straightforward manner and expect it to be believed. That history must have a shape. It must have direction and movement.

Of course I am a romantic. That is my curse; it italicizes all my observations. Always at the book review I am being asked to tone down if not my opinions, then my prose. But to be a romantic, doesn't that mean seeking and even finding connection among apparently random phenomena? There must be pattern. The events of a life are not a series of scattered actions like dust thrown into the wind. Something must link them. And so in writing I am not merely giving the history of one evening at Dr. Pacheco's but of our lives as influenced by Pacheco. Detachment, I struggle for detachment. Those hours

46

with the whore had linked us together. We did not brood about this event. It was hardly mentioned between us and if someone did mention that Saturday afternoon it was casually and certainly without shame or guilt. It had pleased us all. That is why it seemed such a pity to begin our group without Pacheco, and why, once he had joined, I felt he should give the next dinner. Our meetings had in a sense begun with him and so I had waited impatiently for his turn. Yet how unfair, now that his turn had finally arrived, that only three of us would apparently be his guests.

Constantly nagging me as I write is how to give a true sense of that evening. The violence in the city, the soldiers, the shooting made those few hours seem unconnected to the normal course of our lives. We had not just gone to Pacheco's for dinner, we had stepped outside of time and reality as we knew it. Although we had some anxiety, we felt safe at Pacheco's, partly because we had always seen him as a leader, someone who was never in doubt what to do next. His admission about the photograph—that he kept it on the mantel "to remind me of the woman I chose to destroy"—was startling not just for what it said, but also because of the careful way he said it: that he didn't accidentally destroy, but chose to destroy. And then to have this followed so quickly by the arrival of the soldiers led me to think, foolishly of course, that they had come to punish Pacheco and that suddenly he was not in control.

My misconception lasted only a moment, but it should be emphasized that we were not men accustomed to violence. The interruption of these soldiers, even for the most mundane reason, was frightening. I myself have never owned a gun, have never been hunting or even fishing, and all at once here were automatic weapons being waved about and a man screaming out in the hall. Really, my impulse was to scream as well.

47

In the world of violence, it was something quite small. A soldier had been shot and wounded, apparently by a sniper. The lieutenant heard that a surgeon lived nearby and had the man carried to Pacheco's house. But even this, that a man lay on the marble floor of the hall writhing in pain from a bullet wound, even this made us afraid—partly because of its own violence and partly as an interruption of our sedate and sedentary world. At the same time, the fact that a soldier needed help was—and this seems almost comical—reassuring news, since, originally, when the soldiers burst into the library, I had felt in mortal danger. After all, these were young men, inexperienced and extremely nervous. Wasn't I right to be frightened? And I'm positive that Malgiolio and Dalakis were frightened as well.

Later, Pacheco poked fun at my response, saying I must have a guilty conscience. "About what?" I asked.

"Some little thing. Perhaps you ate too much or went out with a girl too young for you or had a spiteful thought. And when the soldiers arrived, you thought you had been found out." And he laughed again.

My first sight of the wounded man was a great pair of black boots, one of which seemed wet, and a smear of blood on the floor around him. Blocking me from the rest of him were the green-clad backs of half a dozen soldiers as well as Pacheco himself down on his knees investigating the man's wounds. But though I couldn't see the wounded man, I certainly heard him as he continued to scream, a short, barking, indignant sort of noise which he made over and over. Because of all the marble, his screams seemed almost theatrical as they echoed off those cold surfaces and mixed with the thick smell of the flowers.

"Get my bag and some sheets," Pacheco told Señora Puccini.

Although I was astonished at the blood, the furor, the ner-

vous soldiers, Pacheco seemed entirely calm. He knelt by the
injured man, discovering the degree of his wounds and talking
to him quietly. Three soldiers stood at the open door with their
weapons pointed out at the street, which was now nearly dark.
Other soldiers, perhaps seven or eight, stood around the hall
watching their wounded comrade but, even more, staring at
the grandeur of the hall itself, gawking at the bawdy tapestry
and the Roman busts, gaping up at the chandelier. As before,
I was struck by their youth. They looked like teenagers just
out of school, and very briefly I had the impression that these
were the comrades we'd been expecting for dinner, yet cast
back to that time when we were all classmates and just beginning our explorations of the world. But then they stood aside
and I saw the boy on the floor. He was dark and black-haired
and his mouth formed a perfect "O" as he continued his astonished protest. Although his body was still as he lay on his
back, his head swung violently from side to side as if he were
scanning the room for the source of his pain. Indeed, at one
moment his eyes fastened on mine and I thought he would
speak, but then he again jerked his head and I stepped back
out of his vision.

Dalakis and I stood by the library door. I suppose he was
as amazed as I was. In his clumsy and bearlike way, he kept
jostling me as he peered at the wounded man through his thick
glasses with a mixture of repulsion and grief. Looking back
into the room, I saw Malgiolio smoking a cigarette by the
fireplace. He seemed still to be studying the photograph. I
didn't realize at the time that he was frightened as well.

Señora Puccini reentered the hall from a door on the right,
carrying a battered-looking black leather bag and several white
sheets. Even in the midst of this clamor she appeared cold
and distant. She made her way between the soldiers without
even glancing at them. As I looked at her, I couldn't help but

see the beautiful face of the girl in the photograph imposed over hers. But what had been confident and even brazen in the photograph now appeared hard, as if she aspired to the condition of stone. After giving Pacheco the bag, she didn't linger but left the hall to return to the kitchen. A sergeant began tearing the sheets into strips. Pacheco took a syringe from his bag and gave a shot to the wounded soldier, who was still screaming, but more faintly, almost mechanically. Then Pacheco began to investigate the man's wounds, which were apparently in his leg and shoulder.

"Can't you get an ambulance?" Pacheco asked the lieutenant.

The officer seemed embarrassed by the wounded man, as if the presence of so much pain were distasteful. "I sent someone to locate one, then a policeman said that you lived nearby. The medics should be here shortly." The officer was also very young, no more than twenty-one or -two. "I couldn't leave him on the street," he added apologetically. "He would have been murdered."

Pacheco glanced around the hall, then caught my eye. "Batterby, go to the kitchen and ask the Señora to bring me several pans of water. Tell her to make it as hot as possible."

"What do you plan to do?" asked the lieutenant. With his good looks and detached manner, he appeared more suited for parades than violent action.

"There is a bullet in his thigh and there are some bone fragments," said Pacheco. "I'll do no more than I can."

Crossing the hall, I opened the door to the back part of the house, happy to be of use. Like many older houses, Pacheco's formed a square with the rear three sides being only one story and surrounding a large garden. On the left of the corridor were a series of small rooms and on the right was a courtyard with a great bougainvillaea, its purple flowers rising to the roof.

Hung along the inside wall were about twenty nineteenth-century prints of the sort found in old newspapers. All showed the various activities of Reynard the Fox, preening his whiskers, fleeing the hounds, and luring chickens from the safety of their coops. The tiles on the floor were covered with a woven mat and my feet made no sound as I hurried forward on my errand.

The kitchen stood at the very end of the corridor on the far side of the garden, but instead of just bursting in, as is my usual clumsy manner, I felt uncertain of the door and stopped to peer around the corner. Only a few feet inside were Señora Puccini and an old woman who I correctly assumed was the cook. They were facing each other and both stood in profile to me. Neither noticed me. I describe this in detail because really the first thing I saw was that Señora Puccini was holding a pistol. It lay in the palm of her hand and she stared down at it. The cook appeared to be looking at it as well. It was a shiny little thing, hardly more than four inches long and, as I watched, she slipped it into the side pocket of her skirt. Quietly, I stepped back from the door and retreated several feet. Then I coughed once or twice and again moved forward.

I'm not certain why I did this. But I didn't want Señora Puccini to think I was spying and I didn't want to embarrass her. As for the pistol, I'm sure I thought little of it. There was trouble in the streets, soldiers in the house, and the weapon probably made her feel safer. Also, the fact that she had been showing it to the cook made it seem rather innocent.

When I entered the kitchen, the cook was on the other side of the room and Señora Puccini stood facing me. It was a large and very long room, taking up the whole back part of the house. From the beams crossing the ceiling hung copper pots and bouquets of herbs. Everywhere there were signs of food being prepared and filling the room were the most wonderful smells imaginable. I looked into Señora Puccini's face for some trace of nervousness, but there was none. It held its normal passive expression. But perhaps that is not right. Although passive, her face also showed indifference, as if nothing I could say or do would affect her. In any case, I told her that the doctor required hot water and she nodded.

"Do you want me to help you carry it?" I asked.

"It's not necessary. There's a boy."

On a table in the middle of the kitchen stood an invalid tray with four little legs, and on it was a bowl of steaming soup and a plate with several pieces of black bread. I wondered about it briefly, but then, eager to get back to Pacheco, I turned and hurried out of the kitchen. As I walked back along the hall I looked out at the garden, part of which had a trellis roof covered with grape vines. In the dim light, I saw there were many bird cages, several being at least ten feet tall. I stopped at a doorway to look more closely. There must have been over a hundred tropical birds, ranging from the tiniest finch to large toucans and cockatoos. Presumably because of the hour they were standing quite still. I say presumably because as I stood there I again heard gunshots in the distance and the stillness of the birds seemed to reflect my own anxiety. I was greatly impressed by the size of the collection and that Pacheco had never mentioned it before—beautiful, fragile creatures in ornate cages, motionless on their perches.

When I returned to the hall, the situation was more settled. The wounded soldier appeared to be sleeping, while most of the other men were out on the street. Pacheco was talking with the lieutenant and both were smoking Pacheco's awful Gauloises. Dalakis had returned to the library. I told Pacheco that the hot water would be there shortly.

"Go to the library," he told me. "I'll join you in a moment."

"Is there anything I can do to help?" I asked. The wounded

soldier lay at my feet and the tips of my shoes barely touched the small pool of his blood. Although I am ashamed to say it, this excited me, reminding me of those few years when I worked as a reporter before being transferred to the book review.

"No, no, this is a dinner party. It may be occurring under peculiar circumstances but it's still a party. We have a duty to the others to enjoy ourselves." Pacheco said this very seriously and the lieutenant looked at him with surprise.

Returning to the library, I found Malgiolio and Dalakis in the midst of an argument. It appeared that Malgiolio wanted some of the soldiers to be kept in the house for our protection. Dalakis said it was unnecessary, arguing that the soldiers had better things to do.

"What's more important than seeing to our safety?" said Malgiolio. "We could be killed here." He stood by the liquor cabinet, slapping his fist into the palm of his left hand.

"Absolute foolishness. We're perfectly safe as long as we stay inside." Dalakis laughed and shook his head, as if he found something lovable about Malgiolio's fear. "Explain it to him, Batterby. Nobody's going to burst in here, although I expect we should close the curtains."

So often had I been the butt of Malgiolio's jokes that his fear gave me a little twinge of pleasure. "Carl's right," I said. "What danger is there? Certainly, I'd prefer to be home, but here at least we'll be well fed."

As I spoke, Dalakis crossed the room and closed the drapes, which were made of a dark blue material with pictures of birds, much like the tropical birds in the garden. "See," he said, "now we can't even hear the gunshots."

"I'd feel safer if I was armed," said Malgiolio.

I started to make some light remark about Señora Puccini's pistol but decided against it. Most likely it would upset Malgiolio even more. The door opened and Pacheco entered.

"I've come to escort you to the dining room. Everything is a little disturbed, as you can imagine. I'm afraid you'll have to start your soup without me. I must do a bit more work on that fellow's leg."

We passed through the hall in single file. Several soldiers looked at us sullenly. Here they were risking their lives while we were about to sit down to dinner. They'd probably had little to eat all day. The wounded man remained unconscious, his face so white that he appeared dead. We entered the dining room, which was next to the library. I was expecting it to be elaborate and so was not surprised, but behind me I could hear Dalakis catch his breath.

It was a long room with a crystal chandelier suspended over the table. But what was particularly striking was that the table was set for the entire group—not only for us but for the six who hadn't come and the other six who hadn't even been expected. It was set for sixteen: a seat on either end and seven on each side. And there were flowers everywhere. The long table had four different vases with complicated arrangements of at least a dozen different flowers. Unfortunately, I have never been an admirer of cut flowers and yet the extravagance of color as well as the palpable weight of their scent took one's breath simply as spectacle. A second door at the far end of the room opened onto the corridor that ran along the edge of the garden, and through a window I could see the cages of the tropical birds.

"As you can see, you have a wide choice of seats," said Pacheco. "Sit where you wish. I'll return as soon as possible."

We watched him leave, then looked back at the table, which was covered with a thick white cloth. Each place setting included four separate wine glasses and eight pieces of silver. Malgiolio picked up a knife, felt its weight, then returned it to the table. The napkins were dark blue linen.

"Shall we all sit at one end?" said Malgiolio, and immediately took his place at the far end opposite the open door giving a view of the garden. I sat down across from him and Dalakis sat on my left. The place at the head of the table we reserved for Pacheco. It was odd to look past Dalakis at that vast expanse of table with those flowers and elaborate place settings and think no one would be sitting there.

As soon as we were seated, a young man entered through the open door with a tray of oysters. Really he was a boy, hardly more than fifteen, and he seemed extremely nervous. Faint patches of black whiskers spotted his face like dark islands on a pink sea. He was quite thin and awkward and wore a black suit that was too small for him. His large pink hands extended from the sleeves like skinned rabbits. He looked very much like one of the boys at my orphanage, a boy who has faithfully listened to me read every Sunday for at least eight years. They had the same thin face and narrow brow, the same unruly shock of black hair. After serving us each a dozen oysters, the boy took a bottle of champagne from the ice bucket and looked at it doubtfully. Removing the wire, he began to twist off the cork as if twisting a screw top.

"Not so fast," said Dalakis, "You'll get it all over yourself."

The boy thrust the bottle away from him and at that moment the cork exploded with a loud pop and ricocheted across the room. Champagne began spewing out of the bottle onto the floor. Malgiolio reached forward with a glass and then another as the boy stood looking confused. Abruptly, the door to the hall opened quickly and the lieutenant glanced into the room. Seeing our little party, he retreated.

Dalakis burst out laughing. "He thought it was a gunshot." He had a low laugh like someone banging on the bottom of a metal drum. The boy was also grinning. But the speed with which the lieutenant came to the door impressed me, and a few minutes later, when they decided they needed another bottle, I opened it myself and the cork made no noise at all.

Dalakis was a very hearty eater. Watching him made me remember those films showing bears scooping grubs from a dead stump or tearing into a honeycomb. In no time, his smiling mouth was shiny with lemon juice and horseradish and juice from the oysters. As he ate, he made small contented noises, sighs that were close cousins to the grunt. Glancing at him, I saw there were gray cat hairs on the jacket of his brown suit.

Malgiolio, on the other hand, ate almost furtively, positioning himself with his elbows on either side of his plate, both to protect it and to make no unnecessary movements. He was also very methodical and moved his hands with such speed that all I could think of was a conveyor belt. Although Dalakis made several remarks on the quality of the champagne and the oysters, Malgiolio hardly spoke until his plate was empty.

As for myself, my diabetes and occasional ulcers have caused me to so regulate my diet that I have become no friend to food. I rarely eat out or eat in the company of other people. Indeed, I find something almost disgusting in watching my fellow creatures insert soft globs of animal tissue and vegetable matter into their open mouths, then chewing and smacking their lips as they make a sound closely resembling that of a boot being extracted from thick mud. Another phrase of Diogenes came to mind: "If only I could free myself from hunger as easily as from desire." Sometimes I have thought that our sole purpose on earth was to produce excrement for a perverse god who uses it as fertilizer for his beloved garden. But I do not mean to be antisocial. I enjoy the company of my friends and even ate several oysters before letting Dalakis and Malgiolio divide my remaining nine or ten between them.

When he had finished, Dalakis leaned back and glanced around the room as if he might try nibbling it as well. In the bright light of the chandelier, I happened to notice his hands. Even though his wife deserted him many years before, he still wears his wedding ring, which has grown into his finger much in the way a wire can be embedded into the tree it surrounds. Turning to me, Dalakis put his right hand on my shoulder. "You know, Batterby, I heard a story recently about a writer that might interest you."

"Oh?" I said somewhat pessimistically, afraid that I'd hear about someone who had experienced great good fortune with little effort.

"Yes, this man was in prison, a political prisoner somewhere. I don't know the country. It turned out that the next cell was occupied by a Yugoslav, at least he said he was a Yugoslav. The two men couldn't see each other but they could whisper back and forth. After a few days, the writer asked the Yugoslav to teach him a little Serbo-Croatian. You see, he was so bored, nothing to do, nothing to read. The Yugoslav refused but the writer kept asking him and after several more days the Yugoslav agreed. . . ."

"Is this going to be a long story?" asked Malgiolio.

"Not particularly. I just thought Batterby might be interested."

The oysters finished, we were sitting back drinking the champagne. Malgiolio chewed on a bit of lemon. "I was wondering if you knew where Pacheco got those oysters." Malgiolio has very small teeth, almost like the teeth of a child.

"Why don't you ask Pacheco when he returns?" I suggested.

"I expect I will, since you can't tell me. But what I mostly want to know about is the picture of the woman on the mantel. Do you think she's his housekeeper?"

"He said she was," said Dalakis. "Why should he lie?"

"But why keep her picture on the mantel?" asked Malgiolio.

"Carl, go on about the Yugoslav," I said.

The boy reappeared carrying a tray with three bowls of a clear soup, which he set in front of us. He spilled a little on the tablecloth and for a moment we were distracted as he hurried to clean it up. Whenever he saw us watching, he blushed.

Malgiolio tasted his soup, rolled it around in his mouth, then began to eat it rather quickly. I sipped a little. It was turtle soup with some sort of sherry. I didn't recognize the kind.

Dalakis glanced at Malgiolio with friendly exasperation. "The writer," he said, continuing his story, "had a piece of chalk, or maybe it was charcoal. The Yugoslav would tell him a word and the writer would print it on the wall. Maybe ten words a day. Neither man knew how long he would be in prison and of course each expected to be released quite soon. In the meantime, they continued this course of instruction in Serbo-Croatian. Additionally, the Yugoslav began to tell the writer about Belgrade. He described the turrets and churches, how the city was built upon three hills. He talked about the rich houses covered with delicate tile mosaics and the ancient part of the city with its narrow winding streets and high white walls. He described the parks and lakes full of little boats and the profusion of flowers and the small bands of musicians that wandered through the outdoor cafés. He described the smell of cinnamon and bread baking and flowers and the smell of some sharp spice that one found everywhere."

I glanced at Malgiolio, but he was giving the same attention to his soup that he had given to his oysters and seemed unaware of our presence at the table. As for Dalakis, he occasionally took a spoonful of soup, spilling a little on his tie, a little on his chin, then dabbing at himself carelessly with his blue napkin.

"As months passed, the walls of the writer's cell began to fill with words, and he and the Yugoslav began to have very simple conversations in this language, this Serbo-Croatian. The writer, who was a sort of wanderer, began to develop a passion to visit Belgrade, to see these places the Yugoslav described so vividly. And he felt that in this acquisition of language and by obtaining an exact description of the city, he was creating for himself a place to live, even a homeland.

"A year went by, then a second and a third. At last the Yugoslav and the writer held all their discussions in Serbo-Croatian. Furthermore, the writer had managed to get paper and began to write poetry in this language, for you see he had made up his mind that when he left prison, he would go to Belgrade and work there and try to be happy and knit together the fragments of his life. And so he wrote and read his work to the Yugoslav, who praised it and made suggestions and would help him with some difficult idiom. And then the Yugoslav would tell more about Belgrade, about its boulevards and streets, until along with the thousands of words which covered the walls, the writer also began to draw a map of the city and would ask the Yugoslav just where this cathedral stood or the palace or the municipal gardens or the train station or the circus which was open every day of the year."

"Did he get out of prison or didn't he?" asked Malgiolio, who had finished his soup and was lighting another of his colored cigarettes, a green one. His tone was hardly polite.

"Yes, of course he did."

"Then what happened?"

The door opened and Pacheco appeared, walked to the table, and took his seat at the head. "I'm not quite finished but I wanted to stop in for a moment." He rang a little bell by his plate and immediately the boy entered with a cup of soup.

"Dalakis has been telling us an endless story about a Yugoslav," complained Malgiolio. "Do you know anything further about what's going on?"

"The lieutenant didn't know much. He wasn't certain who

59

was firing at them. He said there was still fighting at the university and he had heard a story about the air force taking over a garrison in the southern part of the city. It was his idea that the air force had supplied weapons to the factory workers, but I'm not sure he had any real evidence of that."

As I had noticed Dalakis's hands, so I looked at Pacheco's, which were long and narrow and very pale, almost as if he powdered them. The nails were perfect and I thought they must require a lot of attention. I found myself thinking of Baudelaire, who, at the end of his life and despite his poverty and ill-health, reassured his mother that he still spent three hours of each day on his toilette.

"And we have to spend the night?" asked Malgiolio.

"Yes, unless you want to be shot. Those are the lieutenant's orders. But don't worry, you'll be well taken care of. Now, if you'll excuse me another moment. . . ." Pacheco got to his feet, patted his mouth with his napkin, and left the room, his rubber-soled shoes making slight squeaking noises on the marble floor.

I expect we felt ready to complain but, really, who was there to complain to? The three of us had been quite eager to visit Pacheco's and had driven through danger to get here. Others of our group had seemingly refused to go out on such a night. But we three had an additional hunger. Malgiolio had his envy and spite, Dalakis had his loneliness, and I my curiosity. I suppose we had other reasons as well, reasons not immediately clear, for certainly we had risked our lives, and who is foolish enough to do that just for curiosity or loneliness or envy?

"So finish your story," I said to Dalakis. "What happened to the writer?"

But Dalakis's feelings had been mildly bruised. "Why should I talk just so Malgiolio can make fun of me?"

"Oh, you know what he's like," I said. Malgiolio wrinkled

his nose, then took his butter knife and mockingly sawed it back and forth across his neck. I pretended not to notice. "Did the writer go to Belgrade?" I asked.

"Well, yes, but he was in prison for over eight years, then he still had trouble with the police and had to settle his affairs, but at last he obtained a visa and eventually he got to Belgrade. But it was all wrong. Nothing was as he expected."

"What do you mean?" asked Malgiolio, who was picking at his thumbnail with the tines of his fork.

"You see, he had gone there with his poems written in Serbo-Croatian and when he got to Belgrade it turned out not to be Serbo-Croatian after all."

"You mean, he didn't know Serbo-Croatian?" I asked.

"That's right. He would speak to people and even write down the words but no one could understand him."

"What language was he speaking?" asked Malgiolio.

"None, apparently. The Yugoslav had invented the whole thing. He must have been writing words on the wall just like the writer and when the writer asked the word for 'cat' the Yugoslav would say something like 'lork' and the writer would dutifully write it down."

"What about the city," I asked, "was that made up too?"

"You mean there's not a Belgrade?" asked Malgiolio.

"Of course there's a Belgrade," answered Dalakis, "but it was entirely different from what the writer expected. The Yugoslav had probably never been to Belgrade. The whole city was an invention. In fact, he probably wasn't even a Yugoslav. God knows what he was. But even worse was that the writer had all these poems written in fake Serbo-Croatian, which nobody could understand except the fake Yugoslav himself. Later, the writer tried to translate them into his own language, but it was no good. He felt that in this false language he had written some of his best work and now it was lost. The translations were pale shadows. What was beautiful in one language was ugly in the other."

"It's impossible," said Malgiolio crossly. "Nobody could invent a language like that."

"Did he leave?" I asked. "What happened?"

"He stayed in Belgrade. He'd left everything else behind and even though this Belgrade was far different from what he had hoped for, it was still the only place he had. So he stayed and earned his money by teaching language classes and tried to translate his poems. Eventually, he even learned Serbo-Croatian, but it was nothing like the language he had learned in prison."

"Carl, is that a true story?" I asked.

"I was told it was true."

"Why didn't he search out that Yugoslav and shoot him?" said Malgiolio, becoming increasingly irritated. "Think of the time he'd wasted, year after year, writing stuff that had no value."

"But it was the best work of his career," said Dalakis.

"So what?" answered Malgiolio. "Nobody could read it. Bah, it's a stupid story."

Dalakis seemed both apologetic and annoyed. "I thought Batterby would be interested. I mean about the writing."

"Why Yugoslavia, why Belgrade?" asked Malgiolio scornfully. "Why not here if you've got to make up a story?"

"But I didn't make it up," said Dalakis, getting angry.

It struck me that Belgrade was more romantic but obviously it could have been any city. I found myself trying to remember that joke about the twentieth-century condition: the marooned sailor sees the bottle bobbing through the waves. Inside the bottle is a sheet of paper. Is there a message? No, the paper is blank. Unfortunately, I'm terrible at telling jokes and anyway no one was in the mood for further stories. But why did Dalakis think I'd be interested? Certainly I didn't believe him any more than did Malgiolio.

The door opened and the boy and Señora Puccini entered. Really, it was impossible to see her without thinking of Pacheco's words. I stared at her pocket to see if she was still carrying the pistol, but her black skirt was so voluminous that I couldn't tell.

Malgiolio tried to get her attention. "The soup was superb," he said. He spoke almost flirtatiously, showing his little teeth as he smiled.

Señora Puccini nodded but made no comment as she and the boy gathered our dishes. After a moment she went out, then returned shortly wheeling a cart containing the fish course: a large cold salmon with crayfish, asparagus tips, artichoke hearts, and what seemed to be deviled eggs. The crayfish were riding piggyback on the salmon, while the deviled eggs, artichoke hearts, and asparagus formed a decorative border. There was more wine, a fine Corton-Charlemagne. The middle portion of the salmon had been skinned and its head and the length of its body were outlined with mayonnaise. The thought of eating this gastronomic phantasm seemed absurd, but after Señora Puccini had given us a chance to admire it she plunged a sharp knife into its body without hesitation.

As we were being served, Malgiolio said rather offhandedly, "By the way, Batterby, Schwab told me you were getting married. Is that true?"

For forty years Eric Schwab has been given to making excessive statements. He is something high up in the police and this evening, I guessed, he was off banging heads, or worse. I couldn't imagine why he should have said such a thing.

"I have no intention of getting married," I said, as I watched Señora Puccini scoop servings of salmon onto three green plates, which were themselves in the shapes of fish. "It wouldn't occur to me."

"He said he saw you with a tall, dark-haired woman at a restaurant downtown."

"That's true enough but I don't plan to marry her. I see many women." I suppose I don't see "many," but there are two or three I go out with occasionally.

"I wouldn't mind being in your shoes," said Malgiolio, "able to chase after anyone. That's the hard part of living with one's mother and being supported by one's wife. There must be many attractive women at the newspaper."

"A few, but they don't necessarily find me attractive."

"And how long's your wife been dead?"

It is typical of Malgiolio that he should find this an appropriate exchange of conversation to be indulged in while waiting for one's food, specifically fish. Besides, he asks me this question every six months, but the difficulty with tonight and there only being four of us was that everything became magnified. In any case, I told him what I had told him before. "Twenty years."

I took a small bite of cold salmon. How impossible it is to describe the taste of food. It's so ephemeral. Once I had a glass of Grand Marnier which had been bottled in the year of Napoleon's defeat at Waterloo. With it I had a glass of more or less contemporary Grand Marnier. Although the older stuff was incomparably superior, I could find no way to describe it. Smokier somehow, and thicker, and multi-layered with lots of little tastes. Well, I tasted it and it was gone. The salmon was like that, more like a color than a taste, a pale yellow, a light green, except that I am not allowed to eat eggs or mayonnaise and crayfish upset my stomach.

"How did your wife die again?" asked Malgiolio.

"It was a skiing accident. We were in Switzerland."

"Did you see it happen?"

"No, I was below. They brought her down on a sled. She was still alive but she died very shortly after. Her neck was broken. If she'd lived, she would have been paralyzed for life."

"You must have missed her terribly," said Dalakis, pausing with his fork raised halfway to his mouth.

"It's over now, fortunately."

As we were talking, Pacheco came into the room behind me. I hadn't heard him. He took his seat at the head of the table and looked at me. At first I thought he was going to speak but instead he poured himself a glass of wine and sipped it slowly.

"The soldiers are gone," he said at last. "The house is ours, at least for a while. How is the salmon?"

"Malgiolio can hardly get enough of it," I said. Then I realized I was upset with Malgiolio.

"It would please my cook," said Pacheco, "to know how you appreciate her hard work. May I ring for her?"

"By all means," said Dalakis. "She must be a wonderful woman."

Pacheco rang the little bell by his plate. "She's been with me for nearly twenty years."

"You must entertain often," I said.

"Dinners for other doctors and people at the hospital, and then I'm on the board of several organizations and the ballet, of course. I expect I give just enough dinners to keep her happy."

Señora Puccini appeared at the door. When talking to us, Pacheco seemed caring and affectionate; talking to her, he appeared to take on her coldness. "Could you tell Justine that the gentlemen are ready to pay their compliments?"

As we waited for the cook, Pacheco ate quickly, giving little attention to his food. Admittedly, it was approaching eight-thirty and he was probably hungry, but I couldn't help thinking that food didn't mean much to him, that he employed a great cook because it amused his vanity. The floor of the dining room was also marble and the outside wall was stone, so that our voices reverberated as in a well. As we waited for the cook, the room was mostly silent except for the echoing clatter of Pacheco's fork against his plate. Dalakis and Malgiolio tried to have a conversation about whom of our group they had seen in the past six months, but it turned out they had seen no one.

I occupied myself by studying the vases which held those huge bouquets of flowers. Each was perhaps two feet high and painted with brightly colored scenes. The one nearest me on my left showed a kind of wedding celebration with people in medieval dress dancing and drinking wine. But most were violent: men fighting in the street, someone sneaking into a darkened room with a dagger. It was only when I saw one with a man speaking to a human skull that I realized they were scenes from Shakespeare. More vases stood on small tables around the room and all told there must have been a dozen: the death of Caesar, Lear mad upon the heath, the murder of the children in the Tower.

After five minutes, there came a little tap on the door, which then opened and the boy entered, followed by the old woman I had seen in the kitchen. But what I had not realized before, yet what struck me now as immediately obvious, was that the woman was blind. Her eyes were solid gray. As she walked, the boy guided her by touching her elbow. She was quite stout and short with a round face and a great amount of white hair tied up in a bun on the back of her head. She wore a long black dress with a white apron. I thought she must be eighty, even though her face was relatively unlined. We were so surprised by her blindness that we stared without speaking. Pacheco introduced her as Madame Letendre and then told her our names. After each name, she gave a little bob of her head.

"Well, gentlemen," she said, "how do you enjoy my little dinner?" She had a high clear voice, more like a child's than an old woman's, and as she spoke, she didn't face us but stood turned away to the right.

We remained silent, still struck by her blindness. Then Dalakis spoke up. "It's the best dinner I've ever eaten. You must have been working for weeks. We are greatly honored."

Madame Letendre began to smile and her smile too was like a child's because of the way it lit up her face. "You don't think I'm too old or too clumsy?" There was a touch of the coquette in her voice.

"It is perfect," said Malgiolio, toasting her with his glass, which, of course, she couldn't see. "I'm only sorry that I'm not in the position to lure you away from your employer."

She began turning back and forth as if looking for something. "And what does the third guest think?" she asked. "Where is he?"

Surprised, I began to cough. "Excellent," I said. "It's really wonderful."

She curtsied somewhat stiffly and continued to smile, but the smile had taken on an ironic quality. "And where is Daniel?" she said to the boy. "Direct me to him."

"Are you going to ask what I think as well?" asked Pacheco, taking her hand and stroking it. He was smoking again and he waved the smoke away from her face.

"No, you too think it the best you've ever eaten. That's what you always say. Never mind your flattery. Grant me a favor instead."

"What is it?"

As I watched the old woman and her employer, I thought that Pacheco looked at her with more affection than I'd ever seen him show to anyone.

"I wish to go home before the dessert. Would that be possible? My dog is alone, she will be worried."

Pacheco continued to hold Madame Letendre's hand. "I'm sorry, Justine, but that's impossible. There's a curfew."

Justine drew her hand away. "But it is only a short distance. Who would bother an old woman? My dog has never been alone all night. What could happen in three blocks?"

"You could be killed. It's out of the question, Justine. There's plenty of room upstairs and Señora Puccini will see that you're made comfortable."

Madame Letendre continued to protest. It was clear she had no idea what was happening in the city except that it was something that might frighten her dog. Pacheco was gentle but firm. She would have to stay in the house. As I listened, I realized I had been wrong about what I'd seen in the kitchen. Señora Puccini could not have been showing the gun to the cook. She had been looking at it herself. It occurred to me to mention the gun but it didn't seem my place. Anyway, how do you work it into the conversation that you have seen the housekeeper with a small pistol?

After another minute of arguing, the cook reached out and touched a hand to Pacheco's cheek. "All right, Daniel, I'll do as you wish. But if my little dog is miserable, then you must comfort her. And now, gentlemen, you must excuse me. It was an honor to make your acquaintance." We, in our various ways, spoke of our pleasure in meeting her and smiled and tried to look agreeable as she turned and let the boy guide her from the room.

Once the door was completely closed, Malgiolio asked, "How can she possibly cook if she's blind?"

Pacheco sipped his wine and studied Malgiolio over the rim of the glass. "The boy helps her, as does Señora Puccini. And of course she knows her way perfectly around the kitchen."

"But how can she remember the recipes?" asked Dalakis, looking at each of us in turn. "It's astonishing."

"The same way that a singer memorizes songs. And then she combines and invents and extemporizes. In some ways, the blindness makes her even more sensitive. Her sense of taste becomes an exact instrument."

"How long has she been blind?" I asked.

"Twenty-five years. Before that she was the cook at the French embassy. When she went blind, they retired her. She had family in the south and that's where I found her, cooking simple meals for people who wouldn't care if they ate cat food. She was literally dying from having nothing to do. I hired her on the spot. The boy is her grandson. And there is another grandson who is my gardener."

"You seem to have brought all your servants from the south," said Malgiolio. "Is Señora Puccini from there as well?"

"Yes, but she wasn't a servant."

"But don't you consider her your servant now?"

"That's our arrangement. In the south, however, her family was quite well known. They were small landowners. She herself had an excellent education and even, at one point, a little money."

Dalakis made an unsettled noise, a kind of growling in his chest. "Why did you say you had ruined her?" he asked. Then he looked embarrassed, took off his glasses, and began cleaning them.

"Because that is what happened." Pacheco said this perfectly calmly.

"Was it money?"

"You mean did I bankrupt her?"

"Yes." Dalakis continued to fiddle with his glasses, blinking his eyes and still looking embarrassed.

Leaning forward, Pacheco stared at Dalakis. His expression

seemed derisive. "When a man is accused of ruining a woman, there is only one way in which the term is meant."

"What happened?" asked Malgiolio.

Pacheco turned his attention to Malgiolio, who had asked the question rather quickly. Instead of answering, Pacheco lit another cigarette. The smoke from the Gauloise mixed with the perfume from the flowers.

"Who was she?" asked Dalakis after a moment.

"She was the girl in the photograph, only prettier, if that is possible. A beautiful girl, eighteen years old, and I was a young surgeon, just twenty-eight."

"And you ruined her?" asked Malgiolio, again pressing him close. His white, puffy face was slightly puckered in the way a fish must look before it snatches the hook.

Pacheco held out the bottle to pour Malgiolio more wine. He looked at my glass but it was still full. "It's not as simple as that. I didn't just pick her up and break her. It wasn't whim or common desire. There have been many women I've taken without wanting, merely out of boredom or to satisfy an itch. This situation was different. First I had to develop a hunger. She had to fill my mind. You must realize, I had seen her often, sometimes walking in the parks with her aunt or fiancé, or in the tea shops or along the esplanade, even in church. I knew that her parents were dead. I knew she was just out of school. But I had no desire. She was simply another beautiful woman."

The door opened and Señora Puccini reentered, wheeling a cart to remove the dishes. Dalakis looked at her guiltily and perhaps I did as well. As she walked to the table, Pacheco said, "The gentlemen are curious about your life with me, Señora."

The woman appeared not to have heard. If she was ten years younger than Pacheco, then she was about half a dozen years younger than she appeared.

"Aren't you curious what I might tell them?"

Señora Puccini paused with several of the fish-shaped plates in her hands. "I expect you will tell them the truth," she said, not looking at him, "or what you think is the truth."

Glancing at her, I noticed she wore no adornments of any kind, no rings, not even a watch, and her face bore no sign of makeup. Her hair was shoulder length and held back with pins. Her black dress had a black leather belt with a dull tin buckle. Her black shoes were more like a man's than a woman's. Black shoes, black stockings, black dress—one imagined that even her underwear was black.

When she had left the room, Malgiolio asked, "How did your feelings change? How did you become hungry?" He tried to ask this nonchalantly, but one could hear his own hunger in his voice. You know those people who go to parties to collect anecdotes, hoping for the worst in order to amuse their friends later? Malgiolio was like that.

Why did Pacheco decide to tell the story? It may have been the oddness of the evening, as if it weren't really taking place within our lives. It may have been because there were so few of us and because of who we were. If more had been there, perhaps he would have kept silent. As for the three of us, we were unimportant. It didn't matter if we knew. Also we were tied to Pacheco, not just by friendship, but by envy or admiration, maybe even hatred, though none of us would admit hatred. But also I think he would have said nothing if it hadn't been for that brief interruption by Señora Puccini and her pretense that she was indifferent to all that happened; and I sensed that Pacheco liked to test this indifference, perhaps from amusement or anger or perhaps something else. Also, I'm sure the story was a great presence inside of him. Not that he needed to unburden himself; but rather, it formed a major part of his life and was something, I feel certain of it, that he'd never told another soul. As for us, we were eager listeners.

We were hungry for his story in the same way we had been hungry for the dinner at his house. Beyond that, we all had major failures in our lives and so were curious about the strife of others. Perhaps that's why he told us, because who cares more to hear about the battle than those who have been wounded?

The three of us waited. Dalakis clasped and unclasped his great hands. Malgiolio plucked a red flower from the nearest vase and idly removed its petals.

"It began at a concert," said Pacheco, lighting another cigarette, "one of those small chamber concerts during late spring where the musicians are made up of one's neighbors. This one was outside. They were playing Brahms's Clarinet quintet and then something by Mozart. The musicians sat in a white gazebo affair with a lot of gingerbread decoration and a little flag on top. The audience, which was rather small, was seated on lawn chairs in a rough semicircle. It was to have been a larger event but it had rained in the afternoon and there was a threat of rain to come and many people stayed away.

"I had a seat to the side by myself. I'm not even sure why I went. Restlessness, most likely. Just before the music began, Señora Puccini arrived with her aunt and a young man. They sat down slightly behind me and to my right—the girl, the aunt, then the young man. She wore a cream-colored dress, very low-cut. Even so, I scarcely noticed her. Of course, my mind registered a beautiful woman, but I suppose I thought her too young and too . . . well, too clean-looking, as if she weren't a woman but a doll. Then, after the music began, I reached down and happened to brush the back of my hand against her shoe. It was quite dark among the audience. There were torches or tapers around the perimeter, but otherwise we were in shadow. At first I wasn't sure what I had touched. I gently felt for it again and my fingers touched the heel, the sole, the narrowness of her foot."

"What's her first name?" I interrupted. "You can't call her Señora Puccini if you are discussing a girl of eighteen."

Pacheco tapped the ash from his Gauloise. "Antonia," he said, "but at that time I didn't know her name. I knew her by sight, but we hadn't been introduced. For that matter, we were never introduced, not properly at least."

"What happened with the foot?" asked Malgiolio, who with his precise sense of value had a way of keeping all conversations on track.

"As I say, I had touched it. Actually, I had squeezed it, trying to determine what it was. Once I realized it was a foot, I moved my hand quickly away. For a few moments I listened to the music. You know the piece, how the clarinet drifts and swirls above the strings like a spirit above the earth? Do you also know the Tolstoy story about the Beethoven sonata? Well, this occasion was nothing like Tolstoy's, yet there was passion in the music. In fact, there was a kind of passion all around us, for in the distance the lightning flickered and there was a faint rumble of thunder and the breeze felt full of distant rain. And then it occurred to me that although I had touched the foot and although she must have felt my hand, she had made no movement."

Pacheco paused to sip his wine.

"And what did that mean?" asked Dalakis.

"Perhaps nothing, but it roused my curiosity."

"What did you do?" I asked.

"I touched her foot again, very lightly with the back of my hand, then I let my hand brush against her ankle. My chair was such that I could sit in that position quite easily. And her chair was such that her foot and my hand were concealed by the folds of her skirt. In any case, I hardly made any further movement, just shifted my hand slightly so I could touch her ankle. She was wearing stockings, of course."

"Did she move?" asked Malgiolio.

"Not a whisker."

"Ha," said Malgiolio with a little explosion of breath, then he lit another of his colored cigarettes.

"I sat like that for some minutes, not turning or giving any sign that I knew she was there. The music played. Out of the corner of my eye, I could see the young man whom I had seen with her before. He was her fiancé—dark-haired and handsome and quite athletic. As I watched him, still without shifting my head, I slowly turned my hand and grasped the girl's calf just above her ankle. It was then that I became aware of her breathing. Absurd, don't you think? A young surgeon taking advantage of a girl at an outdoor concert?

"But there was an intensity both within me and, or so I guessed from her breathing, within her as well. I massaged her calf, took my hand away, then massaged it again. She didn't move, didn't move forward, didn't move back. From the gardens, the wind blew the smell of lilac. I slipped my hand upward to the underside of her knee and thigh. Did her breathing grow louder? Perhaps not, but I could sense her behind me, almost feel her quivering. As I describe it, I realize that it seems that just a few minutes went by, but actually it was fifteen or twenty. But it was like nothing, so intent was I on the touching of her leg in its silk stocking. I was scarcely even aware of the music, just of a swirl of notes, and the rich smell of the blossoms which the wind blew to my face. As I touched the underside of her thigh, I massaged the muscle, squeezing and releasing it, while slowly I continued to thrust my hand further along her leg. She didn't move although I could feel the constant shiver of her muscles. The farther I reached, the more contorted became my arm behind me. I wasn't worried about anyone seeing. There was no one on the other side, and in that darkness I doubt anything would have been visible. At last I stretched my arm as far as I could and with the tips of my fingers I touched the silk of her underwear between her legs, but just barely, just a slight flickering of my fingers."

He fell silent. I glanced at Dalakis, who was making deep lines on the tablecloth with his thumbnail.

"And she didn't move?" insisted Malgiolio.

"Neither forward nor back. My arm by this time was quite uncomfortable. I tried to move it farther without actually tipping in my chair, but another inch and I would have landed in her lap. I had also begun to worry that someone might notice her breathing, which seemed to mix with the strings and clarinet as if it were part of the music itself. And I was struck that she refused to move forward to let me increase her pleasure, that I could only thrum my fingers on the silk above her vagina."

Dalakis sat back in his chair so hard that it creaked dangerously. "Didn't it strike you that she was a child?"

"She had stopped being a child many years before. I could feel her, feel the heat and her wetness."

"What happened next?" asked Malgiolio. There was something repulsive about his eagerness. One imagined his erection.

"Nothing. The music came to an end. I moved my hand and more lanterns were lit. The girl, her aunt, and the young man left during the interval."

"Did she make any sign to you?" I asked.

"None. Perhaps she was a little red in the face. Clearly, she was embarrassed and never once turned in my direction. I, of course, stared at her constantly. How could I not? I had become hungry."

As Pacheco said these words, the room went dark. It was as if I had been struck blind. Our chairs scraped on the marble floor and a fork or some utensil fell, making a clattering which echoed through the room.

"How irritating," said Malgiolio, as the spark of his cigarette

75

moved impatiently through the air. "They've blown a trans-former somewhere."

This was how the radical left often made itself felt, blowing up a generator or overhead power line. Sometimes the lights would be out a few minutes, sometimes for most of the night.

I heard a clinking noise as Pacheco's glass touched his plate. "We'll have light in a minute," he said.

It could hardly have been more than that when the door opened and brilliant light poured in from the hall and moved toward us. It was Señora Puccini. She was carrying two large candelabra held out in front of her, each with at least a dozen candles. Her middle-aged face seemed brilliant and beautiful, like a star within its miniature solar system. I couldn't look at her without thinking of Pacheco's story and it seemed I could almost hear the clarinet from the Brahms quintet swishing through the darkened room like a length of rope being swirled around and around above our heads.

Chapter Three

The meat course was a roast saddle of veal, a great brown log of a thing, half of which rose off its silver platter on the snapped remnants of ten flimsy ribs like a severely mutated praying mantis. Malgiolio ate steadily, his small hands and teeth aspiring to the mechanical, a robot whose sole purpose was the ingestion of organic matter. Yet at the end of thirty minutes, he'd hardly bruised that spaniel-sized slab of meat. Dalakis took a slightly greater than normal amount for the average person, the excess being destined not for his belly but for his brown suit, which was soon flecked with escaped fragments of food. Pacheco ate quickly and without apparent interest. I took two or three bites just to feel myself part of the occasion. With the veal came a vegetable mixture consisting of peas, chestnuts, and something I couldn't recognize. The candlelight reflected off the silver platter making the veal sparkle like the promise of resurrection.

But while the food remained marvelous, our attention had shifted elsewhere. Certainly I didn't announce to myself that I was now more interested in this relationship between Pacheco and his housekeeper, but I was aware that some additional thing was competing for my attention and at first I wasn't sure what it was. Then I realized. Partly it was the discrepancy. On one hand was the description of Antonia Puccini as she had been twenty years before and on the other was the Señora Puccini who kept bringing us mountains of food without seeming aware that we were in the room. I felt that if I collapsed at her feet, she would step over me without once looking down.

Beyond that, the evening was too peculiar to let me concentrate on my food to the exclusion of all else, although that would have been unlikely in any case. I admired the food as a piece of theater more than as something to eat. Malgiolio, I think, would have kept eating in an earthquake. Perhaps Dalakis as well. But I am easily distracted. The lights, for instance, never came back on and soon we were surrounded by half a dozen great candelabra which threw light and shadow over our plates, the table, and our faces as if paralleling the emotions going on underneath. Then there was the trouble in the city. Occasionally we heard sirens, even gunfire, although the stone walls of the dining room almost completely excluded the outside world. Also, the fact we were so few was a constant reminder of the disequilibrium of our times, that we were only one quarter of our usual number with no sense of the future, how we would get home, or what we would find when we got there.

Additionally, we were curious. Pacheco said how he had developed a hunger for this girl and, as he talked about that evening at the concert, we developed a hunger as well. All of us responded differently. Dalakis, for instance, was quite disapproving. Yet he knew well enough what Pacheco was like. His own wife, the woman from whom he had been separated for seventeen years, had once been Pacheco's lover and presumably she had told him stories. At least Pacheco never tried to appear better than he was. If he wanted something, he pursued it. Dalakis's wife had been only sixteen when she had taken up with Pacheco, who was perhaps eighteen at the time. Her parents tried to stop them from meeting but after a month or so Pacheco and the girl just ran away. Three months later she returned home without Pacheco or any explanation. Of course, the parents wanted no part of her. She went to live with an aunt or older cousin, I forget which, and about two years after that she married Dalakis. It was doomed from the start, one might say.

Malgiolio, on the other hand, was eager for the story, and throughout the meat course he kept pressing Pacheco to say more. Pacheco would smile and change the subject but I didn't have the sense he was refusing to tell, just that he was teasing Malgiolio. Indeed, I thought he wanted to tell his story just as much as Malgiolio wanted to hear it. Malgiolio's interest was partly prurient and partly because he likes to collect bad marks against people. He is a man who has thrown away his life, who is manifestly imperfect, and whose main ambition in middle age is to seek out imperfections in others. Of course he thinks everyone reaches for the biggest piece of cake and would steal from the church poorbox if they could be sure not to be caught. For him to believe that men are not motivated by selfishness, greed, and spite would, I think, make his personal failure more difficult to bear.

I hardly know why we put up with him except that in his cynicism he's extremely hard to deceive. Oddly enough he was once a poet. True, he wasn't a good poet, but he attacked his art passionately, and in his youth, much like Rimbaud, he hoped to embrace the unknown through a total derangement of the senses. You know that letter of Rimbaud's where he says that in order to become a seer and a poet he has been degrading himself "*le plus possible*"? That was also Malgiolio, and he had terrible experiences—raped in jail when he was

79

seventeen, thrown out of the army for theft—and gradually whatever ability or interest he had in poetry just slipped away. His last poems, again like Rimbaud's, were completely incomprehensible; but while Rimbaud's were obscure, Malgiolio's were just gibberish, an accumulation of words without meaning. Sometimes, however, I feel he really did become a seer, but instead of using his ability as a poet it turned him against poetry and he took that job at the hotel, rising in time to become assistant manager before quitting when he won the lottery. So perhaps we put up with him as a failure and a victim, which flatters our magnanimity. Also, to argue against him is often to argue in favor of goodness, altruism, and virtue; and even if the arguer, like myself, doesn't quite believe in those things, defending them against Malgiolio makes them seem true for a while.

And then there was my own interest in Pacheco's story. Why do I find my feelings so difficult to describe? I have always wanted to be a writer, a novelist, but instead I am a journalist. As a matter of fact, I'm not a very good journalist. I tend to be shy and dislike asking people embarrassing questions. So I'm a book reviewer. But I've spent a lot of time thinking about the sort of novels I want to write and what they would be about and how I want them to affect people. In truth, I doubt that I have much imagination, and sometimes I think the effort needed to invent a plot is beyond me. Oh, I could make up a simple enough plot and fill my book with believable characters, but the trouble with being a book reviewer, as well as being a man of taste, as I tell myself, is that even though I can't write great literature, I can recognize it. Consequently, I couldn't stand to write and publish a book, then watch it be pushed aside as trivial. Better to remain silent.

But always I'm keeping an eye out for potential subjects and if a good enough story fell into my lap, then I believe I would begin to write, or at least take notes. As Pacheco spoke of his first encounter with Antonia Puccini, I found myself becoming alert, as if hearing bits of a history that I might use. And so I too was taken up and pressed Pacheco to tell more.

Furthermore, I was interested because Pacheco himself has always interested me. He is someone who makes his own rules and ignores the rules of the world around him. Well, partly we admire that and partly we wish to see him caught. For if he gets away with it and is not punished, then we become fools for pursuing our own little lives and never taking chances. Is any of this true? Am I again deceiving myself? At the moment, however, let it suffice that I thought these to be the sources of my interest.

But perhaps I am saying too much too quickly. We were eating in a large, echo-ridden room lit by candlelight; we had heard part of a peculiar story and wanted to hear more. I didn't say to myself, Aha, here is the story for my novel. But right away I found myself attentive; my curiosity was aroused. Yet even as I put down these words, I question myself. Who knows what all my reasons were or if I will discover them myself? Although I loved Pacheco, I was also one of those waiting for his punishment. No, no, not waiting. Perhaps just listening with half an ear, believing it something that would inevitably come.

As I say, Pacheco seemed to want to tell his story but he also appeared to be waiting. Beyond that, he seemed to dislike Malgiolio's pressure. Malgiolio is the sort of person who, if he says the meat has too much salt, you think it has too little. If he says the room is too hot, then you think it cold. You should see his hands, which are small and white with thick fingers, hands which appear to have grown without the benefit of sunlight, more like tubers than hands. And so I believed that a portion of Pacheco's hesitation was a result of Malgiolio's eagerness. But in retrospect, I think he was also waiting for a sign from Señora Puccini. Perhaps "sign" is too strong a word. But certainly she knew we had been discussing her and I think Pacheco wanted to see some response, some wrinkle in the wall of her indifference.

When Pacheco at last began his story, it was ostensibly in response to questions asked by Dalakis: "Why couldn't you have forgotten her? Why couldn't you have left her alone?" Señora Puccini entered the dining room as Dalakis was still speaking, which made him look embarrassed and lower his head.

Another red wine had come with the veal, I forget what kind, and as Pacheco listened to Dalakis, he tilted his half empty glass, seeing how close the wine could approach the brim without sloshing onto the white tablecloth. Then he abruptly drank off the rest of the glass and sat back in his chair. "Can't you understand, I couldn't forget because the hunger was already within me. I would think of how my fingers had brushed that moist silk and everything else would be pushed from my mind."

And there she was as he spoke—a middle-aged woman in a black dress leaning over the table, replacing the gravy boat with another, picking a yellow blossom off the tablecloth, filling Pacheco's glass with more wine. We all looked at her but it was as if she were alone in the room.

"I slept very little that night," Pacheco continued. "I kept thinking of the girl, seeing her face and dark hair. I indulged in the most extreme sexual fantasies. I would remember how I had actually felt her quivering, yet how she had refused to move either toward me or away."

As Pacheco said these words, Señora Puccini put a few dishes on the cart and wheeled them from the room. The wheels squeaked and the dishes sparkled in the light of fifty candles.

When she closed the door, Pacheco paused, and it was here, I think, that he decided to continue his story, to tell everything, for a whole variety of reasons, to tantalize poor Malgiolio, to upset Dalakis, and perhaps even to give me material for a fiction. He began in a rush, leaning forward with his hands on the edge of the table.

"In the morning there was no question but that I had to locate this girl and have her, over-sweep her if you will. Hunger becomes too trivial a word. I wanted to devour her. I expect this strikes you as excessive, so I will describe it as clinically as possible. Of course, I had desired other women and pursued them with a fair amount of success, but this girl, this Puccini creature, occupied my mind as few had done in the past. I say I wanted to over-sweep her; in fact, I was amazed at having been myself over-swept, at having lost myself in my own desire. It seemed as if my self, my ego if you will, had been pushed aside and all that remained was this extreme sexual tension which left me with a rapid heartbeat and a shortness of breath. Well, this was a new experience, and to some degree I was infatuated with the experience itself.

"Although I didn't know the girl, I had seen her fairly often and I knew where I could learn more about her. My plan was simple: discover her name and address, then find her and confront her. I had enough confidence in my persuasive skills to believe that if I could speak to her, then I would ultimately have my way with her."

"But what if she didn't want you?" interrupted Dalakis, leaning toward Pacheco and bumping me in the process. His tie, I noticed, lay across the gravy in his plate.

"But she did want me," said Pacheco, "or at least she too had felt passion and perhaps even desire. She hadn't pulled away, she hadn't actually said no.

"I had a friend, a lawyer in town, who I believed could give me further information about the girl. He was a bachelor like myself and often we had been interested in the same women. Oddly enough, such competition has never bothered me as long as I get what I want. What does it matter who else has had the woman as well? In any case, I recalled that several times when I had seen Antonia, my lawyer friend had also been in attendance. His nickname was Paco and his business consisted of looking after the estates of people who had little or no interest in handling their own affairs. In this business Paco did very well.

"The morning after the concert I was at the door of his office when he arrived at ten. I'm sure I had patients to see but I simply forgot about them. Paco was a portly fellow with a fondness for blue suits and ivory-handled walking sticks. He's dead now, unfortunately—a boating accident some time after I left the south. He had thick black hair and rosy cheeks that made him look like a schoolboy. On the little finger of his left hand, he always wore a ruby ring.

"He invited me in, obviously curious about what I wanted at such an hour. I tried to appear nonchalant and had worked up a little story about needing his advice about investments. But once in his office, I couldn't be bothered with pretense and I asked him directly about the girl, saying I had seen her at the concert the previous night.

"I expected him to laugh, since even in the midst of my infatuation it struck me as absurd. But Paco took it quite seriously. He knew of course what I wanted and he dealt with the problem as an engineer might deal with the problem of building a bridge. He had an old-fashioned office, meant to soothe his rich and elderly clients, with a lot of brass and leather, ceiling fans, dark woodwork, and shelf after shelf of leather-bound law books, which he never opened. He poured me a small sherry and told me the girl's name was Antonia Puccini, that her parents were deceased, that she lived with her aunt at such and such an address, that she taught at a local primary school and had been engaged to a young man, a second cousin, for the past year and had been inseparable from him for several years previously. He also told me that she had no money. Although the aunt appeared wealthy, she had inherited the money from her husband and it would go back to his estate after she was dead. This young man, this second cousin, also had very little money but he had a good position in the city government, worked hard, was ambitious, and everyone predicted a great future for him.

"As Paco told me this he spoke with great sympathy and concern, as if I were about do something which would cause me harm. Yet, in all that he said there were no words inserted to dissuade me from my attempt. He told me the names of Antonia's friends, what families she knew, where she was likely to be found, what sort of films and books she liked. For a full hour, Paco described her life to me. How she liked this restaurant or liked to walk along the esplanade in the evening. I listened without interrupting. At last he said, 'For a long time I was infatuated with her. Let me tell you, I had absolutely no success. I did everything I could imagine but nothing made the least dent in her defenses. Admittedly, my ways are not yours, but if I were you I would try to put her out of my mind.'

" 'So you don't think I can succeed?' I asked.

" 'She's very much in love with her fiancé. As long as he is there, you will have trouble.'

" 'And this is why you are warning me?' I asked. 'Because of her young man?'

" 'Not just that,' Paco answered. 'She never gave me the slightest encouragement and I even had many other women during this period. Despite this, it took me many months to free myself of desire, to be able to push the thought of her from my mind.'

" 'Is she so special?' I asked.

" 'What do they say? There's no woman so special as the one you can't have? Maybe it's no more than that. But there's something else, a kind of fire. I feel foolish talking about it. She is like a tensed muscle and she is passionate. But how she is exactly, I do not know, since I was unsuccessful. In any case, I was miserable for a long time, and so I warn you only for that reason.'

"Naturally, even as he warned me, I had no doubt about my inevitable success, and so his warning had little effect. It was only later that I thought of it. Actually, given the way she had let me touch her, I was certain I only had to announce myself and she would give herself to me."

As Pacheco spoke these last sentences, Señora Puccini reentered the dining room with the cook's grandson and began clearing the table. I studied her, looking for some response. Although thin, she gave the impression of being a big woman. She was at least my height, only two inches under six feet, and large-breasted, with broad shoulders and solid hips. Certainly she was imposing, both physically and perhaps even in her personality. She paid no attention to Pacheco. Could she be used to his story? And I imagined him repeating it over the years to hundreds of dinner guests. But no, I was sure that this was the first time he had told it. Most likely, had he ever mentioned it to anyone before, then I would have heard rumors already.

As Señora Puccini again began to leave the dining room, Pacheco summoned her over to his chair. She stood slightly behind him and he spoke without turning. "Are you looking out for Justine?"

"She's in the kitchen."

"Be careful she doesn't try to leave the house." Señora Puccini didn't answer, and after a moment Pacheco raised his head and spoke again, still without looking at her. "Do you understand me?"

"Or course," said the woman. Then she continued out of the room.

As the boy started to follow her, Pacheco called to him. "Juan, go up to the roof and see what the city looks like. Can you do that?"

Juan seemed only too glad to get away from his other duties. Grinning broadly, he hurried to the door, skating on the marble as he turned the corner. We sat for a moment sipping our wine. I considered what Pacheco had felt for the young Antonia Puccini and it made me recall my feelings for my young wife and how vacant I had felt after she was gone.

Malgiolio was the first to speak. He had spilled some wine on the tablecloth and I wondered if he was getting a little drunk. "So what happened after you left the lawyer's office? Did the girl topple into your arms?"

Pacheco put one elbow on the arm of his chair, then rested his chin in his open hand and looked down at the tablecloth. Just when I was sure he wouldn't say anything, that he wanted to frustrate Malgiolio, he resumed his story.

"I now knew where she worked, a primary school in one of the wealthy suburbs. I drove there and sat in my car and waited. Several hours went by. The school let out, the children left, then the teachers left. I continued to watch the building. As I was just about to give up, Antonia Puccini came down the front steps. It was a warm day. She was wearing a blue dress and white jacket. She carried several books under her arm. How can I describe her? You're the writer, Batterby. You've seen her picture. Tall and beautifully proportioned, she moved with great dignity and sense of purpose, looking neither left nor right. I got out of my car and hurried after her. When she heard me behind her, she turned with an expression of expectation and pleasure. Yet when she saw who it was her face changed. Rather, it closed, because I had no idea what she was thinking. But obviously she thought I was someone else and just as obviously I knew she had recognized me from the night before.

"She waited for me and I asked if I could walk with her. She nodded but didn't speak, then she turned and continued walking. I walked beside her. 'Did you enjoy the music last night?' I asked. Again she nodded, turning slightly toward me but not looking at me. The sidewalk was narrow and occasionally my arm brushed against hers. I had a huge desire to put my arm around her, but I did nothing. For a moment, I didn't know what to say. All the opening gestures of inviting her for coffee or to dinner seemed inappropriate. Without speaking a word, we had gone past that part of a relationship. At last I decided to tell her what I felt. 'I want you,' I told her, 'I want to make love to you.' She made no response, simply kept walking, neither faster nor slower. She didn't turn, didn't seem nervous; she simply didn't react. Well, that's not entirely true; as I had felt her quiver the night before, so I sensed a similar quiver as I walked beside her. I saw and heard nothing, but there was a slight vibration as when a finger lightly touches a string. 'Did you hear me?' I asked.

" 'I heard you,' she answered, but she neither slowed nor looked at me. 'I want to make love with you,' I said, 'and I know you desire it as well. I want to undress you and lie with you and touch you with my tongue.' Again she didn't respond. 'Did you hear me?' I asked. There was a slight hesitation, then she said, 'Yes, I heard you.'

"I took her arm, quite gently. 'Come with me now,' I said. She pulled her arm free and kept walking. I continued beside her, but now I touched her, touched her arm, her cheek, touched her hair. 'Do you remember how I caressed you last night?' I said, 'I want to caress you again. I want you in my mouth. I want to be inside you.' She didn't answer and after a moment I asked, 'Did you hear me?' 'Yes, I heard you,' she answered. 'Then come with me,' I said. 'No,' she said, 'I don't want to.' Yet even as she spoke she was letting me touch her face and hair. As we walked, I reached out and lightly touched the side of her breast, stroking it. She neither pulled away nor moved toward me, she just kept walking. 'I want to kiss you,' I told her. Again she didn't respond and again I asked if she had heard me and she said that she had. I stepped in front of her, but walked backward so she would have to face me but wouldn't have to stop. She had large full lips, as moist as fruit. She stared into my face as one might stare at a wall. Yet I could still feel that slight vibration, like the ripples on water when you drop a pebble into a pond. Then I slowed and moved my face toward hers. For the briefest instant, she continued to come toward me, then she turned away and raised a hand between my mouth and hers.

"At that instant we both heard a motorcycle and she turned with that expression of anticipation and pleasure with which she had first greeted me. It was her young man. He drew up beside us on a large black Bultaco and she climbed on the back. He was a friendly fellow and nodded to me pleasantly. Then he kissed her and I remember thinking how that was my kiss, how that kiss belonged to me. Then they roared off. Neither, of course looked back."

I tried to remember what Pacheco had been like at twenty-eight—tall, thin, handsome, almost feminine with long eye-lashes and catlike eyes, thick black hair combed straight back over his head just as he combed it now, although now it was gray. While Pacheco was still in medical school, a few of us young men would go to dances together. Usually, they were dances where we knew no one and where we went to meet girls. Pacheco and Schwab had a sort of game they played for money. Schwab would choose a woman, then he and Pacheco would bet on how long it would take Pacheco to convince her to leave with him. Certainly many times Pacheco lost but mostly he didn't and once he convinced a stunningly beautiful blond girl to leave in under two minutes. Later Schwab would try his own luck with these girls but almost always without success. The rest of us, needless to say, would burn with envy. We were normal, run-of-the-mill young men, with two left feet, a stuttering approach, and no confidence. To us it seemed these dances were held entirely for Pacheco's benefit, just to enable him to make a selection. Indeed, often he would come back and leave minutes later with a second girl, while those of us still building our nerve to ask someone to dance would stare at his first conquest and observe her rumpled gown, mussed hair, smudged lipstick, and we would burn.

We might have felt better about these evenings if Pacheco had discussed his conquests, but he rarely spoke of them. The rest of us boasted of our successes, if we were lucky enough to have any, and I remember a complicated system of hand signals we used in school to signify that we had touched a thigh, a breast, or even a vagina the night before. In particular I remember one Friday evening at a downtown café with Schwab parading among us waving two fingers, ordering us to sniff them and didn't they smell like "cherry juice," although who among us could have recognized the smell? But I remember another night when Schwab was poking fun at Pacheco, saying he certainly hadn't had his way with some young lady whom Schwab knew to be steadfastly virtuous. Pacheco made no answer, but continued to smile as Schwab's joking grew more extreme and at last turned to mockery, as if Pacheco had done no more than guide the young woman to the ladies' room, then waited timorously outside. We felt certain that Pacheco would grow angry at such taunting, but instead he reached into his pocket, drew forth a pair of very small red silk panties, and tossed them to Schwab. "Since you know the girl so well," he said, "perhaps you'll return these to her." Several of us swore they didn't belong to the girl, but how could we prove it? Schwab, if not convinced, was silenced, and none of us had the courage to go to the girl and confront her with the panties. I never did learn what happened to them.

As we waited for Pacheco to continue his story, the cook's grandson, Juan, reentered the room, hurried to Pacheco, and whispered something. With us, the boy was nervous and shy, but with Pacheco he was like a pup, unable to stand still and grinning and jerking his hands. I didn't hear what he said. Malgiolio leaned across the tablecloth to listen as well. Dalakis had discovered the cat hairs on his brown suit and was picking them off, making a little gray pile next to his plate.

Pacheco knitted his brow as he bent toward the boy. After a moment he pushed back his chair and stood up. "Perhaps you'd like to see what our city looks like before we have the next course." He didn't allow us a chance to answer but took one of the candelabra and walked from the room. We followed with much scraping of our chairs and a clattering of feet across the marble floor.

Pacheco led us through the great hall, then up the staircase. The soldiers were gone and we were again alone in the house. The candles sent our shadows skittering over the walls as if there really were sixteen of us, or the ghosts of sixteen. Our footsteps on the marble floor seemed hasty and imprecise. Dalakis's shoes squeaked. Reaching the second floor, we turned right down a long corridor. On the walls were pieces of armor and medieval weapons; helmets, breastplates, shields, lances and halberds, axes and broadswords. I hadn't known that Pacheco had such interests. The armor was highly polished and sparkled as we passed.

At the end of the corridor we went up another flight of stairs to what were probably the servants' quarters: a narrow hall with a low ceiling and a series of doorways, all closed. Halfway along the hall a small ladder had been pulled down from a trap door in the roof. Pacheco stopped, set the candelabrum on the floor, then ascended the ladder. Looking up into the dark, I could see stars. Malgiolio went up second, then Dalakis. As I waited my turn, I glanced around the hall. There was nothing on the white walls, no decoration, nothing to relieve the blankness. Under one of the doors I saw a light and assumed this was where Señora Puccini had her rooms, here at the top of the house. Then I followed Dalakis up the ladder.

When I reached the roof, Pacheco and the others were on the far side looking west over the city. We were higher than the surrounding houses and staring out I could see a number of fires, their flames leaping into the dark. Up here the sounds of gunfire, sirens, even explosions were louder and more immediate. Several fires, probably three or four buildings, blazed over by the university. We stood at the low wall at the roof's edge, trying to see across that distance and understand what was happening there. Searchlights crisscrossed the sky, picking out great plumes of smoke like black flowers blossoming in the night. We were in the midst of great change, yet how our lives might be affected we had no idea. I almost envied Malgiolio for seeing it so simplistically, that whatever happened it would mean more jobs and opportunities. Dalakis, on the other hand, as a civil servant, could be out on the street, while Pacheco as a surgeon would have more work than he could handle. As for me, a book reviewer, I could only hope that people would continue to read and take part in their culture. But the change could be far more radical than just changing our jobs. The whole complexion of our city might change, the whole idea of tolerance, forgiveness, and responsibility might be forever altered.

"It's awful," said Dalakis. His voice was choked and I realized he was crying. "They're destroying each other."

I don't know who "they" were, but Dalakis's emotion didn't surprise me as much as Malgiolio's. "I have a cousin who lives over there," he said, "right by that big fire by the university. That could be his house." Then he pointed at a fire in another direction. "And there too, I know people who live there as well! They might be dead! And us, how long will we be safe?"

Apart from an uncle in another country, I have no one who is still living. Otherwise I might have been upset as well. Of course I was troubled, even nervous, but the question of who was battling whom was not as important to me as that the quotidian operation of the city be returned to normal as soon as possible. As a matter of fact, looking out from Pacheco's roof, I didn't feel as if this were my city at all, as if I were just a visitor here. But perhaps that is what I often feel and it is the curse of the observer, as if I were no more than a tourist in my own life.

We stood for some more minutes without speaking. Below us the tops of the plane trees blew back and forth in a wind that bore the smell of smoke. The houses mostly had their shutters closed but I could see candles in some of the back yards. The streets were empty and the city itself, except for the fires, was dark—a few headlights from the highway, army trucks and jeeps; several more searchlights downtown by the government center. From somewhere I heard the whop-whop of a helicopter.

After another moment, Pacheco turned around and leaned back against the wall. I thought he would say something about what was happening in the city, but when he spoke it was again about Señora Puccini.

"Sometimes you pursue a woman," he said, "make love to a woman, just to find yourself again, to be reborn within your own mind, so that it's like making love to yourself. I'm not talking of masturbation but rather of how a whole complex sense of yourself, long forgotten, can rise up within you."

Malgiolio made a snorting noise. He was still staring out at the city. "You'd have trouble selling that to the sex magazines," he said.

"I have no interest in such magazines. I'm talking about how the idea of a woman, her face, her body, your desire for her, your imagining and fantasies about her, how all that can fill the mind like liquid can fill a glass, and how your own sense of yourself, your other interests and ambitions and desires, how even the ego can be diminished and pushed aside. It is like a sickness during which everything disappears except this huge image of the desired creature which is exhausting, irritating, even hateful, so that at last you make love to her simply to get that thing out of your head. Afterward there is a moment while you are still lying with her, still inside her, when your life and concerns come creeping back. You think about what you will do tomorrow and what you will eat and what clothes you will wear. You might think about a book you are reading or a movie or a piece of music. You address the small problems of your life and their solutions seem easy. All is new and different and you are in a sense reborn."

"How long does that last?" I asked. I couldn't see Pacheco's face. He was just a gray shape against the black sprawl of the city.

"Perhaps two or three days, perhaps five or ten minutes. Then it begins again. But there is a point when I sometimes think I am engaged in this pursuit of lovemaking simply to recover myself, to locate myself again. Consequently, if the woman denies me and my desire continues to increase, then my sense of self, my life, my self-respect—all this disappears to be replaced by this double figure, like a pair of entwined

94

snakes, the image of the woman coupled with my desire. And if there's no outlet, then it all grows more desperate, more dangerous."

"Is this a justification?" asked Dalakis with as much sarcasm as he could muster.

"Justification? Why should I bother? I am simply telling a story. You know, there was a General de Caulaincourt with Napoleon, he was in charge of all the horses and transport, and in his memoirs he describes how Napoleon would completely demean himself to get what he wanted. That if he wanted you to do something, he would put all his energy and attention into making it happen. And he had no shame. He would cajole, threaten, flatter, lie. The general said that Napoleon had a little gesture. He would reach up and lightly take hold of your earlobe and give it a little tug and so seduce you to his will. And once you said yes, it was as if he had been freed from a great burden and shortly he would forget you and go on with his life and his empire. I have been that way only with women. Clearly Napoleon's ambitions were greater than mine."

"What about your success as a surgeon?" asked Dalakis. "That must have taken effort and desire."

Pacheco laughed and began to walk back across the roof to the ladder. "That has always been easy for me, mostly because I care little about it. It is where I am mechanical and have no feelings, where I behave precisely. For me it is like listening to Bach—emotion governed by mathematics. You cannot imagine what a relief it is after a night of emotional and sexual turmoil to remove someone's gall bladder. That's why I'm good at it. It's what I do in order to relax."

He descended the ladder and we followed him. One of the doors was open in the narrow hallway and as we approached it I saw Señora Puccini framed by candlelight. Then the door closed and we continued to the stairs.

"Is this where your housekeeper lives?" I asked.

"No, she has several rooms on the other side of the garden. You must come back when we have electricity and I will show you the entire house."

I decided that Señora Puccini must have been preparing rooms for the cook and her grandson and thought no more about it. Mostly my mind was occupied by Pacheco and by whatever was happening outside in the city. As for myself, it was as if I were absent. All my concerns were with things away from my life, as in one of those dreams where you are not part of the story but a camera drifting above the story. I looked ahead at the retreating backs of Malgiolio and Dalakis and wondered briefly what they were feeling, but I had no desire to talk to them. We passed by the medieval armor, which flashed and threw back our reflections. I saw myself, bloated and distant in my dark suit, pass across the surface of a steel breastplate. Then we descended the great staircase. Candles were burning in the four niches occupied by the Roman busts. The flickering shadows made the four bald men with their bruised faces seem alive and attentive. In the dining room we discovered that at each place setting was a raspberry sorbet in a tulip-shaped glass. We took our seats. The room was cold and silent. Suddenly I felt a wave of loneliness sweep over me, although why it should happen I had no idea. I thought of women I had known, I thought of my wife. It wasn't so much loneliness as a sense of being alone, that I would pass out of the world without even a little pop. I hadn't grieved for my wife in nearly a dozen years but at that moment I saw her before me and even imagined her quick laugh. How much simpler the world would be if we had no need of other people.

Malgiolio made short work of his sorbet, then ate mine as well when he saw I wasn't tempted. After he was done, he belched under his napkin and pushed away his glass. He looked very pleased with himself and took out another of his colored cigarettes, a red one this time. "So, Pacheco, what happened? Did you wait for this girl every day after school? Did you offer to carry her books? I'm not sure I believe this business about her letting you touch her breast but I'll accept it for the time being. What did you do next?"

But Pacheco wasn't ready to continue. His mood had changed. He seemed impatient, not just with Malgiolio but with us all. "What do you do for women, Malgiolio? Find servant girls, splurge on the occasional whore? I once had a poor friend whose wife had gone blind, and bit by bit he traded her pretty dresses for the favors of a woman down the street. Then he traded his own clothes, until finally he and his wife were down to one dress and one suit, which the man cleaned and brushed and mended. Then he traded his tables and chairs, pots and pans, until finally he was down to a bed, one straight chair, one table, one bowl, one spoon, and his dreams. His wife knew what he was up to and begged him not to sell the bed. He said he wouldn't but after a while, he sold that too. Every now and then I'd drop by his little apartment. There in the corner would be the piles of newspaper that did duty as their conjugal couch."

"What happened to him?" asked Dalakis, concerned.

"Oh, he died like everyone else and his wife went to live with a niece. By now she's probably dead as well. But answer me, Malgiolio, what do you do for fun? Who are the ladies who console you?"

Malgiolio drank his wine and refused to answer. I was surprised at Pacheco for needling him, especially since he mostly appeared indifferent to what any of us thought, as if none of us could touch him with our words. And while we might all have scorn for Malgiolio, Pacheco had never shown it, had always treated him with courtesy and deference. When Malgiolio was rich and throwing around money, he had bragged about his expensive women, but presumably they had disappeared when the money ran out. As an adolescent he had been like the rest of us, clumsy and yearning. I guessed he had a mistress somewhere, if only because he needed one to maintain his self-respect.

"Yes, I went back to the school the next day," said Pacheco, "but the young man with the motorcycle was waiting as well. We didn't speak but he watched me. It was clear she had told him something. Not that he was worried or felt that I posed any threat. He was too sure of her for that. Then I went to the girl's house, but she refused to see me. The following Sunday I followed her to church, sat behind her, breathed over her shoulder, even touched her once. She didn't appear to recognize me. So I began to haunt her. Whenever she was in town shopping or going to a café, I would be there. I even spoke to her a few times. I would tell her how I desired her, what I wanted to do to her body, how I wanted to kiss her breasts. She would listen and I could just barely sense her breath beginning to quicken; then she would walk away or the young man would reappear.

"The aunt's house where Antonia lived was a large white house set off by itself on a hill. Very soon I knew which room was Antonia's, and late in the evening I would stand out on the street, watching her window and waiting for a light. It was a second-floor room in the front, right above the porch. Of course I hated myself for behaving in such a manner, but that hatred did nothing but strengthen my resolve. Each evening the young man with the motorcycle would come to her house. Sometimes he and Antonia would go out, sometimes they would stay home. Often I would see them walking in the garden. He would have his arm around her waist and they would stop and kiss. Once they lay down on the grass together. She had a large brindle-colored mastiff that she called Caleb, and whenever she and the young man walked through the garden Caleb would follow. After several hours the young man would leave and a little later the light would go on in Antonia's bedroom. I would stand and watch and even when the light went out again I would remain in the street. Then, maybe around two or three, I would walk home.

"Caleb was also the guard dog and would roam loose on the grounds at night. Often as I walked along the iron fence, he would walk along the other side, not barking or growling, but just following me. At first I thought I'd have to kill Caleb and even imagined cutting off his head and sticking it on one of the many spearlike poles which made up the fence. As it was, I turned Caleb into my own little pet, bringing him scraps of meat and talking to him softly, until at last whenever Caleb heard me approach, he would trot down to the fence, wagging his tail.

"It must have been three weeks after the concert that I decided to climb the fence. It was late at night and all the lights had been out for some time. I had saved a little meat just in case Caleb turned out to be difficult. I climbed over by the back gate. Caleb leapt up and licked my face. Then I worked my way around toward the front of the house, being as quiet as possible, which was absurd with this great dog bouncing and being playful. It was a moonlit night and there were also lights from the street. I had no clear plan except that I wanted to get into the house and rid myself of this terrible itch. I hardly thought of the consequences, that I could be jailed and lose my position as well. But each time I hesitated I imagined Antonia in her bed and it pushed away all fear. It was a hot night in late spring. I was dressed in dark clothes. I knew that besides Antonia and her aunt, three servants lived in the house: a middle-aged man who took care of the grounds and did the heavy work; his wife, who served as cook; and a young girl who did the cleaning up.

"Reaching her window turned out to be no problem. I only

had to climb the side of the porch and onto the porch roof. The dog whined a little when I disappeared above him and I tossed him the last of the meat. Antonia's windows were open and I slipped over the sill as if it were the easiest thing in the world. Her room was large with white wicker furniture, white bedspread and rug. Antonia was asleep on the bed, lying on her back. She had thrown off the covers and her nightgown was open. A shaft of moonlight lay across her belly. I stood above her, looking down at her nakedness. Had I chosen to rape her, I could have penetrated her before she knew what was happening. I knelt down in front of her. Reaching out, I brushed her thick pubic hair with the backs of my fingers. My hand seemed on fire. I watched for what seemed a long time, studying her breasts, her thighs, the curve of her lip. It wasn't that I was afraid to rape her. In fact, I had no fear. But I felt unsure that it was in my best interests, since clearly I'd have just one opportunity which couldn't be repeated.

"After twenty or thirty minutes, I stood up. I would defeat her in some other way. I couldn't, however, bring myself to leave empty-handed. Her bureau was right by the window. Going to it, I searched for something I could take. On one corner were several copies of the picture which you saw on the mantel in the library. I took one and put it in my pocket. Then, as I started to leave, I glanced in the mirror and saw Antonia sitting up on one elbow and staring at me, staring at my back. There was no fear in her face and she made no attempt to cover herself. On the other hand, I wasn't sure she knew who I was, that I was the man who had been haunting her for weeks. She stared at my back and I watched her reflection in the mirror. For a moment I almost turned around, but then I knew I wanted her another way. I wanted her to give herself and beg me to take her so that I could amuse myself with refusals before I made love to her. Without looking back, I went out the window and down the side of the porch. I didn't glance back until I had reached the street. When I did, I saw her standing at the window, looking out at me."

The door opened wide and Señora Puccini entered pushing a cart with something in aspic and a salad. I had been watching the door for some minutes because I'd seen it move very slightly when Pacheco was in the midst of his story. Now I believed that Señora Puccini had been standing outside, waiting for him to finish. She gave no sign of having heard anything and seemed as cool as ever. As for us guests, we were in a state of sexual disruption and stared at her, wishing to strip away the years to discover the young woman who had been lying on the white bed.

Señora Puccini put the salad before us, a salad Beatrice with green beans, watercress, and tomatoes. The aspic dish was made up of slices of duck and slices of orange. The food was absurd, an endless progression of comestibles in which only Malgiolio still maintained an interest. We were silent as she put the plates on the table. I nibbled a little aspic and a few green beans. Then, as Señora Puccini was pushing the cart from the room, Pacheco said, "Did you hear what I told them about how I entered your bedroom that night long ago?"

Señora Puccini stood with her back to us, very stiff and tall. At first I thought she wouldn't respond. A draft from the door made the candlelight dance.

"Yes, I heard," she said at last.

"And had you known it before?"

"What does it matter what I knew?" she asked. Then she continued into the hall, shutting the door behind her. Pacheco speared a piece of the duck and lifted it to his lips. Next to me I could hear Dalakis chewing.

"I had the picture enlarged," said Pacheco. "I would stare at it, trying to come to hate that face or at least grow indifferent to it. How is it possible for one person to have such control over another? I would think myself a rational human being, a respected surgeon surrounded by people who admired me, but I would again look at that photograph and all my logic would be swept away.

"A few days after I stole the picture, my friend Paco called to say there was a picnic planned for the following weekend. A mass of young people were going out to some farm where there would be an ox roast and then dancing and general carousing. Paco asked if I cared to go with him. I thanked him but said no. That sort of foolishness has always been immensely boring to me: twenty or thirty people sitting around bonfires singing old songs. But then Paco chuckled and said, 'What if I told you that Antonia Puccini will be there?'

"As you may imagine, I went after all. The farm was about twenty miles from the city, just in the foothills. Over two hundred people must have attended. There were horses and riding paths and games and various sporting activities and these great blackened cows turning over and over on a spit. The young people cavorted. The older guests sat at round tables and talked and played cards. It was a warm, cloudless day and the mountains rose above us to the east like a green curtain. Far up there were still traces of snow.

"Paco and I separated in order to search for Antonia. Shortly I found her near the stable with her fiancé. They were saddling horses. They had a way of always standing close to each other, of constantly touching each other as they talked. I stood back by a tree and watched, and moments later Paco joined me. 'We have to get them apart,' I said. Just then Antonia leapt on her horse and rode off by herself. The boy, her fiancé, was still tightening the cinch on his saddle. 'Quick,' I told Paco, 'run and tell him that his host wants him right away, anything, just get him away from the horse.'

"Paco ran to the boy and blurted out some story. Later he told me he'd said there was a phone call from the city. Someone had had an accident and the boy was needed. Clearly, the boy didn't want to go. Antonia was galloping off across the field, not looking back but certain he'd follow. Then the boy turned and ran off toward the house, leaving his horse still tied to the corral. By the time I got there Paco had the animal ready. 'I hope you can ride,' he said. I climbed into the saddle and as Paco tossed me the reins I dug my heels into the horse's sides.

"Soon I was galloping across the field and there, perhaps a quarter of a mile ahead, was Antonia, still galloping wildly. Looking back over her shoulder, she again urged her horse forward, and I knew she'd mistaken me for her fiancé. I was also certain that she was intending to lead him somewhere into the woods up ahead where they could be alone, and I imagined Antonia getting herself trapped in some narrow canyon, then turning and finding me by her side. How could I not have my way with her?

"When I reached the woods, there was no sign of Antonia. My horse, a huge chestnut, galloped along the narrow path. I slowed a little so I wouldn't miss some turning. It had recently rained and everything was very green. I rode on for some minutes without seeing Antonia. Then off to the left was another path and in the dirt were the marks of a horse's hooves. I followed it, keeping my head down in order to get under the low-hanging branches. After several more minutes, I saw Antonia ahead of me. She had turned her horse around. She was smiling, a wonderfully kind and loving smile. Just behind her was a little meadow between the trees and the cliff face. I still had my head ducked down in the horse's mane and she still mistook me for her fiancé. Then I sat up and nodded to her. Immediately, her face changed. She didn't show anger or surprise or fear. Her face showed nothing. I reined up my horse

103

perhaps two feet from hers. She didn't speak. We looked at each other in silence.

" 'Do you know what I want of you?' I asked.

"She ignored my words. 'That's Roberto's horse,' she said. 'Where is he?'

"I repeated my question. 'Do you know what I want of you?' She wore a white shirt and khaki riding pants. The top three buttons of her shirt were undone, exposing a triangle of flesh. 'Get down from your horse,' I said.

" 'Where is Roberto?' she asked again.

" 'I have no interest in Roberto,' I told her. 'Get down from your horse.'

"She didn't respond or make any expression. Then, unexpectedly, she dug her heels into her horse and it leapt forward, kicking and whinnying. She slapped it with her riding crop and pulled back on the reins so that it reared up, its forefeet pawing the air just inches from the head of my own horse, which shied away. As she came down, she again dug her heels into her horse's flanks and it galloped forward. I tried to catch her bridle but as I reached out she slapped my wrist with her crop and galloped past. I spun my horse after hers. I was furious and I wanted to catch her and strip her.

"We galloped down the narrow path between the trees. Branches kept hitting me no matter how close I crouched over the horse's neck. Still, I kept urging my horse forward and managed to stay about ten feet behind Antonia. My horse was much larger than hers and once we reached the main path I was sure I could catch her. But again I was mistaken. Although I was faster, she was the better rider, and although I gained on her I couldn't quite reach her. She rode beautifully, perfectly balanced, and never once looked back.

"When we galloped into the field, I was perhaps half a length behind her. I still meant to drag her to the ground but as I rode into the high grass I saw her fiancé riding toward us on

104

another horse. She galloped toward him and he, seeing me, charged at me, shouting. Clearly, he knew I was responsible for the little trick about the phone call. I didn't slow but rode directly at him, intending to knock him from his horse. By that point I had worked myself into such a pitch that I was ready to do anything. Unfortunately, he saw my intention and as I leaned out to strike him, he grabbed my arm and dragged me from the saddle. I fell heavily in the grass, rolled, then got to my feet. But immediately he charged down on me with his riding crop, and as I looked up, he struck me across my face and I was knocked to the ground. This time I got up more quickly but he was faster still and was again upon me. I jumped to avoid being trampled, and he struck at me and missed.

"All this time I was aware of Antonia sitting on her horse and watching, not with pleasure or distaste, just watching. Again I got to my feet and again this boy, this Roberto, struck me with his riding crop. By then I was bleeding. I got to one knee and buried my face in my hands, but it was all pretense. As he rode at me I stayed down till the last possible moment. Then, as he swung the riding crop, I leapt up, grabbed his arm, and pulled him from his horse so he fell into the grass. I had no wish to struggle with him. Near me was a large stone and, as the boy fell, I grabbed it and lifted it above my head intending to smash out his brains. Just as I was about to send the stone crashing upon him, Antonia screamed, 'No!'

"I looked up. Her face was full of terror. I realized I was wrong, I was only thinking of the moment, and that perhaps I could use this boy to get what I wanted. I threw down the stone and walked to my horse, which stood cropping grass about thirty yards away. Antonia ran to her fiancé, who was sitting up looking rather dazed and stupid. Mounting my horse, I rode back to the farm. Then I hunted out Paco and we drove back to the city."

Pacheco sat back and began poking at the food on his plate

with a butter knife. I stared at him, trying to guess his thoughts. His expression seemed one of anger, of relentlessness. Dalakis had made a small ball of wax from the candle drippings and was rolling it between his palm and the tablecloth.

"Why didn't you give up?" asked Malgiolio. "Or did you?"

"Give up?" asked Pacheco. "Believe me, if anything my resolve was even greater."

I glanced at the door and wondered if Antonia Puccini stood behind it. Never had I experienced a passion such as Pacheco described. Even though I loved my wife, I dislike those emotions which over-sweep you and leave you beaten.

"You've had many women," said Malgiolio. "Why didn't you just leave this one and find another?"

"Because I'm not interested in whores, my friend." Pacheco's tone was cool and Malgiolio assumed he was suggesting something about his own tastes. He leaned forward and stared at Pacheco across the tablecloth. How foolish Malgiolio appeared, with his strings of black hair artistically arranged in little swirls across his bald head.

"Are you suggesting that I am?"

"You seem to have a preference for bought flesh."

Even though I was surprised by Pacheco's rudeness, I expected nothing to come of it. If Malgiolio wasn't used to insults, then he should be. But this occasion was different. Malgiolio bent his head and sat hunched over his plate. A few seconds went by. Abruptly he sat up and surprised us all by hurling his glass to the floor, where it smashed, sending splinters of glass skittering across the marble.

"I resent what you say about my relationships with women. You know nothing about me!"

Without glancing at Malgiolio, Pacheco lit a cigarette from one of the candles, holding it to the flame without moving from his chair. It was only later that I decided that he had some purpose in upsetting Malgiolio. Perhaps he already knew what Malgiolio was about to tell us and was even forcing him to say it. Perhaps in revealing his obsession, Pacheco also wanted to shake us free of our own.

"You think my feelings are not as strong as yours?" Malgiolio continued. He had gotten to his feet and stood with his hands on the edge of the table. Not only was his blue suit old, but it was slightly small on him. "Look at the two of us. You are wealthy and respected. I am poor and full of spite. Yet I too can burn for a woman. In fact, I burn daily."

I watched how Dalakis stared at Malgiolio. He has endless capacity for empathy. His thick glasses were perched on the tip of his nose like a potential suicide. I thought of the poetry Malgiolio had written as an adolescent. It was a poetry of complaint.

"We all have stories," said Pacheco with a degree of kindness. "Who is this woman, Malgiolio, who makes you burn? Perhaps I can buy her for you."

"Don't mock him, Daniel," said Dalakis, quietly.

Pacheco looked back at Dalakis, then nodded his head. Malgiolio had resumed his seat at the table. He was angry, but whether at himself or Pacheco I wasn't sure. I kept reminding myself that here was a man who had squandered a fortune, who could have made himself comfortable for life but had thrown everything away. I remembered stories about Malgiolio buying a car in the morning, then selling it at a great loss in the afternoon. He had grown tired of it; he desired a change. He had wanted to be someone who never had to think about money and as a result he'd tied himself to it forever.

"It's no story," said Malgiolio in a low voice. "I met a woman when I was wealthy. I gave her gifts and she gave me favors. Then I became poor again and the favors stopped. How simple

107

a situation could you ask for? It's like your story of the man with his blind wife. Did you know about me, Pacheco? Always I am collecting money. I steal it from here, borrow it from there, maybe I even earn a little. And I go to her again with another gift which she is kind enough to accept. She is a tall blond woman, maybe Scandinavian, maybe Dutch. Perhaps she is eight or nine inches taller than I am. She lets me walk with her in her garden. But she is not kind. She laughs at my gifts and says they are too small. If I beg her for something, just a touch of her hand, she slaps my face. If I complain, she tells her servant not to let me in the house. Is it not comical? She makes me lie down on the patio. She makes me lie on my back and she stands above me. And do you know what she does? Never have I told this to anyone. She urinates on me, she pees and laughs and as she laughs the urine snakes back and forth across me. And do I complain? Not a sound do I make. Then I go back home and steal and finagle and borrow until at last I have a little money and again I return to her house with a gift and again I lie out on the stones of the patio as she stands above me. When she stands there she digs her heels into my ribs and kicks, then she squats down and I feel the urine spatter across my clothes, the clothes that my wife later washes."

"Don't you make love to her?" I asked, astonished at his story and even more that he was telling it.

"Sometimes she will lie down on the grass and pull up her skirt and tell me to show her my little thing. She thinks that such talk will stop me. She'll take my prick and twist it and slap at it. She wants me to be impotent with her but my desire is too great. Even so she will often push me off before I'm finished, then watch me spurt my seed into the grass. Then she'll laugh and tell me to go home. So I go home and again I begin to steal and finagle. . . ."

"Stop!" said Dalakis. "Why are you telling us this?" He had gotten to his feet and stood surprised, as if wondering what he was doing so high above the table.

"We were talking about passion," said Malgiolio, "and Pacheco was telling us his grand story. What do any of you know of me? I'm the one who squandered a fortune. Well, I too have a passion. You know, I stand down the street from her house. Not too close because if she saw me she'd be angry. Maybe fifty yards away. I stand under a tree and watch the cars come up and the men get out. There was one man who came all the time. He drove a blue BMW. One night I followed him and discovered who he was and where he lived and I went and I destroyed his car. I slashed the tires and smashed the windshield and gouged the metal with a screwdriver. And after he had the car fixed, I did it all again. Smashed and broke and gouged the metal until his servant heard me and chased me down the street. Then I found out where the man worked. He was an insurance executive. I told stories about him, told how he let women piss on him. Not that it made any difference. I had no power, no way to hurt him. But sometimes I would steal from these men, these other lovers. I would steal from their cars or their houses if I could find them. And with the money I would again buy little gifts and my tall blond woman would again lead me out to the patio. She would take hold of my tie and pull me as if it were a little leash. Then she would push me down and laugh and dig her heels into my sides and squat above me. She would call me her little pig and order me to squeal and say oink, oink; and as I made these noises her urine would splash over me and soak through my clothes and burn."

"That's enough," said Pacheco. "Your story is sordid."

"And what's yours?" answered Malgiolio bitterly. "You ruined some girl, wrecked her life, and I let a woman pee on me. Does that make you better? In fact, why should we believe you? This woman comes in and out and you claim to have ruined her. Why should we believe that you've ever touched her? This could be a fantasy of yours, some sort of craziness."

"Is that true, Daniel?" asked Dalakis, as if he hoped it were so. "Is this just a story you are telling to amuse us?"

Pacheco picked up the small bell that stood by his plate and rang it sharply. Moments later Señora Puccini entered, and again I thought she must have been nearby in the hall. Pacheco got to his feet, took Señora Puccini's arm, and slowly led her over to Malgiolio. Standing behind her, he began to unbutton the buttons of her dress. She jerked and tried to pull away but Pacheco said something I couldn't hear and she stopped. I was right across from Malgiolio and could see as well as he. Pacheco unbuttoned her dress, then yanked it down over her shoulders to her waist. Then he yanked down her slip. Beneath it was an old-fashioned white brassiere, more like armor than clothing. She stared directly at Malgiolio but her face was wooden, almost as if dead.

"Daniel!" said Dalakis, "leave her alone, please stop this!"

Pacheco ignored him. He too was staring at Malgiolio. Slowly, he unhooked Señora Puccini's brassiere, stripped it off, and tossed it onto the table in front of Malgiolio so it fell on his plate. The woman had large firm breasts and dark nipples. Standing behind her, Pacheco lifted her breasts with the flat of his hands, pushing them up toward Malgiolio, then dropping them and pushing them up again. Her breasts were very white, as if never touched by the sun. Looking over at Dalakis, I was surprised to see tears on his cheeks. Malgiolio was staring down at the great brassiere on his plate. Señora Puccini turned from Malgiolio to Dalakis to me. Her eyes were bright and animal, and she had sucked in her belly till I could see her ribs. I must have looked shocked, since that was certainly how

I felt. Pacheco leaned his head forward, resting it on her shoulder and against her mass of graying hair. I couldn't see his eyes. As I was the only one still looking at her, she stared back and began to smile, a smile without humor or warmth or affection. I wondered about the gun in her skirt pocket and if it was still there.

Chapter Four

I had left the dinner table to find the bathroom, or at least that was my excuse for absenting myself moments after Pacheco discontinued his mauling of Señora Puccini to let her return to the kitchen. I watched her retrieve her brassiere from Malgiolio's plate, then hurry to the door, pulling up her slip and pushing her hands through the sleeves of her black dress. I do not like emotional scenes. I do not like the way strong feeling can sweep through a civilized gathering in the way a strong wind sweeps across a pond where children are sailing their paper boats. An orderly life requires detachment. If someone wanted to suggest I had fled the dining room, that would be correct.

A few years ago, shortly after the newspaper published my interview with Borges, a Borges-type story occurred to me. It was based on the idea that when something truly horrible happens, the mind goes into shock and engages in amnesia to shield itself from the awfulness. In my story, a smudge would suddenly appear on the floor of a college classroom and the professor vanish. The man assigned to investigate at last determines that the teacher was a victim of spontaneous combustion, which was so horrible to witness that the entire class blocked it out, leaving only the smudge as evidence that the professor had gone up in flames. Many respectable people have believed in spontaneous combustion—look at Dickens and Balzac.

The difficulty with my story was that the idea was more interesting then the story itself, and I could never really hit upon anything awful enough, or upon a situation in which the witnesses might in fact forget. At the same time, I began to think that perhaps such a phenomenon was quite common, that I myself might have experienced it, say, a dozen times over the years, and never realized it; that the only evidence might be something incredibly small, like an empty glass on a table where I had thought there was nothing, or a strange shoe appearing in my closet, or a smell of lilacs in mid-winter—that these might be the only snippets of evidence proving the existence of who knew what, some horrible thing. Yet just how awful would it have to be? Because certainly I had seen awful things and instead of forgetting them my mind brought them back again and again. How preferable to find a white brassiere upon the table and know this was evidence that something dreadful had just passed, than to see Pacheco paw his house-keeper's pale breasts and watch what I thought to be the animal flutter behind her eyes.

Yet perhaps one does forget. Perhaps even in that scene there was something much worse which I am not relating, which I am unable to relate. Perhaps I have forgotten her pleasure or pain or indifference, or even evidence of our own inappro-priate feelings. Perhaps we howled with laughter. After all, we are creatures of self-deception and it is possible that several things occurred that night which were so unbearable that my mind has entombed them. Yet how terrible they must have been, considering the terror I recall so vividly.

In any case, I fled to the bathroom, which was on the second floor at the very front of the house. On the far side of the bathroom was a pair of French doors leading to a small balcony that projected over the sidewalk. I did no more than wash my face in cold water, then glance at myself in the mirror. The candles on either side of the glass seemed to distort my image, causing me to see myself afresh. How unmuscular my face looked, and I wondered why I'd ever felt pleased about my little gray moustache or why I affected the bow ties that I wore as a kind of trademark. I looked at my watch; it was just past ten. Blowing out the candles, I went to the French doors on which the shutters had been closed. I wanted to know what was happening outside and, in retrospect, it seems almost comical that I sought out the physical chaos of the city to escape from the emotional chaos of the house. Like a thief I made my way onto the balcony. I knew that if there were soldiers about I stood a fair chance of getting shot.

The street was deserted. I crouched down with my head above the low wall of the balcony, one of those cement walls with Grecian balusters two feet high and set about every sixteen inches between an upper and lower rail. The night seemed even hotter. A broiling wind blew out of the west and with it came a mixture of smoke and the perfume of hundreds of flowers, the two smells being as intertwined as melody and harmony. To my left was sporadic shooting. The houses were dark and their shutters closed: two- or three-story houses with whitewashed stone fronts and black wrought-iron bars over some of the windows. A few houses had ivy or flowering vines or large potted plants on their balconies. Although the street lights were out, there were two kerosene lanterns, hardly more than smudge pots, on the sidewalk about twenty and thirty yards to my right. And of course there was the moon, three quarters full and somewhere behind me over Pacheco's house.

Although the houses seemed empty and their facades anonymous, I knew that most had enclosed patios with gardens, grape arbors, fig and orange trees; and that, despite the apparent barrenness of the street, the rich perfume of the flowers was rising up from these hidden centers. Furthermore, even though the houses looked empty, I occasionally heard, mixed in with the gunshots and sirens, the sound of laughter and glasses clinking together or the sound of silverware clicking against plates, as if in some of these houses were private feasts like our own, hidden celebrations.

Several blocks away was a major highway and I kept hearing the noise of heavy trucks, military trucks, and once I heard the clanking rumble of a tank. These deep-throated roars reminded me of nothing so much as wild animals. Often there were sirens, police or ambulance, as well as the high squealing sirens of the police motorcycles, large white BMW's. Sometimes I also heard running footsteps, although I never saw anyone. And often there were gunshots, both the single shots of a rifle or pistol and long bursts from automatic weapons. As I knelt on the narrow balcony I felt great waves of movement sweeping from one spot in the city to another, in the same way great formations of cloud can be gathered and dispersed about the sky, while my own street—the street of Dr. Pacheco—remained quiet.

It was just as I was sensing these waves of movement that I heard a noise that was so common yet so out of place that at first I couldn't recognize it: the hollow, almost syncopated clopping of a horse's hooves far down the street to my right. I looked but saw nothing. Then, as I continued to peer into the dark, the horse came into view, an old white horse, almost pink, walking slowly down the center of the street with its head hanging so low that its muzzle was only a foot or so above the cobblestones. And as I stared at it, I realized I knew the horse, that it was a horse I'd been seeing for nearly half my life.

My own house, as I may have said, was situated on a similar

residential street about a mile away, and for years, every two or three days, there came an old man who sold vegetables from a horse-drawn cart. Certainly the horse now clopping its way down the street was the same horse. It had the same pinkish color, the same sway back and black mane. The wagon had been black with a tattered black canvas roof and an axle and wheels taken from an automobile, something ancient like a Model T Ford. The old man sat up in front while piled behind him were vegetables, potatoes, fruit; and as he moved slowly from one street to the next he would call out his wares: Onions, tomatoes, apples, fresh lettuce, eggs!

Even though the man's produce was more expensive than the market's, certain women always bought from him, perhaps from convenience or laziness or charity or because they felt his produce was fresher than what they found at the store. I had purchased apples from him, and eggs, and tomatoes in late spring. Although we knew each other, we rarely spoke. His own comments were limited to climatic descriptions. "Weather's changing," he'd shout, or "Rain gathering," while I would praise his pears or the firmness of his tomatoes—not a strong bond but a bond nonetheless. The man and his wagon had looked old even twenty years ago. In fact, I'd come to think of the horse, the wagon, the old man, and his produce as a single entity, as one creature who showed up every few days, ambled through the neighborhood, then disappeared. And now here was the horse by itself. What had happened to the man and his wagon? How had they become separated?

When the horse passed the first kerosene lantern or smudge pot, I saw that it still wore its bridle. It swayed from side to side as it moved into the dim light, becoming a vague white shape, almost a ghost-horse, then into the darkness again, clip-clopping at the same slow pace down the center of the street. Obviously something had happened to the old man, and the horse, now lost and ownerless, had fallen back into the pattern of meandering through a thousand suburban streets. When the horse moved into the second small pool of light about twenty yards away, I saw that red flowers were caught up in its black tail, but whether by accident or if someone had put them there I had no way of knowing.

All this time I was increasingly aware of shouting and running in the area to my left. There were also more gunshots as well as the rattle of automatic weapons. The horse passed beneath me. Its ribs stuck out like barrel staves and its head didn't seem to hang so much as dangle as it swung back and forth. When the horse had gone about ten feet past the doctor's house, a figure came rushing around the corner to my left and halted some yards ahead of the horse, which neither stopped nor slowed but continued its steady pace. The figure wore a dark hooded sweatshirt and carried a small machine gun or machine pistol. At this distance it was impossible to tell what side it was on or even if it was male or female. Then, with one smooth movement, the figure raised the gun and shot a short burst at the horse, the noise echoing violently against the stone fronts of the houses.

At first I thought the horse hadn't been hit since it continued to move forward, but then I saw that very slowly its legs were beginning to buckle, but so gradually that the horse first appeared to be making its way into a ditch or into deep water or was simply getting shorter. Then its legs buckled completely and bit by bit the horse rolled over on its side, but still with the same slow speed, like a loaf of bread rolling over, and never with any protest or even seeming to notice that it had been shot. It rolled half onto its back and lay motionless in the street, a small white mountain. No blood was visible but perhaps it was too dark to see any. The person who had shot the horse walked around it in a quick, businesslike manner, prodding its belly with his or her foot. Then abruptly the figure sprinted around the corner and disappeared.

To say I was stunned would be incorrect. The whole progression of the horse and its subsequent shooting was so dreamlike that the force of its death hardly touched me. Also I worried that the hooded figure might see me and take a shot in my direction. But a heavy mixture of sadness and regret settled like a flat stone on my chest, not just sadness for the horse but for that greater creature of horse, man, wagon, vegetables, which, no matter what happened in the city, no matter who won, was now gone forever.

I had moved to my house two years before my marriage, and I'd known the old man and his wagon since that time. "Weather's changing," he'd say, "clouds heaping up." But the sadness I felt was for more than the old man and his vegetables. It was for my life, marriage, my whole youth, as if to see the old man every few days was also to be in touch with my departed wife; and with his passing another mode of access to those memories was shut down. But as I thought this, I began to remember a particular event that occurred during those first years. To say "began to remember" is perhaps inaccurate. Rather a picture took shape in my mind and around it I had to reconstruct the events that led up to it. How clumsy is language. How many words it takes to convey what happened. First the horse was shot, then came the sadness, regret, and the sense of another door closing upon my marriage; and then this image, this picture, for which I had to remember a context in order to understand. Even this brief summary gives no idea of my violent feelings, and perhaps this is why I recall my Borges story, for surely this image was horrible enough for me to block it from memory.

There had been a party and I was on the balcony. Not a small balcony like the one at Pacheco's but a great balcony that led off to a series of terraced gardens and lawns where a dozen young people were playing croquet illuminated by a string of ornate gas lamps bordering the grass. The house was one of those imitation French châteaux that the rich liked to build for themselves toward the end of the last century. I was looking for my fiancée, Cora. In some rooms people were dancing, in others they were playing cards or eating. Someone, a younger cousin, had just turned eighteen and all this was for her benefit—over a hundred and fifty young people between eighteen and thirty as well as several dozen parents. Twenty years ago this sort of party was quite common.

I had looked for Cora through most of the house and was going along the balcony trying to see if she was in any of the rooms opening onto it. We had not quarreled and all seemed well between us, which made her absence something of a mystery. The band consisted of a dozen middle-aged men who specialized in songs that were many years out of date, and I remember the aggressive blare of the horns as I looked in one set of windows after another. Placed along the wall of the balcony were black metal pots full of red geraniums. It was summer, the same time of year as this night at Pacheco's, and the air was full of the smell of flowers and fresh-cut grass.

The corner room at the end of the balcony was some kind of study and it was there I found Cora with Daniel Pacheco. They were talking, standing quite close together. I was about to tap on the glass when Pacheco grasped Cora's shoulders and very slowly eased her backward over the top of a desk. She put up no resistance. Reaching under the long dress he pulled down her panties and shoved them in his pocket. I stood paralyzed as Pacheco moved between Cora's legs and began to make love to her as she lay back on the desk. She was wearing a long yellow taffeta gown. The window was partly open and I could hear the gown rustling as he kept moving against her. I remained at the side of the window and watched. There was very little light and I'm sure no one saw me. Cora's head was turned toward the window. At first her face was blank, almost sad, but then there appeared an almost bestial expression, half anger, half hunger, as slowly she lifted her legs and linked them behind Pacheco's back. She seemed to be looking straight at me. I had known her for many years, both at the university and before. There was nothing in her behavior which would have led me to anticipate or expect what I was now watching. Pacheco stood erect, just kept pushing himself against her while she, as she grew more excited, clutched at his dinner jacket and shirt front and tried to lift herself up from the desk, as she continued to stare toward the window where I stood. When Pacheco was done, he stepped back, then took a white handkerchief from his breast pocket and wiped his penis. Cora sat up and reached out her hand for her panties. Pacheco took them from his pocket. They were light blue with white lace around the edge. Then he shrugged, returned them to his pocket, and walked from the room.

I hurried back along the balcony and took my place with the group playing croquet. A little later Cora joined me. She appeared flushed and kept laughing. She wanted me to go with her out onto the dark lawns. She kept touching me and stroking me but I refused. Not long afterward I took her home. For some reason it never occurred to me not to marry her. I mean, the arrangements, the dates, the invitations, that whole process had already begun, and I didn't have the energy to stop it even if I wanted to. And then, I was very much in love. When she was killed during our honeymoon I had a kind of nervous breakdown and went away for several months. When I returned, my house was empty of all trace of her except for a few photographs. It was spring again. I resumed my work at the newspaper, became accustomed to my bachelor life, my solitary house, my neighbors, and to the old man selling his vegetables from the back of his wagon, shouting as he went up and down the street, "Onions, fresh tomatoes!" or turning to me and saying, "Wind coming, cold nights ahead."

I find it difficult to give an accurate account of what happened that night at Pacheco's and an accurate account of what I felt. The professional reporter, of course, maintains his objectivity, but I was to some degree a participant. To crouch on Pacheco's balcony, to see the horse shot and lying dead in the street, to think of the old man and his tomatoes and the history we had shared, then to have this image, this picture leap into my mind—my fiancée lying back on the paper-littered desk, staring through the window into the night, staring in fact at me, while the expression on her face changed from utter passivity to passion. Truly, what first leapt into my mind was just this image of her face, then it was as if the camera drew back and I saw Pacheco, the room, the huge house, and me standing out on the balcony. To have this picture appear in my head was horrible and if I could have swept it away, leaving me with the equivalent of a dark smudge on the floor—the evidence of horror without the horror itself—then I would have done so without hesitation.

But perhaps that image of Cora was in fact the smudge on the floor, perhaps it concealed something even more awful. It is no great difficulty to relate most events—the tree fell, the house burned, the dog died—but the causality of human events is emotional and submerged, as subterranean as the pressure creating a volcano. "Pursued by threat of war and violence in the streets, we came to a friend's house for dinner." What lies behind those words? What was the emotional event? And did I want to know? That is the question that the reporter must ask himself: Does he really want to know? Which returns me to my pseudo-Borges story: Even if he wants to know, is he in fact capable of knowing?

That party at the country estate occurred long before we

ever decided to meet as a group. Pacheco was living in the south and rarely came to the city. Malgiolio worked near the paper and sometimes we would have lunch. He was a clerk in a hotel and felt certain he would someday become manager. In the classified ads section of the paper was a woman, a typist, whom Malgiolio was rather excited about, and I often felt he came to see me just so he could see her as well. Not that she was attractive: tall and overweight with a square, pock-marked face. I never knew what he saw in her. He would bring her flowers and write her poems. She thought him ridiculous but I believe she went out with him two or three times.

As I sat on Pacheco's balcony, I found myself thinking of Malgiolio's admission, his infatuation with this woman who would piss on him. I tried to imagine him standing outside her house staring at her windows. I realized that here was a man I'd known for forty years and really I hadn't known him at all. It's not just that he let a woman urinate on him. It was winning the lottery, quitting his job, squandering the money, and being unable to find work. It was cheating and stealing and borrowing money so he could be with this other woman. Certainly Malgiolio had felt passion, and his love, no matter how sordid, was as fierce as any of the romantic stories one finds in history books. Indeed, perhaps it was hardly different from Pacheco's feelings for Señora Puccini. Although I thought myself fortunate not to have experienced such a feeling, it made me wonder if I had any knowledge of these people. I had known them all my life, yet they were strangers.

I am trying to set down the exact progression of my thoughts. It was not Pacheco's story and the violence in the city that made me decide I wanted to write, but Malgiolio's story. At first I didn't want to write specifically about this evening but to write a story about betrayal in which these people would occur. But then I decided to write it out as it happened, to

122

describe the evening as a long process of discovery—discoveries about what was going on in the city, in the house, with Pacheco and his housekeeper, with Malgiolio and Dalakis and even myself. Really, I had entered this evening in a state of ignorance and now my mind seemed changed. How could I ever look at Malgiolio again without thinking of that blond woman squatting over him and digging her heels into his sides? But perhaps it wasn't even Malgiolio but my own memories which were the beginning. Perhaps it was that damn horse. Because aren't we always writing about ourselves and our obsessions? I had gone through great danger to come to Pacheco's house. I had thought I had come for one set of reasons, then I saw I had come for another. And because my greatest desire was to be a writer, I decided to take paper and pencil and set those reasons down. But is any of this true? Could it not be just some great piece of papier-mâché machinery designed to convince me of my own correctitude? Wouldn't Dalakis and Malgiolio write entirely different stories in which I might figure badly?

As these ideas gathered within me and my perturbation increased, I heard a noise at the door. Turning, I saw Dalakis stepping onto the balcony. He stood with his hands in his pockets and looked like a tourist gawking at the view. He had no sense of the danger and with more exasperation than I cared to show, I told him to crouch down and not reveal himself.

He squatted down perfectly amicably but with a slightly worried expression, like someone who has left home and is certain he has forgotten something. "So there you are. We've been searching for you all over. The cook and her grandson have disappeared. Pacheco is awfully upset." He settled his glasses more firmly on his nose and leaned over the balcony to take another look around.

123

"I was just clearing my head," I told him. "I keep sensing great waves of movement occurring throughout the city. There's fighting here, fighting there, yet it's all a mystery."

But Dalakis wasn't listening. He was staring down at the dead horse. I have tried to show something of his natural sympathy but his expression at seeing this dead animal, which I had almost forgotten, was one of such shock and dismay that at first I thought he was looking at something else, and without thinking I reached out to touch his arm.

"That horse," he said, "what happened?"

"Somebody shot it. It belongs to an old fellow who's sold vegetables around here for as long as I can remember."

"I've never seen it before," said Dalakis. He continued to stare at the horse, until I began to feel impatient. Was this his first awareness that awful things were occurring in the city? Had he no imagination? But it turned out he wasn't thinking of the events of this night but of another violence entirely.

"You know," he said, as he leaned out over the balcony, "I once killed a horse that looked something like that—a white horse, although mine also had a white tail and mane."

I didn't know what he was talking about. "You mean because it was old?" I asked. As a child I had sometimes watched farmers kill their old horses. They would dig a hole, often using the horse itself, then the farmer would shoot the horse so it would fall into its own grave. I assumed this was what Dalakis was referring to and was about to add that it must be difficult to kill an animal one has grown fond of.

"No," said Dalakis. "I was walking across a field and the horse just happened to be there. It was a young horse. I walked up to it and when it started to move away I shot it, not killing it but crippling its rear legs so it fell. Then I walked around to the front and shot it in the head. I was twelve at the time. It was the only animal I've ever killed."

"But why did you do it?" I asked. Dalakis is such a gentle person that his confession quite startled me.

"I had gone hunting with my father. As a matter of fact, we'd gone out hunting about a dozen times and I'd never killed anything. I'd taken shots but I always aimed to miss. This particular day there'd been a deer right in front of me and I had refused to shoot. My father was about ten yards behind me and watched me raise my rifle, then lower it again. He tried to get a shot but I was in the way. He asked me why I hadn't fired and I said I hadn't wanted to hurt the deer. So he cut a switch from a tree and beat me. Then we walked back through the woods and across the field toward his car. He stayed ahead of me, not wanting to have anything to do with me.

"When I saw the horse and got up close to it I just raised my rifle and shot. It collapsed but it wasn't dead. It was making the most awful noise. My father came running back. When he'd almost reached me, I shot the horse in the head. My father couldn't believe it. 'Why'd you kill that horse?' he shouted. But I didn't know why I'd shot it. I'd just done it, that's all. 'Why'd you kill the horse?' he shouted again. And I told him I'd done it because he'd wanted me to kill something and so there it was and he should feel proud. So he beat me again, not with a switch but with his hands. Then he tried to get out of the field but the farmer came riding up, and my father had to explain what had happened, that his son had accidently shot the horse, mistaking it for a deer. Shot it twice. I don't know if the farmer believed him but he made my father pay for the horse and of course he had to pay far more than the horse was worth. Then we went home and he beat me again. But that was the last time I had to go hunting and I've never fired a gun since."

As Dalakis talked he sat back against the wall with his legs crossed Indian-style and his hands in his lap. His shoulders were hunched forward so that his whole body resembled a great sloppy ball. I remembered his father as a big gruff man who always wanted Carl to do well in sports. But Carl had been terrible at sports, falling over his feet and getting in everyone's way. In fact, Carl wasn't good at much of anything, except at not being cruel and caring for things no one else could be expected to care about. I recall once being surprised that he had given a relatively large amount of money to protect some bird from extinction. Or maybe it was a rodent or lizard. The plan was to improve its natural habitat, grow the sort of little weeds it liked to eat. Carl took the project quite seriously and we all laughed at him for it. But later I thought if it weren't for people like Carl, who knew how many little creatures, how many of the useless, the weak, and unfashionable would slip away into oblivion. He was the enemy of evolution. And if there were a fund for the preservation of the tonsils or the appendix, Carl would surely contribute.

As I was thinking about Carl and the quirks of his character, he had turned to look again at the horse. All of a sudden he stood up and pointed.

"There's Juan!"

I looked over the balcony and off to my right I saw the cook's grandson running along the sidewalk, crouched down and trying to stay close to the house fronts. The boy had heard Carl's voice because he looked up and called, "Get the doctor, quick, open the door!"

I hurried through the bathroom. It was pitch black but then I saw the candlelight from the great staircase. Dalakis came stumbling after me. I ran down the stairs and as I reached the hall, Pacheco and Malgiolio came out of the dining room. "It's Juan!" I called as I ran to the door. Pulling back the bolts, I yanked the door open. Juan half fell into the hall and I caught his arm. He was sobbing and seemed unable to catch his breath.

"Madame Letendre, she's been shot. I can't carry her. I left her around the corner. You must come. She's still alive."

I found myself thinking of the figure who had killed the horse. I had no doubt that he or she, or even the soldiers, would shoot me just as readily if I ventured outside. Pacheco, however, didn't pause. He told the boy to get the wheelbarrow from the garden. As the boy disappeared, Señora Puccini hurried into the hall. Her mouth was half open in alarm and she held up a hand to cover it. She ran to the door.

"No," said Pacheco, grabbing her arm. "I'll get her and one of my guests will help."

I happened to be looking at Malgiolio as Pacheco spoke, and saw how he stepped back and seemed to fold into himself. But Dalakis volunteered even before Pacheco could make a specific request. The boy returned through the hall, wheeling the barrow, which made a great racket on the marble floor. Pacheco opened the door, looked out for a moment, then motioned to the others to follow. It was clear he was risking his life but he didn't hesitate and neither, it should be said, did Dalakis. I glanced at Señora Puccini but her face was again without expression.

"Come upstairs," I told Malgiolio. "We can watch from the balcony."

"Is it all right?" he asked uneasily.

"It's certainly safer than the street. No one can see us if we keep our heads down."

I led the way upstairs and through the bathroom. Malgiolio followed nervously as if expecting to be hit over the head. Once on the balcony I again felt the great disparity between the apparent calm of the doctor's house and the city where large and mysterious events were happening. Beneath us we saw the boy, then Pacheco, then Dalakis carrying the wheelbarrow, presumably to keep it from making any noise. They stayed close to the house fronts and paused only to glance at the dead horse. Dalakis said something and Pacheco looked up at the balcony from where we were watching. Turning, he again ran up the street and we lost them at the corner.

"You didn't seem very eager to risk your neck," I said to Malgiolio.

"And neither did you." He was crouched down with his eyes barely above the top of the wall.

"We book reviewers lead sedentary lives," I said. I don't know why I decided to bait him. Probably I kept thinking of his female friend and wondering why he didn't take a stick to her.

"What'd you think of the housekeeper showing her tits?" asked Malgiolio.

"I thought you'd been wrong to assume he'd never touched her."

"Oh, I knew he'd touched her all right. I just wanted to see what would happen. I'd hate to live with someone like that, someone who I knew despised me."

"And did you want to maul her breasts as well?" I said.

"Of course. D'you know, Pacheco would probably have given her to us if we'd asked."

"You mean let us make love to her?" I was rather shocked.

Malgiolio laughed at my discomfort. "Pacheco has so much anger it would probably amuse him. But she seems dead, no life, no feeling, although there was a moment she stared at me when he was touching her breasts . . ."

I waited for him to continue but he remained silent. Briefly, I thought of mentioning how I had seen Señora Puccini with a pistol and how I was certain I had seen it again outlined against the fabric of her skirt. But just as I decided to tell him, Malgiolio pointed up the street.

"Here they come!"

I heard the rumble of the wheelbarrow, then I saw the boy dashing toward the house. Behind him came Dalakis and Pacheco pushing the barrow, rushing with it along the sidewalk. The old woman lay sprawled with her slippered feet sticking out in front, bouncing up and down as the barrow passed over the cracks and faults in the concrete. Every few yards Pacheco would reach out a hand to steady her. The woman's white hair had come loose from its bun and trailed over the back of the wheelbarrow. As the boy reached the house, Malgiolio and I turned and hurried back through the bathroom and down the stairs. They were just easing the wheelbarrow through the front door when we got to the hall. The boy slammed the door fast and shot the bolts. Very carefully Dalakis and Pacheco lifted the old woman out of the wheelbarrow and laid her on the floor. Señora Puccini hurried toward us from the dining room.

"Batterby," said Pacheco, "go out to the garden and get the mattress from the chaise longue."

As I ran across the hall, I heard Pacheco telling Señora Puccini to get sheets and pillows. The door to the garden was to my right off the corridor leading to the kitchen. Candles had been lit there as well, and the front part by the patio was filled with the wicker bird cages I had seen earlier, some quite small and others a dozen feet high. The birds were awake and seemed frantic, chirping and twittering and rushing about their cages. Perhaps it was the candlelight that disturbed them. A yellow finch kept fluttering against its bars, flying against them as if it might break them. In another cage, a black crow rapidly paced back and forth along its perch like a sentry on duty. The chaise longue was right beneath it. The crow watched me but didn't pause in its hurried perambulation. The disturbance of the birds was quite unnerving, as if they knew of some awfulness that hadn't yet occurred to the rest of us.

I grabbed the mattress off the chaise longue and ran back into the house.

Madame Letendre was alive, but she had been shot several times and her black dress was soaked with blood. We got her onto the mattress. She lay on her back groaning with her face turned toward us. Her blind eyes seemed to take us in, almost to focus on us although there was no pupil or iris, just a flat gray surface like the surface of an egg. Really, she made the most horrible noise, a great stertorous breathing somewhere between a gasp and a shout. Pacheco had unbuttoned and cut away part of her dress to inspect her wounds. He had a pail of water and one of the blue linen napkins with which he kept wiping away the blood, then dipping the napkin in the water and wringing it out. Apparently, one bullet had passed through her lung, another had struck her shoulder, and a third was somewhere in her abdomen. Señora Puccini brought Pacheco his bag and he prepared a shot of something. In the candlelight the blood was dark, almost black. Although the sight horrified me, it was impossible not to look.

"Why did you leave the house?" Pacheco asked the boy, who stood behind him holding one of the candelabra.

Juan was staring at his grandmother with a kind of breathless surprise. "She thought we could get home."

"But I said it was dangerous." Pacheco turned to Señora Puccini. "Weren't you watching them?"

She didn't answer but knelt down on the other side of the cook and began stroking her forehead and whispering to her. Pacheco stared at her furiously. I wondered if she had encouraged the cook to leave, perhaps in order to hurt Pacheco. But that may have been mistaken because certainly Señora Puccini appeared fond of the cook. The boy, however, seemed confused, and I felt his puzzlement came from being advised to do the wrong thing by someone he trusted. Again, I thought how closely he resembled the boy in the orphanage to whom I read the Brothers Grimm each Sunday. Both had the same black, wondering eyes. In any case, Pacheco asked no more questions but continued to tend the cook's wounds. She grew calmer as the shot took effect, although her breathing was still that dreadful rasping which echoed throughout the hall. Dalakis stood next to me; Malgiolio stood over by the fountain.

"Did you see anyone out there?" I asked Dalakis.

"No one. She was lying half in the street. There was no one else around."

Pacheco stood up. "There's nothing more I can do," he said.

"Will she be all right?" asked the boy.

Glancing at him, Pacheco took the candelabrum and held it over the cook. "She's going to die," he said, "but at least she's in no more pain."

"Can't you do anything else?" asked Señora Puccini. I was struck by the emotion in her voice.

"You don't think I'd save her if I could?"

"I don't know," said Señora Puccini.

"Why weren't you watching her?" Pacheco asked again. He looked at the housekeeper but she was staring down at Madame Letendre. "She'll be all right here," said Pacheco. "To move her would only make it worse." Apart from the rasp of her breathing, the cook lay quietly. The only other noise came from the boy, who had begun to sob, as if the cook's injuries hadn't become real until Pacheco had spoken of them. Pacheco turned to us and took my arm. "Let's return to the dining room," he said.

We followed him across the hall. Along with the candles in the niches containing the Roman busts, about twenty more candlesticks had been placed on the stairs and on the balcony above. The hall was drafty and the flames kept flickering, which made the large hall quiver with shadow and sparkles of light as if the air itself were in turmoil. The boy and Señora Puccini remained behind with the cook.

In the dining room, the remains of the salad had been removed and in its place were several bowls of ripe peaches, a Camembert cheese, and two bottles of sparkling Burgundy. We took our seats. Pacheco had closed the door, but even so I could hear the rising and falling gasp of the cook's breathing. I thought how she had designed this meal and how there was even more food to come. Not that I would take another bite. How could I eat under that canopy of groaning? Dalakis and I looked at the cheese. I sipped my wine. Malgiolio was peeling a peach. Pacheco was slouched down in his chair with his arms crossed and his chin on his chest. He was smoking and his mind seemed a thousand miles away.

"So tell us," said Malgiolio, cutting a slice of peach, then eating it off the blade of his knife, "what made her change her mind? You've shown us that you were finally able to have your way with this woman. How did it happen?"

Even though I have been long aware of Malgiolio's dogged sense of the inappropriate, I was surprised that he could so casually sweep aside what had happened in order to urge Pacheco to return to his story. I'd noticed that on the other side of the vase showing the wedding celebration was a scene depicting a man stumbling along with a donkey's head on his shoulders, the afflicted Bottom from *A Midsummer Night's Dream*, so the wedding must have been that of Theseus and Hippolyta. But I couldn't see the man with the donkey's head without thinking of Malgiolio, so foolish did he sometimes seem in my eyes.

"You mean you aren't satisfied?" said Pacheco. "I can make her strip in front of you and you still aren't satisfied?" He looked at Malgiolio in such a way that I felt he hated him.

And really it seemed particularly insensitive of Malgiolio to act as if the brutal assault on the cook meant nothing, that we could just continue as before. But I had observed his fear and I wondered if Malgiolio wasn't insisting on the story partly because it made the violence outside the house seem more distant.

"I'm simply curious," said Malgiolio, cutting another slice of peach. "What did you have to do to get her? How low did you have to go?"

Pacheco started to speak, but then the door opened and Señora Puccini entered. The sound of the cook's breathing grew louder, then quieter as she opened and closed the door.

"You're continuing with your dinner?" she asked, as if startled.

Pacheco turned in his chair. I'm absolutely certain that her surprise pleased him. I also feel that Pacheco's decision to continue with both the dinner and his tale stemmed to some degree from a desire to manipulate her surprise and further affect it. "I see no great evidence of hunger but, yes, we'll proceed with the meal. After all, this is Madame's very last dinner. She wouldn't want us to interrupt it for her death." Glancing at Señora Puccini, he took a peach from the bowl, tossed it into the air, and caught it. Then he bit into the peach so the juice ran down his chin. "Besides, my friends remain interested in your story. Would you like to tell it?"

She didn't look at us. "The past is nothing to me. We had a bargain and I have fulfilled my part."

"And have I?" asked Pacheco.

"You've done many things but you have at least done what I asked you to do." With that rather mysterious statement she passed through the door to the hall.

We watched her go. She seemed changed from the rather dowdy woman who had admitted me over four hours earlier, as if she were younger and more beautiful. But perhaps it was an effect of the candlelight. I noticed she had not completely shut the door and I wondered if she left it open so that she might listen.

"And so finish," said Malgiolio, "what is the rest of your story?"

Pacheco looked at Malgiolio as if considering his scraps of hair, his pale face and little hands, his old but well-brushed blue suit. Then, picking up a silver fruit knife, Pacheco idly tapped the tip against the stem of his wine glass and began again. "Over the next year I continued to pursue Señora Puccini, but let me describe just three occasions. The first was a few days after that party in the country. I realized of course that my behavior had become excessive, but I still hoped that if I simply talked to Antonia I might in some way sway her mind.

"The very first of the week I went to the school where she was teaching. I knew people on the school board and was even acquainted with the principal. After all, I was a doctor, a surgeon, one of the very few in that city. It was as if people were obliged to think well of me. I saw the principal and told her it was important that I talk to Antonia Puccini, giving the impression it was some medical matter. I said I would wait in an empty classroom. I asked her not to tell Antonia who her visitor was but that she should come right away. As I say, I knew this woman. She was attractive and middle-aged and I am sure she knew that my interest had little to do with medicine. Even so, she didn't hesitate but immediately led me to an empty room, then went off to fetch Antonia.

"You may imagine I was in a state of extreme nervousness and anxiety, yet I knew I had to behave with perfect calm. I happened to have my briefcase with me and I sat down at the teacher's desk, took out a sheaf of papers, and pretended to read through them. Moments later Antonia hurried into the room. When she saw me, she stopped. The principal was behind her. 'I'll see that the two of you aren't bothered,' she said. Then she shut the door, leaving us together. I glanced up, asked Antonia to take a seat, and went back to the papers for a few seconds, after which I took a pen and signed my name at the bottom of what was probably a laundry bill. Then I put the papers back in my briefcase and looked up. Antonia was sitting at one of the desks in the front row. The desks were meant for children and it was much too small for her.

"I told her I wanted to apologize for the other day, that I had wanted a chance to talk and things had gotten out of hand. She stood up. I remember she was wearing a blue dress with thin white stripes and I kept being aware of her body beneath it. 'We have nothing to talk about,' she said. 'You've behaved brutally every time I've seen you and you tricked me into coming here.' Then she told me that if I didn't leave her alone, she'd file a complaint.

"I asked her to hear me out, then said that I wanted her to come live with me. 'I'll marry you,' I told her. 'I'll do what you wish, give you as much money as you require or want.' "

Pacheco's admission amazed me. I leaned forward, nearly upsetting my wine glass. "How could you imagine that she'd marry you?" I interrupted. Even Malgiolio seemed startled.

"Of course it was absurd," Pacheco continued, "but I knew that I couldn't appear hesitant. In any case, she looked at me with what might be called an uncomprehending stare. 'You're insane,' she said. 'I don't like you, I don't find you attractive, I have no interest in you. Besides, I'm in love with another man, whom I intend to marry and make a life with.'

"Then I too stood up. It was extremely difficult to talk to her coolly. 'I can't help the other man,' I said, 'yet if you come to me, I won't interfere with your being with him whenever you wish.' I told her that I doubted her lack of interest in me and asked why she had let me touch her at the concert. 'You were as much caught up as I was,' I said. 'And if I were to kiss you now, you would again be caught up.'

"But she claimed it wasn't true, that I'd embarrassed her greatly at the concert, that she hadn't known how to react. I said I didn't believe her. I took a step toward her to see what she'd do, but she stood her ground. 'I could feel you trembling,' I said. 'You weren't indifferent.' And I asked if she would feel nothing if I were to kiss her now.

"She thrust her chin out at me. Although she was defying me, there was still something else. 'I despise you,' she said, 'and feel nothing for you. You think you can make me want you?' She was only a few feet away. I walked to her slowly, keeping my eyes on hers. Then, reaching out, I gently took hold of her chin and kissed her, lightly at first then harder as I tried to prize open her lips with my tongue. Her hands were at her sides. I put my right arm around her waist and pulled her to me. Her lips were very soft and although they resisted at first, I felt them begin to open. But I was impatient. As she began to respond, I lifted my left hand to her breast. For a moment she accepted it. It was as if she were balancing on a high place. Then she tore herself away and left the room without another look at me. The principal was waiting in the hall. She smiled and it was as if she knew exactly what had happened."

Pacheco paused to light a cigarette. It wasn't until he stopped speaking that I was again aware of the noise of Madame Letendre's breathing. Malgiolio had begun to peel another peach. I dug my pipe from my pocket, then started looking for my pipe cleaner. Dalakis sat with his arms crossed, facing away as if he wanted no part of us. Even as I glanced at him, I had an image of him at age twelve shooting the horse. How astonished his father must have been.

"Oddly enough," continued Pacheco, "I left the school feeling encouraged. Despite her words, I had sensed in her a trace of the hunger which obsessed me and I had no intention of giving up. During the next weeks I tried to see her as much as possible; that is, I put myself in locations where she would see me. I went to her church. I got myself invited to parties where I knew she would be. Often I ran across her fiancé but he ignored me. I can't tell you how much I was galled by his self-confidence, that he knew Antonia Puccini was his no matter what I did.

"The most important fact I learned was about Antonia's aunt. I happened to talk to her doctor, who was a colleague of mine, and found out that in the past several years she had twice been operated on for cancer, was still having treatments and that he, the doctor, was quite pessimistic about their result. Though I was sorry for Antonia's sake, I had gotten into such a state that I saw everything as being either helpful or harmful to my cause. And this information seemed decidedly helpful.

"As weeks, then months went by and I continued my haunting, I watched the aunt and saw how she seemed to diminish. She grew smaller, paler, as if all her attention were directed inward at the trouble within her body. From her doctor I knew the cancer was spreading and it was only a matter of time before she went into the hospital and never came out again.

"During this period I also saw other women, but my feelings for Antonia remained undiminished. Of course I knew I was in the grip of an obsession but it didn't matter, the words right and wrong no longer held any meaning for me. Finally the aunt entered the hospital. Antonia came each day after school and stayed late into the evening. Often her fiancé came as well. I had patients on the same floor and many times I would go by the aunt's room. Antonia would be reading to her aunt or just sitting. As often as possible I made certain that she saw me.

She would look, then look away as if she had seen nothing. Several times I entered her aunt's room and would feel her aunt's pulse or look at her chart. Of course I had no business there but I knew her doctor and, obviously, I wanted to keep my presence alive in Antonia's mind. She rarely looked at me. Sometimes I went in while her fiancé was visiting and once I took him out in the hall and told him it was important that the aunt get as much rest as possible. I had to laugh. To him I was an important doctor. To me he was just an obstruction.

"As the aunt's condition worsened she was kept more and more sedated. Many evenings when Antonia visited, her aunt would remain unconscious for the entire time. Winter approached and the aunt grew weaker. One rainy evening I happened to be on the floor and saw that Antonia and her aunt were alone in the room. I went in, looked at the aunt's chart, and took her pulse. It was very faint and I doubted she would last much longer. Antonia was reading in a chair and hadn't looked up. 'Have you had anything to eat?' I asked her. 'I can order something for you from the kitchen.' But no, she wasn't hungry. She thanked me and returned to her book. 'You know,' I said, 'your aunt could easily die in two or three days, perhaps even tonight. What do you plan to do after she is gone?'

" 'How is that any business of yours?' she asked.

"Of course I thought it was deeply my business but I wanted to appear to some degree contrite. I said that I still loved her and worried about what would happen to her. She again repeated it was none of my business.

" 'But once your aunt dies,' I said, 'her property will revert to her husband's family. I doubt you have much money of your own. The offer I made still holds. If you agree to be my wife, you can have whatever you desire and also continue to see that young man.'

"But Antonia would have none of it. 'I don't like you,' she

said, 'I don't want you and I don't need you. I have a job and I am engaged to be married. Even if those things were not true I would still refuse to be with you.' At that moment her young man entered the room. He was not happy to see me and asked Antonia if I had been bothering her.

" 'It's nothing,' she said, 'don't concern yourself with it.'

"I walked to the door. 'Remember my offer,' I said.

" 'What offer?' asked her fiancé. 'What's he been saying?'

" 'I want her to marry me,' I said. 'I will give her anything she wants and she can continue to see you as well.'

"Of course he was angry. He pursued me out of the room and grabbed my jacket. 'Be careful,' I said, 'you're in my territory now. One word from me and you'll be expelled from the hospital.' He let go rather quickly. 'Apologize,' I told him. He refused and I shouted the word at him. After another moment he said he was sorry. I was watching Antonia as he said it. She looked furious."

Pacheco paused and in the silence I was again aware of the sound of the cook's dying. Her breathing was so loud, so violent that it didn't seem like a person at all, and I had the impression it was the house itself that was breathing, that we were caught within the body of some living thing, but nothing healthy, nothing with the prospect of long life before it. But isn't it always the case, when you go into another person's house, that you are so surrounded by their choices, by examples of how they see themselves and want to be seen, that to some extent it is like being inside their brains? I glanced at the door but there was no sign of movement. For a moment, I wanted to throw it open, just to see if she was there, but I kept my seat. On my left Dalakis was staring down at the tablecloth and I could hear him breathing as well, a frustrated, angry sound. Across from me Malgiolio was helping himself to a bit of cheese. On my right Pacheco was again drawing the blue pack of

Gauloises from his shirt pocket. I took my tobacco pouch and began filling my pipe.

"As I predicted," said Pacheco, "the aunt died a few days later. The funeral was a big affair and I made certain to attend. A few weeks after that Antonia packed up her things and moved to a small apartment in town. Her cousins came from the north, took over the house, sold whatever they didn't want, and eventually sold the house itself. Antonia was by then nineteen. I had learned that after a period of mourning, probably six months, she intended to announce her wedding, which would occur several months after that.

"The aunt died in mid-winter. During the spring there were a number of meetings of the school board. It seemed there were fewer students, decreased funds, and cutbacks were necessary. Clearly, I'd lost any moral sense of my actions. I passionately desired Antonia Puccini, was in a constant state of agitation, and it seemed that anything I could do to alleviate my discomfort was to the good. Besides, part of me despised Antonia for rejecting me, and so any pain I inflicted on her in return was also to the good. As I've said, I knew Antonia's principal and I also knew several members of the school board. By using my influence and demanding favors and winning people to my side, I was able to make sure that Antonia lost her job. It was necessary that a number of positions be erased and with them went Antonia's. Don't think it was easy. She was a popular teacher and very good at what she did. Be that as it may, at the end of the school year she was told there wouldn't be a place for her in the fall.

"Although she had some money saved, she began right away to look for another job. There too I interfered. For instance, she was nearly hired by the bank until I talked to the manager. She was nearly hired by the city government, until I talked to one of the counselors. After a month or so she got a job as a clerk in a shop that sold fabric and sewing materials. There too I could have had her fired but I decided to let her stay. Her fiancé during this time was doing work in the capital and was supposed to return in about six weeks. Again I interfered, seeing to it that he was forced to stay even longer. More than that, I had people tell him that Antonia had been seen with me, that I'd spent the night in her apartment. My friends would tell me how he'd laugh, so confident was he of his success.

"Antonia was quite poor. Just after taking the job as clerk, she moved to an even cheaper apartment. She was nearing the end of her period of mourning and in several months she would marry. Despite the distance, her fiancé had made several trips down from the capital on his motorcycle. I would sometimes see them walking in the evening, looking into shop windows, sitting on a park bench. With me, her face was always closed, as if time stopped until I left her presence. But with him her face was like water with sunlight reflecting upon it, always moving, always bright and excited.

"She knew, or course, that I hadn't given up my interest. Now and then I would go into the sewing store to buy some small article. It was an ironic gesture and I joked with the woman who owned the store, saying this was where I bought the needles and thread to sew up my patients. I found it very easy to charm these people and yet Antonia remained cold and suspicious.

"After Antonia had been working at the shop for about two months, I decided to visit her apartment. I'd noticed that when her fiancé came down from the capital on his cycle it was always quite late on a Friday night, perhaps eleven or eleven-thirty. So I decided to go to her apartment at about that time and she would open the door, thinking I was he. She had no phone, of course, and I doubted she actually knew when he was coming. My intention was just to talk, to make another offer. I told myself I wouldn't try to touch her or molest her in any way.

"Around midnight Friday, I went to her apartment and knocked on the door. As I anticipated she opened it without thinking, assuming it was her fiancé, and I, very quickly, entered her living room. She was furious and ordered me out. She wore a blue bathrobe and had recently come from her bath. Her dark hair was piled high on her head and the little neck curls were still tipped with beads of water. I told her I only wanted to exchange a few words. She said there was nothing she wanted to hear and if I didn't leave immediately she'd make a scene. Again, I had made sure that I knew her landlord and one or two of the other people in the building, but despite these acquaintanceships I didn't want a disturbance.

"So I threatened her back, saying if she made any noise I'd rape her. 'You know I don't particularly care what happens,' I said. 'If you make a scene, then I'll take you. What I am asking for is a minute of talk.' She didn't respond but neither did she start screaming, so I repeated my offer. 'You are poor and I can make you rich. I want to marry you.'

" 'I despise you,' she said.

" 'I don't care about that,' I told her. 'I know you desire me and I want to make love to you.'

" 'I don't desire you,' she said. 'I hate you.'

"I asked her why, just for loving her? After all, she knew nothing about me except that I was persistent. Surely that was a commendable quality. I promised to honor her, cherish her. What more did she want? But she grew angry. 'Can't you understand,' she said, 'I'm engaged to marry someone else and even if I were not I have no feelings for you at all.'

" 'That's not true,' I told her. 'You too have some of the hunger.'

" 'That's a lie,' she said.

"So I offered to show her, offered to kiss her again. I walked toward her but as I approached she snatched a pair of scissors from a table and slashed at me, actually cutting the fabric of my jacket. Even while doing that, her face held no expression. I stepped back. As a matter of fact this evidence of strong feeling made me want her even more, and I was on the very edge of brushing aside the scissors and pushing her to the couch. But that wouldn't have satisfied me. I had too much anger.

" 'At least you've heard my offer,' I told her. She didn't speak but stood holding the scissors. One of her scarves was on the table, a blue silk scarf. I took it as a souvenir, sniffed it, and put it in my pocket. Then I left."

Pacheco reached over for the box of matches next to my wine glass, struck one, and held it to his cigarette. Exhaling a small cloud of smoke, he waved his hand to disperse it.

Dalakis had been fussing with his napkin, fussing with his glass. He was obviously unhappy and when he spoke it was as if the words burst from him unwillingly. "Why couldn't you have left her alone?" he demanded.

"I wanted her. I've already told you, right and wrong didn't enter into it. I simply wanted her."

It struck me as interesting in the scene that Pacheco had described how his desire was its own justification for action; that if he wanted something, then it was as if that thing were owed to him. Normally I believe he was a very moral man, whatever that means, but he'd always been someone who helped the poor and unfortunate, who spoke of himself as a liberal, even a socialist, with a strong sense of responsibility for his fellow creatures.

"But you didn't love her," said Dalakis. "You had no feeling but this hunger."

"That's not quite true," said Pacheco. "Clearly, my passion was what motivated me, but I also admired the way she refused me. You see, so few women did. It's almost amusing. I had no respect for my own behavior and neither did she, which led me to admire and desire her even more. Beyond that, I liked how she was her own creature. Most women take their identity from what they imagine men want them to be. That's not very interesting. You scratch the silver surface and find lead. But Antonia was entirely honest. She would never act in any way contrary to her nature, and, of course, that is what I was asking her to do, which again was one of the reasons I desired her."

"So you decided to ruin her life?" asked Dalakis. "You had this desire and the consequences meant nothing? She was no more than a snippet of food?"

Dalakis leaned toward Pacheco and kept jostling me with his shoulder. I was surprised at the degree of his anger. As for Pacheco, he seemed to regret it, almost to feel embarrassed by it, but he didn't retreat.

"I wanted her," he repeated.

"In the same way you wanted my wife?" asked Dalakis. "You hungered and so you took her?"

Pacheco didn't answer right away. Since Pacheco and Dalakis's wife had been involved some years before Dalakis appeared on the scene, it seemed inappropriate that he should be so upset. After all, how many men marry virgins? Looking up, I saw Malgiolio's moon-shaped face pulled into a grin.

"Your wife I wanted only once," said Pacheco. "That wasn't a hunger, it was an itch."

Dalakis threw his napkin down on the table. Even though he is the most nonviolent person I've ever known, he is still a large man, much larger than Pacheco, and I had no wish to see them fight. But my fear was wrongly placed. After this gesture of frustration, Dalakis returned to his point.

144

"Still, you took her."

"It's not as simple as that," said Pacheco in a softer voice. "She too had her hunger, her desire. One doesn't simply rape people."

"There are different degrees of rape."

But Pacheco had grown tired of the discussion. Removing the orange handkerchief from his breast pocket, he shook it several times and replaced it so that one point flopped over the top like a dog's ear. Dalakis remained angry, huffing and puffing beside me. Thinking again of the afflicted Bottom on the vase of flowers, it occurred to me that perhaps Dalakis was the one with the donkey's head. Malgiolio watched him with a little smile as if waiting for him to make a greater fool of himself. From the hall came the sounds of the dying cook. I was surprised how I seemed to be getting used to it, even though her breathing had grown more choked and ragged. Pacheco, however, continued to listen carefully and after a particularly loud gasp he got to his feet. "Perhaps I should take a look at her," he said.

He pushed back his chair and as he walked to the door, Señora Puccini entered wheeling the cart. They passed without glancing at each other.

Dalakis watched Señora Puccini put the plates on a tray and fill our glasses with the last of the Burgundy. Then he got to his feet and reached out a hand so that she stopped. "You've been listening, haven't you," he said. It wasn't a question. Señora Puccini looked at him, not angrily or harshly. It seemed even a glance of some understanding. "Why have you stayed with him? Why did you come in the first place?"

She shook her head, then put the cheese and bowls of peaches on the cart, moving almost mechanically.

"He got you fired from your teaching position," continued Dalakis, "kept you from getting another job, interfered with your friends. You knew all that and still you came to him."

She again looked at Dalakis, stopping her work and standing with a silver bowl between her hands. She didn't seem to be looking at him as much as into him, almost as if she knew him intimately. "Some of it I only learned tonight," she said, "but still I would have come."

"But why?" I asked.

She didn't give me the smallest glance, but kept her eyes on Dalakis. At that moment, Pacheco appeared in the doorway and stood watching his housekeeper. Apparently without seeing him Señora Puccini put the bowl on the cart and pushed it to the door. I realized the wheel was no longer squeaking; someone must have oiled it since the beginning of the meal.

"So you want to know why she came to me?" said Pacheco, after she had gone. "You think perhaps I was able to talk her into it, even make her love me. Is that right, Carl?"

"I don't know," he answered, not looking at Pacheco. "Earlier you said you'd ruined her and apparently that's what you have done. But how or why she permitted it I have no idea."

"You don't think she could have liked me for myself alone?" asked Pacheco. He had remained by the door and I had to turn in my chair to see him. He was so far from the candles that his face was in shadow. Even so, I thought he was smiling.

"How could she? Obviously, she was forced to come here, and obviously she hates you." Dalakis's voice was so controlled that I wondered if he didn't hate Pacheco as well.

Pacheco was silent a moment. He was smoking a cigarette and its smell blew toward us in the draft from the door. It was uncomfortable twisting around to look at him and I wished he'd return to his seat.

"You think how we grew up," he said at last, "well loved, well cared for, going to good schools and surrounded by people who were kind to us, always having enough money and enough to eat. If you took the thirty of us at the age of fourteen and sat us down and asked us individually whether or not we were good human beings, then I am sure we'd have said yes, while also being mystified by the question. We might have elements of greed or selfishness or envy or spite but in general, yes, we were pretty good boys. After all, we were the future middle class.

"But then let's say we were called together at twenty and asked the same question. What would have been the result? By then some of us had behaved badly. There were illegitimate children, petty theft, various forms of betrayal. But, even so, I think we would have called ourselves basically good. And if a few of us had gotten into trouble, we could point to complicated circumstances, weaknesses, errors of judgment; yet even with these lapses we would still have claimed a certain morality. We were decent, or hoped we were. But where does it change? You, Malgiolio, with your squandering of that fortune and the wreck of your family and the woman who pisses on you whenever you scrape together a little money, do you still call yourself good? Or take Schwab. I've seen quite a few people in the hospital who've just returned from being questioned by him or his men. Does Schwab call himself good? Or any of us? You, Dalakis? You, Batterby?

"It depends on what you want and how much you want it and how you place yourself in relation to the generally accepted system of morality. You know that old argument, that some people have the right to set aside conventional morality because of their superiority or whatever? Clearly, there are people who do terrible things and are able to justify their misconduct by need or superiority or by saying that they weren't responsible. But if these things continue and if you're unable to avoid self-deception, then you reach a point where you have to say, No,

I am not a good person. I have behaved badly. That is the first admission. The second admission is that I will continue to behave badly.

"Until I met Antonia Puccini, I was able to convince myself I was a decent human being. Yes, I had caused trouble for many women, but I could argue that they had wanted it or that it didn't do them harm. But with Antonia I came to a point where I no longer believed in my own decency, and furthermore I had no wish to be decent. Most of the time I behaved quite well. I am not mean-spirited or envious or cowardly. But I realized when I behaved well I was doing so only because I had no good reason not to. By good reason I mean my own self-interest. Give people enough to eat, a warm place to live, and some amusement, companionship, and general safety and they are basically good human beings who eagerly claim to believe in traditional Judeo-Christian values. Take something away or make them want something they can't easily have and those values become a trifle shaky."

"Why are you telling us this?" asked Dalakis. He too had turned in his seat to look at Pacheco. His glasses had slipped down to the tip of his nose and he roughly shoved them back.

"You were asking Señora Puccini why she'd come to live with me, why she'd given herself to me. I'm just making a few prefatory remarks before I show you something."

"What're you saying?" asked Dalakis. "What justification can you possibly have?"

Pacheco grew suddenly angry. "Not justification! Why should I care to justify myself to you or anybody? I wanted something and I wanted it badly enough that I took it. Only those who still believe in their own decency attempt to justify. I simply describe. Now, if you gentlemen would be good enough to come with me, I will show you the nature of my final argument. Ready, Dalakis? Malgiolio, Batterby?"

Pacheco took a candle and passed into the great hall. We followed with more haste than was perhaps decorous and jostled each other at the door. I kept trying to imagine what Pacheco intended to show us but my mind ran on as fruitlessly as a squirrel on a wheel. Pacheco walked directly to the stairs. I looked over at the cook lying on her back on the small mattress. Her grandson sat on the floor beside her, wiping her forehead with a cloth. Her harsh breathing echoed so against the stone walls that again I had the sense of listening to the house itself. But I didn't want to think of her then, didn't want her dying image to intrude on whatever Pacheco intended to show us, and I hurried up the left bracket of the staircase. Malgiolio and Dalakis were right behind me. None of us spoke.

Pacheco turned right down the hall and we again passed the medieval armor, the battle axes and swords. I wondered whose job it was to polish it all so carefully. A helmet with the visor down seemed to watch us from its shelf. I had an impulse to pick up a particularly vicious-looking mace with four sharp spikes, just to hold it and feel its weight. Pacheco didn't turn to see if we were following. I looked at his narrow back, his well-groomed gray hair. I thought of all the escapades I had followed him on as a youngster, even as a young man, how many back alleys I had gone down with him only a few feet ahead. I remember once when we were both eighteen he led me up a fire escape and across one rooftop after another, steep, slate-covered roofs, until we reached the dormer window of a girl who cheerfully made love to us both. Her name was Katrina and she had crossed eyes. She had been locked up by a father who would have killed us had he known we were there. I could hear him banging around downstairs drunkenly breaking the furniture and shouting at his wife.

We climbed the smaller staircase to the third floor and for a moment I thought we were again going up to the roof, but then Pacheco paused by the door to the room from which I had seen Señora Puccini emerge about two hours earlier.

"Ready, gentlemen?" he asked. "At least do me the favor of remaining silent."

He opened the door and entered a room that seemed lit by a hundred candles. I felt immensely curious and almost pushed around Pacheco to see what was there. Against the far wall was a bed with its foot pointing toward the door. But before I even describe it or what lay upon it, I should say that every square inch of the walls was covered with bright colors, not only orange and red and yellow paint but colorful posters and pictures, that even the woodwork was painted in bright colors, that even the ceiling was covered with pictures and reproductions of famous paintings—Breughel and van Gogh and Monet—and that hanging from the ceiling were various mobiles and little airplanes and tiny figures on trapezes and colorful stuffed birds, so that one had to be careful not to get tangled up in something. And even the surfaces, the tables and bureau, were covered with ships in bottles and oriental carvings done in ivory and jade, and interesting shells and even more pictures. There were also bird cages and a large tank of tropical fish, while on one table a stuffed snake, a cobra, was half coiled around and poised above a stuffed mongoose that reared up on its hind legs, baring its teeth and ready to fend off attack.

We crowded into the room, ducking away from the mobiles, trying not to bump into the table. The room was very hot and there was only one small window, which was closed. There was a smell of lavender and sweat. I looked over the footboard. On the bed lay a man covered with a white sheet. His age was hard to calculate. Perhaps he was seventy, perhaps only thirty. He was extremely thin and his face was sunken and gray, although relatively unlined. The sheet was pulled up right to his neck and his body was a narrow ridge beneath it. His eyes were open and he stared at us. They were very blue, a light blue like water in a blue basin. His hair was dark but streaked with gray. The thinness of his face and his sunken cheeks made his eyes seem huge.

We stood at the foot of the bed and stared at him. Certainly, it was strange that a man should be lying in one of Pacheco's upstairs rooms, but what made it so striking was the eccentricity of the room itself, with its colors and pictures and every surface jammed with objects. It was so hot that after a moment we were all sweating.

"Who is he?" asked Dalakis, as if the man weren't really in the room, for although we'd been staring at him and he apparently had been staring back, he made no sound or gesture.

"His name is Roberto. Roberto Collura," said Pacheco. "He is Señora Puccini's fiancé."

"Can he speak?" asked Malgiolio, almost breathlessly.

"He used to be able to, or at least he could a little. Now I'm not sure whether he refuses to or if he has lost the ability. You see, he's paralyzed from about the nose down."

"But what's he doing here?" asked Dalakis.

"He lives here," said Pacheco. "He's lived in this house for as long as I have. He's been with me for about twenty years."

Truly this Roberto Collura was a pathetic sight, made even more pathetic by the riot of color which surrounded him, but equally remarkable was Pacheco's voice. How cold it was and full of scorn. How much he seemed to hate the man who lay on the bed. We all wanted to ask why he was here, and in fact the question was about to explode from each of us, but then we heard rapid footsteps in the hall and Señora Puccini hurried into the room.

"What are you doing here?" she demanded.

The doctor looked at her coolly. "I was showing them Ro-

151

berto," he said. "After all, how can I explain your life with me unless they meet Roberto Collura?"

"You said you wouldn't bother him," said Señora Puccini. "That was part of our agreement."

"Agreements change," said Pacheco.

How can I describe Señora Puccini's anger? I had been used to her face as smooth and expressionless as the front of a building. To say it was contorted would be to say nothing. It was dark red. Veins stood out at the temples. The skin was stretched as if the whole under part was about to burst through the surface. It reminded me of magazine photos of space pilots forced to undergo extreme gravity. Both Malgiolio and Dalakis stared at her with alarm and apprehension. I glanced at Pacheco and saw he was smiling. It wasn't a mocking or cynical smile but one of true pleasure, as if she had done something particularly to gratify him.

"Get out!" she demanded. "I won't stand for your being here!"

Pacheco walked to the door and held it open for us. "We were just leaving," he said.

Chapter Five

As we descended the stairs from Roberto Collura's room, I trailed behind, letting the circle of light thrown by Pacheco's candle get about twenty feet ahead, separating me into the dark. Do you remember being caught by your parents doing something you shouldn't? That's how I felt when Señora Puccini had discovered us, and I wished to disassociate myself from my comrades. Not that I was less interested than they, but my interest, as well as theirs of course, felt slightly improper. It seemed unclean.

Naturally, it wasn't, unless curiosity itself can be called unclean. But her anger and the way she had surprised us made me think I had behaved badly and so I hung back and watched my comrades descend the great candlelit staircase—Pacheco first in his gray suit, then Malgiolio short and rotund several steps behind, then Dalakis shambling and bearlike and rubbing his head. I paused at the top and once more had the sense of the layered quality of time and memory so that I wasn't looking at my friends at just that particular moment but at many moments stretched over our boyhood. Always Pacheco was in the lead and too often we were returning from some deed that would have been better left undone. Then once more I pushed those other occasions from my mind as I watched Pacheco make his way across the hall to the cook, the noise of whose breathing still filled the house as water fills a cup. Juan sat cross-legged beside her, stroking her brow. Malgiolio paused by the fountain. I continued my descent and had just joined him and Dalakis when there was a great booming knock on the door.

The knocking was so aggressive that all three of us grew as nervous as forest creatures poised on the brink of flight. Is the comparison hyperbolic? Possibly in memory I had inflated an innocent reaction into a guilty one, although I am certain that emotionally, even irrationally, I tied the loud knocking to our expulsion from the bedroom of Roberto Collura. Let it be enough to say we were in a nervous state, which perhaps stemmed from no more than the night itself. Pacheco, who had been kneeling beside Madame Letendre, got to his feet. "Go into the dining room," he said. "I'll join you shortly."

We didn't run, but walked briskly. Why did I feel we would be called to account for our behavior? The image of the paralyzed man kept returning to me and I thought of him lying there year after year in the midst of that glittering clutter which existed not just to entertain him but to take the place of the world. We resumed our seats. My wine glass was full but I didn't want any more. I found myself desiring sugar, chocolate, anything sweet, but surely that was the temptation of my disease, more aptly described by its German name: *Zucrekrank*, sugarsick.

The others turned out to be thinking about Roberto Collura as well. Dalakis leaned toward me and began to speak in a kind of urgent whisper. "He brought her with him from the south. That's why she's here, just so she can take care of her fiancé."

"But why is he paralyzed?" asked Malgiolio. For the first time the table was empty of food and Malgiolio glanced about him with the expression of a child who has misplaced a favorite toy. He drank a little wine.

"Do you remember that story years ago that Pacheco had shot somebody in a duel?" asked Dalakis, still in hushed tones. "I can't remember the details, but perhaps that is what happened to the man upstairs. Perhaps Pacheco fought him and this was the result."

Malgiolio made an amused chuffing noise through his nose. "Really, Carl, why do you need to improve on everything? He might simply have been sick, some lingering disease that has reduced him to that condition."

Together they had articulated our main question: Could the man have ended up in that state without Pacheco being responsible? How far might he have gone in his pursuit of Antonia Puccini? Of course, I refused to believe that Pacheco could be blamed in the matter. Malgiolio was probably right; and as for Dalakis, he had shown himself not entirely objective in his feelings toward the doctor.

"We should never have come," said Dalakis. "This is an evil house."

Again Malgiolio made his chuffing noise. It wasn't like laughter so much as like blowing his nose. "We have done what we ought not to have done and we have not done what we ought to have done. Is that how it goes?" He somewhat condescendingly reached his little hand across the table to Dalakis, who ignored it. "You've spent your life in a cave, my friend, I can tell you far more sordid stories than this one."

I was afraid we might be forced to hear a couple, but at that instant Pacheco walked briskly through the door. "Schwab's here," he said. "He's starving. I've told Señora Puccini to bring back the food."

Eric Schwab entered immediately after. He paused to take in the room, then smiled and opened his arms in an expansive gesture. He was a large blond man dressed in a blue uniform that had been so carefully tailored that it didn't seem to be clothing as much as an extra layer of skin. Usually when I saw him he was wearing a suit and tie. In fact, I don't think I'd ever seen him in uniform. He was a high-ranking official in the police department, although I never really knew what he did. People said it was something in counterintelligence. That was perhaps the politest description of his job. Whatever it was, many people were afraid of him.

Schwab walked rapidly to each of us and we stood up and embraced. He had a red bricklike face, as if his collar were too tight, and a large muscular chest and shoulders. He smelled of talcum powder and leather. Schwab has always struck me as someone entirely without a moral sense. Even as a child his behavior seemed governed by the prospect of punishment or reward. Once, when I asked him why he had taken a job with the police department, he told me, "I have a skill and my skill is for sale." And when I asked him what he meant, he gave me a smile that seemed to indicate that I was an innocent fellow who shouldn't ask such questions. Somehow it seemed typical of him that he should be five hours late for dinner and still expect to be fed.

There were four times the number of empty places as occupied ones at the long table, and Schwab took the seat beside Malgiolio and across from Dalakis. To each of us he said some small personal thing. For instance, to me he said how much he enjoyed my reviews in the paper, particularly a recent piece comparing several books about show dogs. We have never been close but Schwab is one of those people who treats everyone as if he were a best friend. I find it amazing that he can decide upon each of his potential actions entirely according to its effectiveness. Never would he behave, as it were, accidentally. Despite his apparent delight in our company, these dinners are the only times that any of us ever see him.

"Well," said Pacheco, pouring Schwab some wine, "tell us what's happening in the city. We've been unable to get any news."

"Pah, a few students, a few malcontents. It's nothing, just a lot of noise."

"But what are the fires we've seen from the roof?" asked Dalakis.

Taking some wine, Schwab let it slosh back and forth in his mouth, breathed across it, even chewed it, then looked at Pacheco and winked. After this demonstration of pleasure, he tapped one finger to the side of his nose and smiled at Dalakis benignly. "There was a little trouble at the university. Several buildings were seized and some fires started. Also some cars were burned. A few students even had guns. These were joined or aided by a mutinous air force regiment. For a while, yes, there was a bit to excitement, but how could they do anything against the combined force of the police and military? The city is full of unhappy people and at a time of instability there is always a certain amount of trouble-making."

He spoke as if the subject were inconceivably minor.

"But what is this continued shooting?" asked Pacheco.

"Curfew violators, a few would-be rebels with guns, perhaps even fireworks . . . Ahh," he said, as Señora Puccini entered wheeling a cart laden with food, "now I can eat. I can't tell you how sorry I was when I thought I would have to miss my friends for another six months. So there are only four of you?"

"We're all that came," I said, "and we live nearby."

"Yes, of course," said Schwab, shaking his head, "the road-blocks. What a nuisance." He began eating immediately and continued talking with his mouth full, swallowing rapidly and

157

washing down the food with more wine. While we had had our various courses in succession, Schwab's came all together, so that he was surrounded by a dozen heaping plates, including even the oysters. "My dear Pacheco, this veal is tremendous. And the salmon!" Scooping up an oyster, he dabbed it with horseradish and tilted it high over his mouth so it slid half off the shell, hung for a moment, then dropped. It seemed like an immoral amount of food. Even Malgiolio appeared impressed. I felt sure that Señora Puccini was engaging in a kind of bitter joke. She poured him a second glass of wine, then went out to the hall. Schwab never once looked at her. Again the noise of the cook's breathing grew louder as she opened the door. Schwab took a mouthful of this, then a mouthful of that, turning quickly from plate to plate, then glancing up at us, dragging his napkin across his shiny and food-smeared mouth, then smiling.

"What a feast!" said Schwab. Truly, he held a fork in each of his great red hands. "When have we last eaten like this, Batterby?"

"I really can't say." I was struck by how healthy and happy Schwab looked, as if he had just returned from a week at the beach, instead of forcing his way through whatever violence was occurring in the city.

"They don't eat like this anymore, that's the sad truth. Do you remember that party in the country we went to as young men? It must have been over twenty years ago. They had tables and tables of wonderful food. Some pretty girl had come of age and her parents were rich."

"I don't think I was there," said Dalakis.

"I remember it," said Malgiolio suddenly. He had been staring at Schwab not exactly with awe but as one might stare at a television personality. "And Pacheco was there as well. Fillet of beef Wellington. How could I ever forget. An endless supply of food and drink."

"That's right," said Schwab, "and I remember that Vicuña and Machado were there, as well as Kress and maybe Shapiro. And Batterby was there with his wife. And poor old Keester, he was killed about a year after that."

These were all members of our group. "No," I told him, "I remember the party, but it was before my marriage, about six months before." Malgiolio had taken a fork and was helping himself to some of Schwab's veal. Some people have no shame.

"I was sure it was after," said Schwab, "because it was in the summer and your wedding was the previous fall. That too was a wonderful feast. How perfect to relive the great feasts of one's life. I've always regretted not keeping a culinary diary to describe those wonderful meals. Then when I was old and without teeth and half a stomach, I could read about those days and all those wonderful tastes would come back to me."

"What makes you think you'll reach old age?" asked Pacheco, rather tonelessly.

Schwab laughed as if the joke were the funniest he'd heard in weeks, then he choked on some succulent morsel, coughed until he turned purple, and drank down more wine. His blond hair was cut short and his forehead was a perfect rectangle. All in all he seemed composed of rectangular slabs of pink flesh.

"How true," he said, smiling kindly at Pacheco. "But then my children could enjoy it. That beef Wellington, for instance. And do you remember the lobster thermidor, Malgiolio, and the salmon? I'm sure it was after your wedding, Batterby. Ah, Pacheco, I can't tell you how I regret not having gotten here earlier, that we all couldn't have been here. The veal is astonishing. What a memory it would have been for the group. Now, if we all live, we'll have to wait another seven or eight years for your turn to come again."

As I watched Schwab stuff himself, I felt somewhat disappointed in him. If I couldn't hear the rest of Pacheco's story, then I wanted to know more about the violence we had seen from the roof, even from the balcony outside the bathroom. Schwab was an emissary from that violent world. Surely there were stories he could tell.

"How did you get here?" I asked. "Isn't it dangerous?"

Schwab took a moment to swallow his food. As he looked at me with those pale blue eyes, I felt he disliked my question. Not that he frowned, rather he smiled a trifle less. "The streets seem quiet, but even so I was able to commandeer an armored car."

"But what will we find tomorrow?" asked Dalakis. "What will the city be like?"

"How can we ever know that, my friend?" asked Schwab, wiping his face with his napkin. He seemed charmed by Dalakis's question. "Isn't the future in doubt even in the most peaceful times? I look at it this way: It takes the light of the sun eight minutes to reach the earth. So if the sun blinked out this very instant, we would have eight minutes of warmth, eight minutes of further life. And who's to say? Maybe it has already been out two, three, five minutes. That's how I live, as if the sun had already blinked out. As for tomorrow? Events have taken the city by the neck and shaken it a bit. The dust is resettling. You have to be patient. Who knows, perhaps tomorrow we'll all be lying in the morgue." Here Schwab laughed again, a mixture of coughing and laughing, and I watched several small particles of food shoot from his mouth back onto his plate and the surrounding tablecloth. "But truly this is a busy time and I can only stay a few minutes. Just long enough to take a few bites and run. I wanted to pay my respects, that's all, and to taste what your marvelous cook has prepared."

I don't think Schwab realized that the woman who had cooked the meal was noisily dying out in the hall. But even had he known, I doubt it would have affected him. At one time I thought Schwab rather callous, but then I decided he had entirely no sense of other people, as if they were like abstractions to him. He had never married and because of that some people liked to say he was homosexual, but I gather he had a mistress and saw other women as well. When we were teenagers and even later, he loved to go to whorehouses and knew dozens of them. I have no idea where he got the money. Even though his parents were not well off, Schwab never seemed to go short. And he was generous with it, I'll say that for him. If he had the money and you were with him, he'd pay all the bills.

I remember once running into him with Cora a few months before our marriage. We were in a women's clothing store and she was trying on a hat. In fact, there were two hats and she was completely unable to decide between them. Schwab saw us through the window and came in. She told him her problem and Schwab laughed and bought both hats. Then he took us out to dinner, to a rather strange private club in the old part of the city with private dining rooms and waiters who must have had a million secrets. We ate in a little room by ourselves. There was a big fireplace and old etchings on the walls. From nearby rooms I kept hearing hysterical female laughter. The meal was extremely lavish with course after course of fish and beef and fowl and complicated arrangements in aspic. When it was done we went into another little room and Schwab drew back a curtain and we saw we were in a private box above a stage. A man and a woman, both practically naked, were doing a wild dance. Each had a whip and as they circled one another they pretended to lash each other's faces and bodies. I say pretended, but really it was hard to tell and right at the end I remember seeing a great red welt appear across the woman's breast. The music was Arabic or Greek. During the whole performance, Schwab laughed happily and pointed out to Cora intricacies of the dance. Although fascinated, I found the whole thing rather depraved.

I was about to ask Schwab about the roadblocks and if they

weren't still in place when Señora Puccini reentered the dining room and went to Pacheco. "I think you should look at her," she said.

Without glancing at us, Pacheco stood up and walked rapidly into the hall. Even though he was intent on doing his duties as host, I felt most of his mind was on the cook and her dying. But no matter the degree of his grief, Pacheco would have hidden it from us. That was his way. Sometimes I even felt he flirted with strong emotion just to show he was immune from it.

"The pity about these disturbances," said Schwab, letting the smile slide from his face, "is that so many innocent people get hurt. But what can you do? It is like those porpoises that get killed in the tuna catches. The poor things just get in the way." Saying this, he sipped a little water, then looked thoughtfully at his empty fork before jabbing it with renewed vigor into the veal.

"Do you think it would be all right for us to go home tonight?" asked Dalakis, reassured by Schwab's descriptions of the city. "Pacheco has said we can stay, but of course I only sleep well in my own bed."

Schwab had continued to look somber, sitting very straight in his chair and rising about a foot above Malgiolio on his left. "No, there are too many fanatics about. You should stay until tomorrow at least."

"But you said the city was safe," said Dalakis.

"There you go again, my friend," said Schwab with the beginnings of a smile, "pressing for safety in a helter-skelter world. Remember what I said about the sun? Safety is relative and while it's relatively safe there are still a few malcontents. The army wants to make certain they're out of the way before trying to put the city back together. Surely you can see that."

"I saw someone shoot a horse a little while ago," I said.

Schwab happily clapped his hands together. "Yes, I nearly crashed into it. I'm afraid there'll be a lot of cleaning up to do before the city is fit for normal life. I'll tell you what. If there is any chance of the curfew being extended, I'll return tomorrow and take you home myself. It's quite convenient having an armored car." He took another huge bite of veal, then washed it down with more wine. He didn't chew his food so much as float it into his stomach.

Wiping his mouth, Schwab pushed his chair away from the table, got to his feet and stood smoothing down the front of his blue tunic with both hands. "Now, back to work," he said.

We were surprised and spoke all at once. "You're leaving already?" I said. Really he'd hardly come.

"You've still given us little idea what's happening," said Malgiolio.

"What about the government," asked Dalakis, "will it survive?"

Schwab sucked thoughtfully at his teeth as he turned to look at us. "I wanted to see how you were. You're my friends, all men I've known for forty years. What does the city matter? I'm not a newspaper. Yes, it has changed, but what it is and what you will find is not for me to say. I'm your old friend who has gone through much trouble to spend time in your company. You should say, 'Here's Schwab. How good to see him well and healthy.' You should see this as possibly the last moment of our world. We must drink to it." Here Schwab lifted his glass and motioned to us to follow his example. Only Malgiolio raised his glass, although hesitantly. Dalakis assumed he was joking and I had had enough.

Then Schwab did an astonishing thing. Drawing his pistol from the holster at his belt, he held it over his head.

"Drink!" he shouted.

"Really, Schwab," protested Dalakis.

Of course he was joking but we drank nonetheless, even though I'd already had more than was good for me. Emptying his glass, Schwab stared at us critically, then turned and threw his glass against the wall. It made a little flash of light and the fragments scattered every which way. We watched, then Schwab raised his pistol again, pointing it at the ceiling.

"Throw them," he ordered, grinning.

We all threw our glasses, although tossed would be the more accurate word. Dalakis actually missed the wall, bouncing his glass off the back of a chair so that it fell to the floor, where it shattered. To tell the truth, I found Schwab's conceit almost impossible to stomach.

Pacheco had just reentered the room and was standing by the door. If he thought anything about our toast and the damage to his stemware, he gave no sign of it. "What have you been doing out in the city that has caused you trouble?" asked Pacheco, walking to his chair.

"Patrols, mostly. The city has been divided into sectors and we were assigned to this particular area. That's how I was able to stop by."

"Have you seen anyone?" asked Pacheco.

"What do you mean?"

"Rebels or troublemakers or curfew violators, whatever you call them."

"Some."

"And when you catch them, you question them. Is that right?"

"Yes, if we're able to catch them. Usually they run or shoot back at us." Schwab stood by his chair, still smoothing down the front of his uniform. He seemed to have little interest in Pacheco's questions.

"And when you're finished with them," asked Pacheco, "what do you do with them then?"

164

"Often they go to one of the neighborhood jails."

"You don't just kill them as curfew violators?" asked Pacheco. He was also standing by his chair and the two men were speaking back and forth over Malgiolio's head.

"Some have died, yes."

"So you kill them?" Pacheco asked again.

"It has happened. Why do you care?"

"They are my neighbors. Malgiolio was earlier praising the disturbances by saying it would give him more opportunities to find a suitable job. And I just wanted to see if they would be hiring grave diggers."

Schwab laughed heartily, apparently deciding that Pacheco was having a joke. "Yes, they'll need lots of grave diggers."

"What about Kress," asked Dalakis, "have you seen anything of him?" David Kress was a colonel in the army who was also a member of our group.

"No, his garrison is in the southern part of the city. I know there's been a lot of shooting down there but I haven't been able to get news. I'm sure he's all right. You know Kress, he's a survivor."

Schwab walked out to the hall and we followed him. He was quite tall and walked as if his back were held straight by a brace. Standing by the door were four uniformed policemen. When they saw him, they stood quickly to attention. I was struck that they seemed frightened of him. Schwab glanced at the cook lying on her mattress, then continued to the door.

"Too many casualties," he said, "too many hurt people." Turning, Schwab shook our hands, then embraced each one of us. "I hope our next meeting is more cordial. We need to remember that we have two lives—those we had when young and our present ones. We can't let the latter interfere with the former." He smiled, then straightened the patent leather holster attached to his belt. "After all, these current lives are not why we meet. They are trifles and exist to keep those other lives bright and shiny in our minds." With this Schwab turned away and one of his men opened the door. They all ducked down and ran for the armored car which was parked at the curb. Schwab didn't look back. Considering his claim that the streets were safe, I thought he ran rather quickly. As Pacheco shut the door, I heard the armored car roaring its motor, then accelerating down the street.

"He's a cheerful man for a torturer," said Pacheco.

Dalakis turned to Pacheco in surprise. "How can you say that about a man who's your friend?"

"As I said earlier, I've had to treat the men and women whom he's questioned."

I was struck by what Schwab had said about our having two lives and equally struck that Pacheco had either chosen to ignore it or hadn't noticed. And I wondered if that were true, as if our group when it first decided to meet was no more than a fan club for the boys we had been, boys and young men; as if as adults we could in no way compete with those past selves, so much more alive and interesting. And perhaps that was why Pacheco hadn't seemed to notice Schwab's comment, just because his life as an adult, his affair with Señora Puccini, was larger than any life he'd had as a boy or young man. With me the reverse is true because often it seems that my life stopped with the death of my wife. And the reverse may also be true with Malgiolio and Dalakis. Here then is another explanation why we took such a chance to travel to Pacheco's house that night—that it formed an avenue to reach the important parts of ourselves: those boys we had been.

Just then the cook's grandson called to Pacheco. There was such fear in his voice that I hardly wanted to see what was wrong. We turned to find the cook arching her back high off the mattress, almost like a gymnast. All the veins seemed to stand out on her face and her blind eggshell eyes bulged from their sockets. She reached out toward Pacheco and I had the impression she could see him, although that was impossible. The gasping grew louder, like a machine breaking itself apart. Señora Puccini hurried in from the corridor. The cook kept arching her back, bending as if she would break, then she collapsed to the floor. Pacheco knelt down and felt her pulse. He let go of her hand, and it fell to the mattress. There was no need to say she was dead.

The boy burst into tears. When Señora Puccini stood up, I could see that she too was crying. She put her arms around the boy and embraced him. I had become so accustomed to her blank stares that to see her eyes full of tears was tremendously affecting. I looked over at Dalakis and Malgiolio. Dalakis had taken a rather gray handkerchief from his pocket and was blowing into it. Malgiolio stood with his head bowed.

Pacheco continued to kneel beside Madame Letendre, stroking her forehead. I thought how her skin was growing cold and stiff and how he could probably feel the change. I couldn't be sure in the dim light, but it seemed her eyes were still open.

"I'd like to carry her to the garden," said Pacheco. "Perhaps you'll be good enough to help."

We each took a corner of the mattress from the chaise longue and lifted. The cook was a big woman but with the four of us and the boy at the back we had no trouble except for gripping the canvas surface of the mattress itself. Señora Puccini went in front holding several candles. I was carrying the rear right corner and the cook's head kept lolling back toward my hands. For some reason I had an absolute terror of her gray hair brushing my wrists and I almost dropped the mattress as I tried to keep from touching her. Her eyes were half closed and her mouth was open. If it hadn't been for the boy holding the rear of the mattress between me and Malgiolio, the whole business would have fallen to the floor.

We made our way to the corridor, then turned right through

the door to the patio. As we passed the dining room I glanced in at the remnants of food that Schwab had spared, crumbs mostly, bones, oyster shells. The five of us carrying the cook made quite a bit of noise and our entrance disturbed the birds, which began chirping and fluttering in their cages. Señora Puccini placed the candles on a chair. There was a long wooden table, a sort of picnic table, at the back of the patio and we put the mattress on top. The bird cages were all around us and the air was filled with nervous twittering. Malgiolio stared at them as if frightened. Some people, I know, have quite a terror of birds. Señora Puccini lit more candles. Their flames flickered in the slight breeze.

"I'll get something with which to cover her," said Pacheco, and he hurried off, leaving us with the cook. Although he was certainly fond of the dead woman, he showed a casualness with death that came, I supposed, from being a surgeon. Señora Puccini approached the cook's body, then reached out and touched her face. She did this with great tenderness and I couldn't help but be surprised at her loving expression, particularly when I considered that she might have purposefully done nothing to keep the cook from leaving the house, that she might even have encouraged her to leave.

Dalakis stood beside her. "Had you known her for many years?"

"We all came at the same time—she and the man upstairs and myself."

"You must have loved her very much," said Dalakis. He reached forward and closed the cook's eyes. I shuddered. The idea of touching that dead flesh was horrible to me.

"She knew all my secrets," said Señora Puccini.

Dalakis put a hand on her shoulder. "If there's any way I can help . . ."

Señora Puccini shrugged away from his touch, then glanced at the three of us. Her face grew cold again; it was like seeing curtains being pulled across a window. Without another word, she walked toward the kitchen, passing Pacheco as he came out with a white sheet. I followed her part of the way through the garden. The rich smell of the flowers, the smell of herbs, mint and dill and basil, seemed to push away the smoky smells of the city, the smells of death and blood that surrounded the cook. I started to light my pipe, then stopped myself. How odd, I thought, that in the very midst of enjoying this perfume, I should decide to violate it with my tobacco.

To my right the great bougainvillaea rose up against the side of the house huge and voluptuous, with its purple flowers resembling decadent kisses as they crowded together from ground to roof. Then, after several seconds, I saw a movement, then another. Taking a few steps toward the bougainvillaea, I noticed a small pair of eyes which, when they saw me, darted away with the flick of a brown tail. There were rats running along the branches, behind the leaves and purple flowers. Maybe five, maybe twenty, darting, jumping, peeking out from the darkness, so the great flowering shrub trembled as if alive. I turned away, disgusted, and was about to rejoin the others when I saw Dalakis approaching me along the stone path. He had taken off his glasses and was rubbing a hand across his eyes.

"It's so sad," he said.

Of course he meant the cook but I could think of nothing but that beautiful shrub swarming with rats like a kind of purple madness. I started to point it out to him, then stopped. Why upset poor Dalakis any more than he was upset already? I looked up at him. He has a long rectangular face that seems to have too much skin, hanging jowls, bags beneath the eyes, so the whole impression is of an unmade bed. As he returned my look, he pushed his glasses back up his nose and blinked. How unhappy he seemed. Even so there was something repellent about his emotion.

"Do you mean the cook?" I asked.

"The cook and everything. Think of that man upstairs spending his life as a paralyzed guest in Pacheco's house."

There seemed nothing to say.

"Did Pacheco ever know your wife?" persisted Dalakis. "I remember he was in the south at the time of your marriage."

"He'd met her several years before our wedding." I couldn't imagine why Dalakis wanted to talk about my marriage. The trouble with people like him is that their natural sympathy becomes an excuse to pry into the lives of others.

"It was all so long ago," he continued. "You know, of the thirty in our class, I wonder how many wives and girl friends he was involved with. My wife . . . we weren't married then, but she laughed when I grew angry. She was still a child and there was that trouble with her parents. What do you think makes a woman go with a man like that?"

"I have no idea. Maybe he spends a lot of money on them," I added, jokingly.

"But don't you wonder about it?"

"Not if I can help it." I put my arm through Dalakis's and led him back across the patio to where Pacheco was talking with Malgiolio. Yes, I had lied, but I told myself there was no reason to stir up the past, that what my wife had done was nearly forgotten. The white sheet lay spread over the body of the cook so that she looked like no more than a long white hill, something snow-covered and wintry.

"Let's go back inside,"said Pacheco. "Our meal isn't quite over."

In single file, we followed him down the corridor. I came last. Behind me I could still see that white mound lying on the table surrounded by many candles. Then I turned away.

When we had nearly reached the dining room there was another loud knock on the front door. Perhaps it was just the echoes in the large hall that made these arrivals dramatic and almost frightening. Not that I felt fear this time; rather, it was irritation at the further interruption.

But my irritation was misplaced. Fear would have been the correct response. It was more soldiers—suspicious and aggressive, secure in their bullying. They pushed their way in, a dozen of them, stamping their feet and swinging their weapons in all directions, their faces smeared with camouflage paint. They were like rough dogs ready to attack at the slightest provocation. Seeing them, I held back by the door to the dining room. How does one describe fear? Rapid breathing, a pressure in the chest, tensing of the muscles. I kept thinking it would be so easy for one of them to make a mistake and start shooting. We three guests stood petrified, careful not to make the sightest movement. Pacheco, on the other hand, became angry.

"What is it now?" he asked, standing by the doorway. "What right do you have to push your way in here?" The soldiers had spread through the hall, hardly paying attention to him.

A captain stopped in front of Pacheco, a small and dark young man looking somewhat electric and almost twitching with attention as he glanced around the room. In his hand was a large pistol.

"There have been gunshots from the roofs of these houses," he said, "and we must make a search. Do you have identification?"

"I am Dr. Daniel Pacheco."

"Do you have identification?"

"Isn't my word good enough?"

Casually the captain raised his pistol and laid its barrel alongside Pacheco's nose. "Don't play the fool with me. I've shot many men tonight and another would mean nothing."

I must say that Pacheco never flinched. As the captain threatened Pacheco, the other soldiers pointed their rifles at us, as if we three middle-aged men might run indignantly to his aid. As I had noticed before, the soldiers were young and rather excited. They were scattered across the hall and one was halfway up the stairs looking down at us. The paint on their faces made them appear particularly inhuman. It was the sort of moment that seems pointed and brittle and I could only shut my eyes. Most likely it was our obvious fear that made Pacheco reconsider.

"Do you think I can reach for my wallet without your becoming upset?" he asked the captain. "And perhaps you can tell me your name as well."

The captain looked at Pacheco's identification without answering. He was at least six inches shorter than Pacheco and had thick black hair visible beneath his cap. I guessed he had Indian blood and felt sure he was offended by the opulence of the hall. Another of Diogenes's remarks occurred to me: "In a rich man's house the only place to spit is in his face."

"Search these men for weapons," said the captain to another officer. "Then search the house."

"No!" shouted Pacheco. "I refuse to allow you to bully me within my own home."

The captain spun around, lifting his revolver, then struck Pacheco on the side of the face, knocking him back. Before I could see more, the soldiers grabbed us, pushed us up against the wall, and proceeded to search us with no attempt to be gentle or respect for our age. I felt myself yanked and then the rough touch of their hands as they prodded and groped, but there was nothing I could do. Briefly I saw Señora Puccini standing by the door to the hall. I wondered about her small pistol and if she still had it on her person. Then she turned and disappeared into the back of the house.

When the soldiers were certain that I wasn't armed, they pushed me toward Dalakis and Malgiolio so the three of us staggered together and my head bumped Dalakis's shoulder. Both of my friends looked terrified. I glanced back at Pacheco, who was getting to his feet. The left side of his face was bleeding but he didn't touch it. Really, I had to admire him. He stood up as if he felt no pain or discomfort and addressed the captain with perfect calm.

"You still haven't told me your name," he said.

The captain ignored him and turned to his men. "Search the house but don't disturb anything. If you find anyone, bring them to me."

"Wait," said Pacheco, "there's an invalid in an upstairs bedroom."

"Can he walk?" asked the captain.

"He hasn't moved for twenty years. Nor can he speak."

"Why should I believe you?" asked the captain.

"If you saw him, you would believe me." Pacheco noticed Señora Puccini standing again in the doorway. "Señora, take the captain upstairs and show him our permanent guest."

"That's all right, my men can look at him." He called over another officer. "Have that woman show you the house. Make sure she doesn't skip anything. I also want her searched. Don't be too brutal. And hurry, we're wasting time here."

Pacheco was wiping his face with his handkerchief. It still appeared to be bleeding. Señora Puccini stared at the blood but I couldn't guess her thoughts. Did the sight of his blood give her pleasure? In any case, she was soon hurried up the staircase by the soldiers while other soldiers fanned out through the downstairs rooms.

"Remember," shouted the captain, "don't touch anything!"

Pacheco took a few steps toward us. Several drops of blood spotted the jacket of his gray suit. "Shall we return to our dinner?" he asked.

Noticing Pacheco walking away, the captain bellowed at all

of us, "You'll stay in this hall until I give you permission to leave! Sit down over there." He pointed toward one of the marble benches bracketed on either side by a vase of red flowers.

Pacheco turned slowly. "Again I ask you for your name, Captain? Are you afraid of giving it?"

Dalakis hurried to Pacheco and took his arm. "Come along, Daniel, they'll be gone in a minute. Let's just do what he says." From other rooms and upstairs we could hear soldiers stamping around and banging the doors.

Truly, I think Pacheco would have preferred being tied up than do anything the captain asked, but Dalakis and I prevailed upon him to sit down. Malgiolio had been silent all this time. Glancing at him, I saw his face was paper white. He appeared to think that at any second he might be shot. I took his arm and led him to the bench. The four of us sat in a little row. What a contrast to the grandeur of our sumptuous meal. Dalakis was trying to look pleasant and obliging. Pacheco was leaning forward with his elbows on his knees as if studying his shoes. Malgiolio was hunched over with his arms crossed. I too felt nervous but my fear wasn't enough to keep me from observing all that happened around me. The captain was over by the stairs talking to one of his men. I noticed he had a limp and the heel of his left shoe was about one inch thicker than the other. Five other soldiers were spread around the hall and three were staring up at the tapestry of satyrs and nymphs. Then they began to poke each other as they took notice of the sort of sexual celebration that was going on there.

After several minutes, Dalakis stood up. "Excuse me," he said, "excuse me, sir." The captain gave him a look which made me guess he was one of those career soldiers who hates civilians. "I wonder," continued Dalakis, "if you could give us some idea what's happening in the city. I'm a government employee and it's difficult to get information."

To tell the truth, I was rather surprised by Dalakis.

The captain seemed surprised as well. "You sit and you do not speak! Do I have to tie you up? Are you a child?" He turned back to say something to the man with him and the man laughed. Dalakis sat back down on the bench. His brow was severely creased and I thought he might cry.

Pacheco patted him on the knee. "They are intent on being animals. Leave them alone."

The captain glanced at Pacheco but made no comment. As for Dalakis, his behavior was only to be expected. Even as a boy he had constantly backed whoever was in power. There were stories that he'd even reported our various pranks to the school authorities, but we never had proof of that.

But there was a time when Pacheco, David Kress, and I had gone wandering in the night. We were seventeen and ready for adventure. Pacheco had led us down to a sort of low-class dance hall that catered to sailors and was filled with prostitutes. The place was extremely crowded and one of the people, surprisingly, was Dalakis's father, dancing rather drunkenly with a fat red-haired woman who wore a shawl of bright purple feathers. At the time we were sure he didn't see us. Then several days later we were called before the headmaster. It seemed someone had reported us. Kress denied being there. Pacheco said the school had no business telling us how to behave outside of school. And I kept silent. The upshot was that we had to do extra work and stay late for about two months. A dreary punishment.

Kress was certain that Dalakis had heard about us from his father and reported us. Of course Kress was furious and within an inch of beating poor Dalakis black and blue. But Pacheco said that many people had seen us and the information could have come from anywhere. I rather sided with Kress but without definite proof we had no case. Actually Kress was quite a gentle fellow but he hated betrayal and hated spies. Sometimes

I've wanted to ask Dalakis if he told, but then I decide I'd rather not know. If he did betray us, even after this much time has gone by I'd have difficulty maintaining a friendship with him.

In twos and threes the soldiers had begun to return to the hall. Presumably they had found nothing to interest them. All at once we heard a shouting from back toward the kitchen which grew louder as it approached along the corridor. Several soldiers burst through the door dragging the cook's grandson, Juan, who was struggling to break free. One of the soldiers threw Juan to the floor, kicked at him, and missed. I had forgotten about the boy. Pacheco jumped to his feet and ran toward him.

"Leave him alone!" he shouted. He pushed himself between Juan and the soliders so quickly that everyone was too surprised to do more than stare. "You've murdered this boy's grandmother and now you bully him. Get out of my house!"

What would have happened I don't know. Certainly the captain was capable of his own fury and seemed indifferent to anything that Pacheco might say. But as Pacheco was speaking several new soldiers appeared in the doorway. They entered followed by an officer, a colonel, who, much to my surprise, was someone I knew. At least we belonged to the same club and even played cards on occasion.

"Carrera," I said, almost without thought, "tell these men to leave us alone."

The colonel looked at me with surprise. "Batterby, is that you? What's going on here?"

"Your captain has gotten out of hand," I said with increasing anger. "First he assaulted our host, Dr. Pacheco, and now he's threatening the servant boy."

Carrera continued to glance around the hall with some puzzlement. He was a man of about sixty, quite thin and with a little white moustache. He looked quick and agile and had always reminded me of a kind of racing dog, a greyhound or whippet. After a moment, his eyes settled on Pacheco.

"You're the doctor, aren't you? We've never actually met but I've seen you at the hospital. I wanted to ask if we could use your hall for some of our wounded. We have several medics to do most of the work but if you could just take a brief look at one or two of the more seriously wounded it would be a great help. We don't seem to be able to get through to the hospital."

With hardly a glance at Carrera, Pacheco walked slowly over to the captain. "I want to know this man's name. He has insulted me, my guests, and my servants."

"My name is Captain Quatrone," said the captain, looking just as angry, "and I have been doing my job."

"Is it your job to threaten and abuse defenseless people? I want you out of my house."

Quatrone clicked his heels and made a sarcastic bow. I doubted he would apologize or that he regretted any of his actions. Colonel Carrera appeared somewhat confused as to what was happening but I felt he cared little for the captain, most likely because of his dark skin. Carrera was a wealthy man whose family has been in the military for generations. He affects a stuttering way of talking, which makes him sound both bored and surprised at the same time.

"Really, Captain," said Colonel Carrera, "I don't see by what right you've threatened these people. Obviously those were not your instructions."

Carrera had crossed the hall and was standing by the fountain with Pacheco and Quatrone. We three guests had remained by the marble bench. About twenty soldiers were scattered around the hall watching the little scene being played out by their officers. Some were grinning.

"Our men were being fired at from the roofs," said Quatrone. "I decided to search the houses."

"I think you had better leave, Quatrone," said Carrera in a low voice.

Quatrone made a sharp salute, nodded to his lieutenant, and walked quickly to the door, his heels clicking on the polished marble.

"Wait," said Pacheco.

Quatrone stopped but kept his back to the doctor. Pacheco walked over and stood directly behind the captain who, after a moment, slowly turned. Pacheco tilted his injured face down toward Quatrone. It had stopped bleeding but the bruise and dried blood looked dreadful.

"You see this?" asked Pacheco.

"What about it?"

"I won't forgive it."

Captain Quatrone glanced at the colonel, then back at Pacheco. He seemed to be trying to conceal a smile. "It's part of the night," he said at last. "There is much danger about. You must be more careful."

"Is this a threat?" asked Pacheco.

"It is a description of the city. As for your warnings or forgiveness, why should I care? I have my own work to do."

"Quatrone," said the colonel, "you had better go."

Without another word, Quatrone turned and left the house. His men straggled out after him, some still smiling, others looking indifferent or uncertain.

Once the door was shut, Pacheco turned to Carrera. "Colonel," he said, "come and drink a glass of wine with us. This was supposed to have been a banquet for my friends but events have interfered."

"Perhaps a small one," said Carrera. He had a little stick like a riding crop that he kept slapping against his leg. "You still haven't answered my question about the wounded men."

By now we had begun to move back toward the dining room. "By all means," said Pacheco, "bring them here. But if Quatrone winds up among them you must allow me the pleasure of letting him suffer."

Carrera appeared embarrassed. "This is a night of great change. Quatrone is very eager."

"Just what's going on in the city?" I asked as we resumed our places at the table. Despite my apparent interest, the outside world, even with the constant intrusion of soldiers, seemed unreal to me, or at least not as real as Señora Puccini, who was even then filling the colonel's glass with wine. Schwab's dishes had been cleared away and Carrera was sitting in his place.

"It remains a confusion," said Carrera, holding his wine glass up to one of the candles. "Did you know that General Colecchia was murdered this afternoon?"

"Not the minister of the interior!" said Dalakis.

Even though Dalakis's response struck me as exaggerated (what other General Colecchia was there?), we were all surprised. There were men in the government one thought of as secure from attack. Always they traveled with an armed escort and were rarely observed in public. Colecchia was one of these. We would only see him on television or when his armed caravan passed rapidly from one part of the city to another.

"What happened?" asked Pacheco.

"He was blown up, or rather his car was blown up and he was inside it. You see, the air force or part of the air force has mutinied in an attempt to overthrow the government. Some army regiments have joined with them, which is neither here nor there, since basically they have been defeated. But arms have also been distributed through the labor unions and they have taken the opportunity to make a little rebellion. They've been responsible for this constant shooting. I'm told there're also students involved." He paused to sip his wine, and gave Pacheco a small but appreciative nod.

"We heard some of this from Schwab," said Malgiolio. "But he implied it was very inconsequential."

"Schwab was here?" asked Carrera in a voice that seemed more attentive.

"We were schoolboys together, all of us," continued Malgiolio. "Schwab was to have come earlier but was delayed. He stopped to pay his respects." It was clear that Malgiolio was proud of the connection.

Carrera carefully set his wine glass back on the white tablecloth. "He is a man with many enemies," he said.

"But what's going on in this neighborhood?" asked Dalakis. "Why can't we go home?"

"There is no way you can leave this house while the curfew is in effect," said Carrera. "All I know is that we've been dealing with snipers and street barricades, most of it pretty minor, but until we can finish with these air force regiments we can't quite wipe up the rest. Even as I say this, I'm partly guessing, because communications are poor."

It turned out that Carrera didn't know much. His own responsibility was this sector of the city, which he and his men had tried to close off, but the result was they knew little about what was happening elsewhere. Because of the mutinous regiments little trust was put in radio communications. Indeed, the military airways seemed crowded with specious orders, claims and counterclaims so that no one knew whom to believe. Several runners had been sent out to other sectors but they hadn't returned.

Dalakis found all this shocking but I felt that his sympathy for the army had been dulled by the abuses of Captain Quatrone, although I'm sure he would have apologized for Quatrone

180

as well if he hadn't been afraid of infuriating Pacheco. As for Malgiolio, his anxiety grew increasingly apparent. From his earlier position that any kind of trouble could only create opportunities for someone like himself, he had retreated to a dull fear for his own life. Pacheco, on the other hand, didn't seem to care one way or the other. He smoked his constant cigarettes and gave only half an ear to what Carrera was saying. It upset him that innocent people had to suffer but as for who ruled the country, he was the sort of person who believed that all the generals, army, air force, or whatever, were cut from the same cloth, while if the labor leaders turned out successful, then that just meant another sort of idiot in power.

As for me, politics is not one of my interests. My free time is spent reading, which means living in other people's worlds. Still, I have known the country was getting worse and that we are saddled with a government which doesn't care for its people, other than the rich, of course. My sense of this comes mostly from the jokes I hear at the club. For instance there was the joke about the president going on a fishing trip. He catches a nice little trout. Grabbing it around the middle, he slaps it two or three times across the face. All right, says the president, where are the others?

In recent years these jokes have increased and grown more bitter, so it seemed that an eruption was inevitable. But is it my solipsism that keeps me from being able to separate the dinner at Pacheco's from the events in the city? Most likely the events at Pacheco's would not have occurred had there not been this upheaval in the streets. The story would never have been told. But it seemed more than that—not just that our lives were the result of that violence, but that the violence was the result of our lives, that this trouble around us had erupted in part from Pacheco's story. It puts me in mind of those lines from *Julius Caesar*:

A lioness hath whelped in the streets;
And graves have yawned and yielded up their dead;
Fierce fiery warriors fight upon the clouds,
In ranks and squadrons and right form of war,
Which drizzled blood upon the Capitol.

My friends at the paper would say I am being too romantic, making connections where none exist. They would say that perhaps I am inventing this to hide from myself my own bad feelings against Pacheco, my wish to hurt him. Of course I only need to express this improbability to show how foolish such an argument would be. Yet there does appear to be a connection between the personal and public. For instance, look at Malgiolio. He takes no responsibility for his personal life and has no interest in the public. In varying degrees this might be true of all of us. If one is not absolutely destitute and downtrodden or physically handicapped, one probably gets the life one deserves. From this it follows that one gets the sort of government one deserves. I mean, if my fellow citizens are fighting in the streets, am I not to some degree responsible?

But perhaps I was being romantic again. Things happen to a person; that is, life deals you a set of cards and you play them as you are able. If I do the best I can and make no trouble for my neighbors, then surely I cannot be blamed either for my existence or my government. There are forces that buffet us through life that no mere individual can withstand. Better to stick to my books and musings about literature and leave the government to those who know best. That certainly was what I'd believed for years, but this evening I had begun to wonder, foolishly perhaps, if it wasn't that sort of thinking which had helped bring about this current state of affairs.

The others had continued to talk about what might be occurring in the city and I listened, occasionally interrupting with a question. Carrera was a very gentlemanly officer, really someone of the old school, and was one of those men who remained polite even if he intended to kill you. Indeed, he was probably more dangerous than Captain Quatrone, because he would speak with great gentleness but if you went against him, he would act without hesitation. This is a trivial example but when we played cards—poker mostly, but also bridge or whist—he was without mercy.

After we had been talking about ten minutes, I asked, "By the way, do you know anything of Colonel David Kress? He's one of our group and was supposed to be here tonight."

Carrera folded his hands before him on the tablecloth and grew more somber. "I . . . I'm afraid I have rather unfortunate news about that," he said in his stuttering drawl. "Colonel Kress's regiment was one of those army regiments that attempted to join up with the air force regiments in the south. I know nothing about him personally but they were blocked just outside of the city and there was some fierce fighting. I don't know the details but I heard they'd been defeated. And even if Kress is alive he'll certainly have to face a court-martial or even worse, that is unless he gets away. But where could he go?"

We met this news with general silence. Kress has always been popular—a kind man who looked out for the men under his command and who has a very strong sense of connection to our group. When one of us needed assistance in moving or to borrow something or needed help in any way, Kress was the person one could count on. The fact that he might be dead seemed to suggest more than anything that the group had been broken asunder, that whatever happened after tonight, it would be different—a different group, a different city. Certainly, much of this destruction was due to the violence around us, but I also wondered if it didn't also stem from ambivalent feelings within the group itself. Maybe this was even what Schwab had been referring to, that we needed to take more responsibility for our past selves, which meant taking more responsibility for our present ones. It was hard to understand that, hard to know what it meant. All we knew for certain was that tomorrow would be different and that what we had taken for granted had become suspect and fragile.

There seemed nothing to say. During the whole evening we had made one exclamation of surprise after another and now here was this information about Kress. Carrera looked at us sympathetically. "I'm sorry to bring bad tidings. I didn't know Kress personally but I always heard well of him."

"I never thought he was particularly political," said Dalakis.

Carrera finished his wine. "It's hard not to be these days."

He got to his feet and there was general talk about whether he would have another glass of wine or even eat something, then further talk about the casualties in his regiment. Several of his men had already gone to see about bringing back a few of the wounded. Pacheco said he would need bandages, antibiotics.

But I continued to think about Kress, whom I hadn't seen since our last dinner six months ago. He had been one of the ushers at my wedding and some weeks later he had met us at that small ski resort in Switzerland where I had gone with Cora to spend our honeymoon. He had been married himself less than a year and his wife came with us. Her name was Dorothy or Delores, I can't remember. We made quite a jolly foursome.

That first evening of his visit we had had dinner in the lodge. It was one of those great pine buildings with a large central hall going up five or six stories and balconies all around. While we were at dinner we talked cheerfully about the next day's skiing. Kress, although affectionate with his wife, was constantly glancing around at other women and actually made

184

contact with one. I have never known whether this was someone he had met previously or if they just made eye contact and came to some agreement. Moments later he excused himself to go to the rest room. In ten minutes he had still not returned and his wife thought he might be sick. Although I had noticed this other woman also leave the dining hall, I went off to the rest room to look for him. Of course he wasn't there. I glanced around through various meeting halls and function rooms, then, looking from a window, I happened to see Kress's rented car down in the parking lot, a large Citroën. And there he was with this woman, making love to her in the backseat. I remember standing by the window and looking down, seeing only a confused tangle of arms and clothing.

I went back to the dining hall and about ten minutes later Kress returned perfectly calmly as if nothing untoward had happened. He said he'd had a headache and had gone to his room for aspirin. A few minutes later the woman returned and joined her friends, three women and two men. She didn't look at Kress and he didn't look at her. You can imagine that I looked at her a great deal, not with desire but with amazement. I intended to ask Kress about his escapade and I especially wanted to know if he'd known this woman before. I also told myself that I had better keep my own young wife out of his way—not that I felt I had anything to fear, since we were very much in love and totally occupied with each other. But as it turned out I had no time to ask Kress about the woman. My wife had her fatal accident the next day and everything else was pushed from my mind.

Colonel Carrera thanked Pacheco for the wine and we walked with him to the front door. "You may start receiving these wounded men in ten minutes or so. I'm sorry about the inconvenience, but there seems no alternative. And by the way, Pacheco, I would be careful of Captain Quatrone. He's not like the rest of us. No loyalties. He only serves himself."

"These are difficult days," said Pacheco, opening the door, "but that's no reason to let everything go. A man like Quatrone is only happy when he holds the stick and even uses it. You showed him a bigger stick. I'm sure he'll behave."

"I hope you're right," said Carrera.

We watched him go, hurrying across the street to his jeep.

Pacheco closed the door. Turning, he seemed suddenly tired. Then, lighting a cigarette, he took hold of himself again. "Well, gentlemen, we still have some eating left. Will you join me for dessert?" His damaged cheek was livid and swollen and I found it impossible not to stare at it.

"Really, Pacheco," said Dalakis, walking back across the hall, "I feel I have eaten enough for a dozen people, but what I am most interested in is that man upstairs. Has he actually lain in that bed for twenty years?"

Pacheco slapped Dalakis on the back and led him toward the dining room. I followed with Malgiolio. I must say I was impressed by Pacheco's insistence that we continue our dinner no matter what. The marble floor was muddied with the footprints of the soldiers and there were spots of the cook's blood, although in the dim light the bloodstains only appeared as a brighter-colored dirt.

"You shall get the rest of your story," said Pacheco. "But you must also have dessert. The cake was my cook's great creation and it is your duty to her to taste it." He glanced back at Malgiolio and me. Malgiolio had been dawdling along but his interest perked up at the mention of cake. He looked at me and grinned so that his whole face grew as round as a bowl.

We again took our places at the table. Pacheco rang the little silver bell and after a moment Señora Puccini appeared at the door.

"Señora," said Pacheco, "we're ready for the cake and you

186

might start the coffee as well. Is everything all right in the kitchen?"

"It appears to be."

"The soldiers didn't do any damage?"

"None to speak of."

She spoke so flatly and seemed so disassociated from Pacheco's questions that I thought something was wrong, but perhaps it was only a matter of her mind being someplace else. Actually I felt our dinner was over and was angry with Pacheco for prolonging it despite the fighting and soldiers and the death of the cook. He seemed absolutely callous. If I have so much as a remote cousin die I'm no good for anything for days.

"And did they search you, Señora?" asked Pacheco. She stood behind his chair and he had his back to her.

"Yes."

"And did they offend you?"

"Why should I take offense? I have no rights over my body."

Pacheco turned and observed her, then made an impatient gesture with his shoulders. I wondered how much of their life was passed in such interchanges. After a moment, Señora Puccini walked to the door and I heard her departing down the hall.

Malgiolio started to pour himself more wine, then apparently thought better of it and drank some water instead. "Well, what about the story?" he asked. "What happened to that fellow upstairs?"

Instead of answering, Pacheco asked a question in return, a peculiar one, I felt. "Have you ever been horsewhipped by a woman? Señora Puccini tried with me once, but I overcame her. What about spanking, Malgiolio?"

"Are you mocking me?"

"On the contrary, I have an endless curiosity. Sometimes I wish I could contain all of humanity's sexual experience within my person. I listen to you describe how your fat whore pisses on you and I think how disgusting, but part of me would like to experience it, to see what it would be like."

"I can give you her address," said Malgiolio, pouring himself some wine after all.

"Perhaps I will take you up on that. The only trouble is that afterward I would probably have to beat her. But tell me about beating, Malgiolio. Have you ever had a woman whip you?"

"With her hand, yes; with a stick, yes; with a Ping-Pong paddle, yes; with a whip, no."

"How bizarre," said Pacheco. "What color was the Ping-Pong paddle?"

"Red, I think. I didn't see much of it," said Malgiolio. There was an expression on his face that I could only interpret as pride, mild pride.

"And did you like it?" I asked.

" 'Like' is not really the right word," he said. "But it was pleasurable, even gratifying."

Dalakis pushed his chair away from the table so that the legs scraped loudly on the floor. "What a disgusting conversation. If I could leave here, I would."

"And you, Dalakis," said Pacheco, "have you ever had a woman mistreat you?"

Dalakis lifted his big hands to his tie and tugged at the knot. He appeared shocked. Since his wife had deserted him, I thought Dalakis knew quite a bit about being mistreated by women. But before he could reply the door opened and Señora Puccini returned wheeling the cart, on top of which was the most amazing cake I have ever seen.

First of all, what made it amazing was that it was basically a wedding cake with eight round layers of decreasing size, ranging from nearly three feet in diameter to about six inches, but instead of having white frosting, it was bright red with a rich strawberry taste, as I was soon to discover. It was the sort of cake which conventionally has a cupola on top with two little figures of the man and wife. Although this cake had little figures, they weren't at the top, nor were they man and wife. Instead there were sixteen little male figures representing the sixteen men in our group of old schoolboys. There was a soldier to represent Kress and a policeman to represent Schwab. There was a doctor with a stethoscope to represent Pacheco and a priest to represent Julio Hernandez. There was a little man in a butcher's apron for Paul Sarno, who owned a market on the other side of the city, and a man in a tuxedo who was probably meant to be Henri D'Arcy, a diplomat stationed in Rome. There was a white coated figure who was probably Leonid Shapiro, a chemist teaching in the south, and a little man in blue coveralls who I assumed was Paco Pezzone, who owned a car dealership. And then there were eight little figures in coats and ties who were meant to be the rest of us—Berruezo, Vi-cuña, Serrano—including a portly gray-haired man with a pipe who I thought was meant to be me. But the fact that it was a wedding cake astounded me, especially since Pacheco had delved into so many of the women that these men were attached to. Even Hernandez, the priest, had a sister whose heart Pacheco was said to have broken. Not that Hernandez was so celibate, for there were many stories about him.

Pacheco had begun to cut the cake, giving us each a large slice. Even the interior was red, with tidbits of strawberries and walnuts and a rich strawberry filling between the layers. I glanced at Dalakis and Malgiolio to see if they thought the cake in any way odd, but they seemed more impressed by it as spectacle than symbol. Between the sixteen figures, which stood on seven layers of the cake, were whole fresh strawberries. Of course such a thing was terrible for my illness, even for my ulcer, but there are times when one cannot help oneself.

I have always loved cake while feeling guilty about doing so. It seems so adolescent, even pre-pubescent, as if cake were something which one should reject after puberty. What a childish pleasure to fill one's mouth with such sweet glop. There even seems something wrong about it, as if it should be eaten in private, and I thought of myself as a child up in the attic with my trains sitting in the half-dark with my fingers covered with frosting and my lips covered with crumbs.

Both Dalakis and Malgiolio were shoveling great forkfuls of cake into their mouths while Pacheco watched. I admit it may have been the best cake I have ever tasted, and even though there was enough for thirty people, I felt a twinge of pleasure that Carrera and Schwab had left before the cake was introduced. How to describe it? Light, sweet, moist with a strong strawberry flavor—the sort of cake made with dozens of egg whites and gallons of cream. I don't know what it reminded me of, sex possibly or the apotheosis of a summer day. You see how foolish these descriptions become. But in its spectacle, it seemed to be a part of Pacheco's story and so it did not seem out of place when Malgiolio began to urge Pacheco to tell us about the man upstairs. At first Pacheco suggested waiting until we had finished, but Dalakis said no, we wanted to hear it now.

Pacheco leaned back in his chair. Joining his hands in front of his face, he made a tent out of his fingers and appeared to study it, or perhaps it was more of a cage than a tent. I should say that he had taken quite a small piece of cake and barely nibbled it. When he had held it to his lips, I noticed that the strawberries and the bruise on his cheek were exactly the same shade of red.

"It was quite simple, really," he began, "yet also astonishing. You know I told you that this Collura fellow, Antonia's fiancé, kept making these trips down from the capital on his motorcycle. Quite a long way, nearly four hundred miles. Perhaps he did it twice a month, rushing down on a Friday after work and getting in quite late. Well, one Friday night or early Saturday morning in early autumn he was brought into the hospital. I wasn't there at the time but I came in a few hours later. He'd had an accident and was unconscious. His neck was broken. It seemed certain he would die.

"Many doctors worked on him and I worked on him too. Someone had notified Antonia Puccini and she arrived at the hospital in a panic around three in the morning, then waited in the hall while Collura was in surgery. She asked the other doctors how he was and if he would live but she didn't speak to me. By mid-morning it was clear he would survive, but it wasn't for several days that we realized he would be totally paralyzed. We tried several other operations but they were useless. Again Antonia would ask the other doctors about his progress but she never said anything to me, even though I was often in his room while she was there.

"He had been unconscious when they brought him in and two weeks later he was still unconscious. Apart from the broken neck, he had a head injury, two broken legs, and some internal injuries. At last he came out of the coma and, although he could speak, it was only with great effort. He remembered nothing of his accident. He lay with his two legs in traction and his head bandaged. The legs were particularly pathetic. It hardly mattered how they mended, since he would never walk again. He lay on his back and Antonia would sit beside him. Often she read to him, novels like Blasco Ibáñez or Dickens. Or they would just talk quietly. If I was on duty, I would see how he was doing. As the weeks went by, his other injuries healed, but nothing could be done for the paralysis. Originally he had a double room, but then he was moved into one of the wards. He had no money and no family. It became clear he would have to go to some sort of charitable nursing home, one of those places run by the church.

"One day I happened to meet Antonia as she was leaving the ward. She pretended she didn't see me but I stepped in front of her. 'Just a moment,' I told her. 'If you come to live with me, I'll see that your friend Collura is taken care of.' You understand, I still thought that if I had the chance to talk to her, even make love with her, or perhaps just be with her for an extended amount of time, then she would choose to be with me—choose without pressure, choose because that was what she would want. She glanced at me, then glanced away and pushed past me down the hall. Need I tell you that I also hated her, that I wished to knock her down and kick at her body?

"Yet I was not without hope. I knew the sort of place that Collura would wind up in. I knew that Antonia had little money and little or no chance of earning more. Many times she would go out to search for a better job, perhaps in an office or working for the city government or perhaps for a lawyer or doctor. But wherever I could I intruded myself. I told stories against her, used my influence to see that she was passed over. After Collura had been in the hospital for six weeks, he was transferred to a nursing home attached to a convent just outside the city. It was clean but very crowded and poor. It was far from where Antonia lived and she had to ride out on her bike, which took nearly an hour. The young man himself was, of course, miserable and despairing. The noise kept him awake. There was nothing he could do. The nuns had no time for him. He was a vegetable and all he wanted was to die.

"Antonia moved so she could be nearer the nursing home, but then she was often late for work and was in danger of losing her job as a clerk in the fabric store. Do I have to tell you that I had gotten to know the woman who employed her? In any case, she soon had to let Antonia go. It wasn't just my doing. Antonia had been late many times. For several weeks Antonia looked for another job and again I made this difficult. At last she was forced to work as a waitress in a tavern, working in the evening from six until past two. Of course it was far from the nursing home and she could only see Collura during the day outside of visiting hours, which the nuns disliked and complained about. As for Collura, he was truly wasting away. I visited him now and then to see how he was doing. Actually, it was he who begged me to help him get out of there. I brushed aside his request and suggested he talk to Antonia. By now clearly my hatred was equal to my passion. As more time went by, I knew he was begging her to do something. She, poor thing, was nearly a wreck, working all night and then with him during the day. One hardly knew why she continued.

"She held out for ten weeks while he was in the nursing home. Then she came to me. Not to my house, of course, but to my office. I had known it was bound to happen and told my receptionist not to give her an appointment right away, to make her wait a week or two, so that when she finally came, expecting to see me, she was sent away for a further eight days, after hearing I was too busy. Of course, during those days I was constantly anxious, dreading she would change her mind. I visited Collura and indeed he seemed worse, weak and listless and with no desire to live. I know if it had been myself I would have preferred death. That's a problem, don't you think? How to commit suicide when you can't move a muscle. On the other hand, I hardly cared about Collura. He was just a tool in gaining Antonia Puccini. You can imagine that by this time I was entirely without moral sense.

"At last it was time for her to come to my office. I think of myself, for the most part, as a calm and controlled human being, yet for the whole day before her appointment I was as emotionally erratic as a schoolboy, elated and despairing by turns, snapping at people around me and constantly nervous.

"Her appointment was in the morning, ten o'clock, and she arrived exactly on time. Of course, I couldn't let her see my eagerness. I kept her waiting for a bit, then buzzed the receptionist to send her in. When Antonia entered my office, I remained at my desk, apparently occupied with papers. She stood in the middle of the room. It was again spring and the windows were open. I remember that she wore a gray cotton coat over a dark blue dress. A white scarf was tied around her neck. She cleared her throat, made a little cough, and I continued to write. Actually, I was writing just nonsense, some poem of Hugo's that I remembered from school. Then I glanced up. She was terrified.

" 'What can I do for you?' I asked.

" 'You wanted to see me,' she said, as calmly and slowly as possible, 'you said you could help Roberto.'

" 'Help him?' I asked. 'In what way?'

" 'To get him out of that place, to find some way I can be with him.'

" 'That was some time ago,' I said. 'I'm not sure I can do anything now.'

" 'But you must . . .' she began, then stopped. She was literally trembling. It was so sweet. I thought of the pain she was feeling and weighed it against the pain she had caused me.

" 'You said you could help him,' she continued. 'There must be some way. I'm ready to do anything.'

"I pretended not to be interested. I yawned and blew my nose and looked at my watch. Slowly, I pushed back my chair and got to my feet.

" 'You're a rich man,' she said. 'You could help him if you wanted. Please, it is not easy for me to be here.'

"I walked toward her, then stopped and looked out the

window toward the main hospital building on the next block. 'I think it's too late,' I said. 'Maybe you should go back to your cripple.'

"She was about five feet away. She hurried, almost fell toward me, and grabbed at my arm. I shook her loose, even pushed her. She collapsed on a chair and began to cry, a fierce silent crying. I watched her shoulders heaving, heard her great intakes of breath. After a few minutes I told her to get up. She remained on the chair. 'Get up!' I ordered.

"She stood up, still crying. Her head was bowed and she dabbed at her nose with a white handkerchief.

" 'Strip off your clothes,' I told her.

"She hesitated and looked up at me. Really, she had no choice. She unknotted the scarf around her neck and dropped it to the floor. Then she unbuttoned her coat and let it slip down to the floor as well.

" 'You can put your clothes on a chair if you wish,' I said.

"She began to unbutton her dress. She was frightened yet, I think, she also had a kind of interest mixed with her fear. I, of course, was fascinated, as you can well imagine. The dress must have had thirty buttons. When she had unbuttoned them down past her waist, she pushed it from her shoulders, let it fall, and then stepped out of it. She wore a necklace of beads of blue lapis lazuli. She removed her white slip, again just dropping it to the floor. She wore a white brassiere with a little lace around the cup, white panties, rather conventional things, and a little belt to hold up her stockings. For a moment she stood like that, as if unable to make up her mind.

" 'Take off everything,' I said. Then I lit a cigarette and again looked at my watch.

"She took off her stockings, unhooked her bra, and let it drop onto the pile of clothes. After a slight hesitation, she removed her underwear and stood naked except for the necklace. At first she had her arms folded across her breasts, then slowly she let them drop to her sides. She stood with her legs slightly apart and stared down at the floor. Then she looked up at me. She was very frightened, as well as embarrassed and humiliated. I stared at her, almost clinically. She held herself rigid and had sucked in her breath so her belly was flat. Actually, I was surprised at how hairy she was. Not like a man, of course, but thick black pubic hair with a little peak pointing up toward her navel. I walked around her, very leisurely, stopping every so often to touch a breast or her buttocks but lightly, just with one finger or a stroke of the palm.

"As I circled Antonia, continuing my inspection, the receptionist opened the door, then began to close it again. 'Wait,' I said, 'come in here a moment.' The receptionist entered, trying not to appear embarrassed. She was a woman of about forty-five who was married to a custodian at the hospital. 'What do you think of this girl?' I asked her.

"The woman glanced at Antonia, then looked away. 'She looks very healthy,' she said.

" 'Anything else?' I asked.

"She looked at her again, almost furtively, a quick little glance, and then looked away again. 'No, she seems all right. Is there something I should see?'

"All this time Antonia had been staring at the floor. 'Don't you find her beautiful?' I asked.

" 'Yes, certainly,' said the woman, even more embarrassed. 'She's very beautiful.'

" 'Was there anything else you wanted?' I asked.

"She had some errand having to do, I think, with finding several X rays, and after she had gotten them, she returned to the waiting room. All this time Antonia stood motionless.

"When the door was again shut, I approached Antonia and stopped a little more than a foot in front of her. 'Look at me,'

I said. She lifted her head. I saw she was shivering, although the room was warm. Very gently I reached out and touched her cunt with the backs of two fingers. She jerked away, startled. 'Look at me,' I said again.

"She looked into my eyes as I gently stroked her cunt, first the outside, then the very lips of the vagina, using just the backs of two fingers. A minute went by, then another. I watched her emotion overcome her, watched her change from being cold and frightened to being obsessed by the same passion that had driven me for so long. There was nothing I couldn't do to her, nothing I couldn't make her do."

Pacheco paused and took a small bite of cake, then crumbled the rest between his fingers. He seemed lethargic suddenly, while we three guests were entirely caught up in his story. The side of his face where Quatrone had hit him looked on fire.

"Wouldn't any woman react like that?" asked Dalakis.

Pacheco started to speak, then touched his fingers very lightly to his bruised cheek. When he looked again at Dalakis, it appeared to be with dislike. "Not at all. Some would be angry, some would feel nothing, some would laugh. That's what is so attractive about women, Carl, that out of a thousand women all would make love differently, like hearing a thousand string quartets or reading a thousand books. When I touched Antonia, she was swept away much in the same manner that she had been at that summer concert almost two years before."

"Isn't your description excessive?" I asked. Why did I feel angry with Pacheco? I had been caught up by his story, even excited by it, and those feelings made me almost ashamed.

"Swept away? Well, she was overwhelmed by her own passion. Call it what you want, but as I stood there gently stroking her cunt her hatred for me and her love for her fiancé were pushed aside and all that remained was desire. Can't I call that being swept away? All reason and moral sense were obliterated. That's very rare. It had been my original sense of that which had helped create my hunger."

"And so what happened?" asked Malgiolio. "Did you make love to her right there in your office?"

Pacheco looked at Malgiolio, and again I had a sense of Pacheco's dislike, really, that he disliked us all. It seemed that Pacheco was telling this story not for us but for Antonia Puccini. Very likely he cared nothing for us, nothing even for the world outside his front door. All his life was caught up with her.

"No, we simply struck a deal," said Pacheco. "I wanted her to marry me but she refused. Nor would she agree to bear my children. She was very adamant about that. The agreement was she should come and live with me as my housekeeper and that I should bring her fiancé Roberto Collura into my house and take care of him. As for our sexual relationship, I could have her at any time. At first she wanted some sort of schedule, but I would have none of it. I actually told her to put on her clothes and get out. Can you imagine a schedule? Forever looking at your watch or counting days on the calendar? Any time, any place, that was the final agreement. But you see, in a way I was very foolish or perhaps I was just deceived by my own conceit, because I still thought I could make her love me, that if she lived with me and had sex with me, then she would inevitably come to love me as well. As for me, I hardly knew her and hardly liked her, but I loved her passionately, have always loved her passionately. That, unfortunately, has been my great weakness. Without that love and desire, I could have come to like her more."

Pacheco tossed his napkin onto his plate and stood up. "I've asked Señora Puccini to give us coffee in the library. Perhaps we can go in there."

Again I glanced at the door leading to the kitchen. It was

open and someone could easily have been standing there in the dark. "And do you still hunger for this woman?" I asked, getting to my feet.

Pacheco gave a kind of humorless smile. "Perhaps not hunger, but there is still great desire. Believe me, I see many women, but she continues to be the one I want most."

"She must be about forty," said Malgiolio.

Walking to the door, Pacheco paused and looked back over his shoulder at Malgiolio. "In matters of desire, age makes little difference. Yes, it is wonderful to make love to a woman who is young and beautiful, but sometimes I think that desire has less to do with the body and more with a quality of the eye, a certain expression, a suggestion of interest. I know many men who can only make love to one sort of woman, but that's like restricting yourself to one sort of food, in which case it's not exactly the eating that one likes."

Pacheco continued out of the room and we followed him through the hall. Just as we were about to enter the library there was a knocking at the front door. Pacheco went to open it, setting the candles all flickering in the draft. A lieutenant entered, then several medics bearing stretchers, then three more men, who appeared to be wounded. The soldiers looked around them at the great staircase, the Roman busts and tapestry. Pacheco rejoined us, then said, "Go in and help yourself to coffee and brandy. There are cigars as well. I'll be with you shortly."

I followed Dalakis into the library. Malgiolio was already pouring himself something to drink. In truth, I felt rather bloated and I went to the window for a breath of air. There were soldiers in the street talking quietly. In the distance I again heard the rattle of gunfire. A sergeant saw me at the window and angrily motioned me away. I let the drapes fall back into place. It would be just my luck to get shot.

Malgiolio and Dalakis were talking by the fireplace and I joined them. I realized both were quite worked up, as if Pacheco's story had physically excited them. That didn't surprise me about Malgiolio, but I thought Dalakis would have more control.

"But why should he get it out of his mind?" Dalakis was saying. "For at least a dozen years I thought of my wife twenty times a day, and maybe now, if I'm lucky, I only think of her once or twice a day. I don't like her, I feel I was betrayed by her, but it's as if her memory has burned a hole in my brain. All this was chance, that I should meet her, that I should fall in love with her. We met at a party to which I nearly didn't go. She too had decided to attend only at the last minute. If she had been standing on another side of the room, if the host hadn't introduced us, my whole life could have been different. I once knew a man who was crippled when a bit of masonry fell on him from a building—a piece of bad luck falling out of the sky. My experience with my wife was the same. So how can I judge Pacheco? Certainly he has behaved abominably, but his obsession with this woman, that is no more than bad luck, a freak of chance which sent him to the concert that night."

Malgiolio had lit a cigar and was tapping the ash into the fireplace. "We become the toys of our obsessions," he said rather ponderously. "You think I don't hate myself for my relationship with my blond woman? Sometimes it astonishes me. I'll be walking down the street in the middle of the day, looking at all the people, and I'll think that I'm actually involved with a woman who stands astride me and pisses on me. I tell you it disgusts me. Yet that doesn't matter. No matter how much I hate it I have no wish for it to stop. Wherever I am, I'll think of her thick shape squatting over me and, well, as Pacheco said, I feel swept away."

"And you pay her for this?" I asked, hardly believing it possible. I had poured myself some mineral water and was sitting on the couch.

"Yes, of course, otherwise she wouldn't permit me to visit."

"Does your wife know about it?" asked Dalakis.

"She knows there's someone I see, that's all. If she heard the details, she wouldn't believe it. You see, in my own house I'm a bit of a tyrant. The food has to be just right, my clothes must be perfectly cleaned. And my wife, she too has sexual desire and sometimes I just laugh at her. I'll see her wanting me to touch her and I'll just laugh."

"You're a commendable fellow," I said.

"I don't make any apologies for my life," said Malgiolio. He was still standing by the mantel, a short, round-faced, pudgy man with elaborately combed wisps of black hair, cigar in one hand, brandy in the other. "I am condemned to live within the limits of my nature. I'm mean and selfish and small-minded, but all on a petty scale. It's like what Pacheco was saying. I grew up thinking pretty well of myself, thinking I was a decent person. Well, there came a day when I had to admit that I wasn't very good after all. What could I do? Die? I had to tolerate myself. I had to go on living. It's like when I had all that money. I knew I should invest it. I could have eked out enough to support me and my family for the rest of my life. But no, I gobbled it down, I deprived myself of absolutely nothing. It was the best year of my life. And now, after all this time of not having a job, of living off my family, of having to put up with constant humiliation, I know if I had it all again I'd do exactly the same thing, just splurge with it, throw it away on trifles."

Malgiolio kissed his fingertips, made a little blowing noise, then looked at us with a foolish grin. He had always struck me as a proud man, but now I saw that what seemed to be pride really existed to conceal his ridiculous obsessions. One asks how it begins, the slightly peculiar taste growing more peculiar with each passing year. After telling us such dreadful stories, I wondered how he expected us to meet him again in six months' time. Both Dalakis and I felt embarrassed. There was coffee on a table by the door, strong espresso, plus a little silver pitcher of hot milk. Dalakis went and poured himself a cup, then poured one for me as well.

As Dalakis handed me the cup of coffee, he asked, "Tell me, did you ever think of your wife like that? I mean, obsessively?"

Although I realized he was trying to change the subject, I had no wish to bare myself as they had done, and Pacheco too for that matter. "I guess I got over it," I said.

"But you never wanted to remarry?"

"I suppose I still might. After all, forty-nine is not so old. But I'm comfortable by myself, comfortable with my habits. And there are women I see." I was speaking somewhat dishonestly and tried to correct it. "The trouble with Pacheco's obsession or even yours, Malgiolio, is that there's nothing comfortable about it. Obsessions are disruptive. After I lost my wife, I thought my life was over. It took a long time to get past my own grief and once I was recovered, I had no wish to lose myself over someone else. I suppose an older man may be just as obsessively passionate as a younger one, but an older man usually knows the pitfalls and so will try to avoid the occasion. I was passionate about my wife. That is a rich feeling, but it's not always a pleasant one."

I reminded myself of an inferior Polonius, but even so Dalakis sympathetically nodded his head.

Malgiolio had sat down on the other end of the couch, still holding his brandy and cigar. "Was your wife buried here in the city?" he asked. "I don't remember the service."

"No, she had no other family, just some cousins and an aunt. I buried her in Switzerland, in that little ski resort town. There was a cemetery on a hill behind the church. Actually, they had to put her coffin in a sort of crypt until the ground thawed. I flew there again in the spring when they buried her. Have you ever seen a ski resort when the grass is green and there are flowers everywhere? All that mechanical apparatus, the lifts and so on, look rather ghostly. It was a pretty cemetery, but I wondered how many had died as she did."

"And how did she die?" asked Pacheco. Without my noticing, he had entered the library and was standing by the door.

Again, it is difficult to remember exactly what I felt when he asked that question. I have to put myself once more in that library, see the three of them looking at me: one kind, one mocking, one clinically curious. What did I feel? Fear and foreboding, I expect.

"She fell," I said. "She hadn't had much experience skiing. There were trees. She was going too fast. We were racing actually. She fell and hit her head against a tree trunk. It knocked her completely unconscious. She never woke up. I remember sitting in her hospital room for one day, two days. Then the doctors turned off the switches."

"And where did you bury her?" asked Pacheco.

"I was just telling Luis, I buried her in that ski town, a little cemetery behind the church."

"Did Kress go to the funeral?" asked Pacheco. "You said he had gone skiing with you."

"Yes, I suppose he must have. I'd forgotten. Both he and his wife came to the funeral."

Pacheco walked to the liquor cabinet and poured himself a thimbleful of Benedictine. From the hall I heard the soldiers, some talking, one making a rather dreadful whimpering noise. My friends continued to look at me.

Pacheco toasted me with his glass, then drank. "Why are you lying, Batterby?"

"What do you mean?"

"Your wife is not dead. As you well know, she's been living in Europe for many years. I saw her within the past six months, as a matter of fact. She was in Barcelona. We had dinner together. She is still beautiful, Batterby. She asked about you. She wondered if you ever thought about your son. He's in the university now. She wanted to know how you've been. I said you seemed fine but that your friends sometimes worried about you."

Chapter Six

So you see, I had lied. For many years I had put it about that my wife was dead, that I was a childless widower. How embarrassing to think I hadn't been believed. Yet in a way I wasn't lying. Of course I've known all along that my wife wasn't killed in a skiing accident, but in her betrayal and desertion it was as if she had died. And so I had come to tell the world she was dead. In fact, I had been talking about her death for so long that she actually seemed not among the living. Consequently, when Pacheco confronted me with my fabrication, my immediate response was to think him the liar. Then there was a moment of true surprise which, even now, looking back, I'm certain I'm not inventing. Seconds afterward I caught hold of myself and realized the sort of deception I had been living and I felt ashamed. Yet I also hated Pacheco for exposing me. Both Malgiolio and Dalakis looked at me with surprise and embarrassment, while Malgiolio even wore a little smile as if to indicate I was no better than he was, even though I hadn't judged him or thought him worse than anyone else. But you see why in this narrative I have been writing as if Cora were dead, because that is what she was until the moment of Pacheco's accusation.

I responded to Pacheco's words with a weak joke: "Well, it seemed she was dead; even when we slept together she seemed dead."

But that particular moment, the moment when my deception was laid bare, seems carved into the very flesh of my brain—Dalakis in the armchair to my left shifting uncomfortably so the leather squeaked; Malgiolio at the other end of the couch on my right with his aggressive smile, his lips slightly parted to show his little teeth; Pacheco with his bruised cheek lighting a cigarette in front of me by the mantel near the photograph of the young Antonia Puccini; and all those thousands of books like a vast symphony of mockery for me, the unwriter. The closest of the Piranesi prints above the mantel showed one of his prison scenes. Surely there was never a prison like that one, with its catwalks and many different levels and great open spaces. The prison I personally felt myself in was much smaller, more like the prison cell of that man in Dalakis's story who spent all those years learning the false Serbo-Croatian—walls covered with meaningless words, men conversing in impossible tongues.

Surrounded by my oldest friends, what I wanted most was to get away from their questions and curious looks. I felt as if I had glanced into a mirror and instead of seeing the face I'd known all my life, I saw another: a meaner, more culpable face. I wanted to be by myself and for the first time the fact of the curfew made me feel trapped and claustrophobic. Wasn't I too a victim of the city's violence? For my lie would not have been exposed had it not been for this evening, these stories, these men.

"But she's not dead," Pacheco persisted, flicking his match into the fireplace.

"She's dead to me," I answered, "and she's been dead for twenty years." I wanted to add that he'd killed her, but I kept silent.

"You've been lying all this time," said Pacheco. "You had a wife who loved you and you damaged her life and your own as well."

It was on the tip of my tongue to say that he was no one to accuse me of damaging someone's life, but instead I excused myself, saying I had to visit the bathroom. Then I hurried into the hall. I did have to visit the bathroom, but beyond that specific need nothing could have kept me with my friends at that moment. Leaving the room, I could feel their eyes like fishhooks gouging my back.

The hall seemed full of soldiers, although perhaps there were only fifteen of them. Four were lying on stretchers, while the others were lounging on the marble benches or gawking at the tapestry. One man was standing in the fountain amusing his friends with some obscene joke that involved the statue of the nude girl. Several medics were tending the wounded. They all looked at me suspiciously, as if I were some criminal or anarchist, and one soldier even moved his rifle lazily in my direction. I hurried across the hall and climbed the stairs. There were candles on almost every step and I made my way around them.

I felt humiliated and craved punishment, something to obliterate my thoughts, which were so confused that I moved forward half unconsciously, like an escaped cart rolling down a hill. Even though my wife wasn't truly dead, I had successfully buried her within my own mind and here she was resurrected again. I entered the bathroom. One candle stood on a shelf above the commode and after I had finished my business I blew it out, leaving me in darkness. Then I opened the door to the balcony overlooking the street and crouched down behind the railing.

The street was full of soldiers shouting and calling to each other. Their rowdiness and the fact that quite a few appeared to be drunk greatly surprised me. Beneath me to my left a soldier was leaning against the body of the dead horse drinking from a bottle which he had tilted up to catch the last few drops. Another soldier began to shoot his automatic weapon up at the leaves, while still another was waving a pistol. In the distance I could see the red glare of fires but the noise in the street kept me from hearing anything from any other part of the city.

Up the street to my right, the soldiers had broken into a house. A second story window had been smashed and clothes and furniture were now being thrown through the opening and heaped into a pile on the cobblestones. Other soldiers were crowding around the doorway with bottles of wine. One raised a bottle and smashed the neck against a railing, then lifted the jagged bottle to his mouth and drank—more accurately, he poured the wine in the direction of his mouth. All those men running in and out of the house, appearing at the windows and even on the roof, looked like ants busying themselves with the carcass of an animal. A soldier began sloshing something from a can onto the mound of clothes and broken furniture. Then there was a great whoosh as the whole pile ignited in flames. In the sudden light I saw Captain Quatrone leaning against one of the houses across the street with his arms folded across his chest.

I knelt behind the balustrade so I couldn't be seen, but even so I had a great desire to attract their attention. I wished they would break into this house and shoot us all. For years I had been living in a kind of eternal present, shutting off all the past which disagreed with me, letting through only the most censored memories. As for the future, nothing was thought out. It simply happened, like the turning of a page. In filling my life with books, I was repeating the existence I'd led as a child when I filled my life with electric trains—surrounding myself with other people's stories in order to obliterate my own.

Again, I began to remember that party in the country where

I had seen Pacheco making love to Cora, my wife. Of course it was after my wedding. Of course I had lied to Schwab and the others. Perhaps they'd even known it. Fleeing the sight of Pacheco and Cora I had joined the croquet players playing a midnight game illuminated by huge flambeaux. At one point I saw Cora looking for me and I hid. Then I began to drink more and more until finally I passed out in one of the many sitting rooms on the first floor of the house. When I awoke it was just dawn. I felt sick, and, as I recalled what I had seen, I experienced a renewed sense of horror. You see, I'd thought we were so happy. Again I remembered her eyes when he had been making love to her, how dead and distant they had seemed. But perhaps I had invented it; perhaps I was the victim of some nightmare hallucination. Hung over and still half drunk, I began to search the house. People were sleeping everywhere—singly and in twos and threes, on couches, chairs, sprawled on fur rugs, upstairs in the bedrooms. I moved with great stealth, as if intent on catching my wife in the commission of a crime, which indeed was the case.

After almost an hour I found them in a maid's room on the fourth floor. Next to the room was a large walk-in closet with a door opening onto the hall. I entered it and stood in the warm darkness, which smelled of wool and mothballs. The door to the maid's room was partly open. Putting my eye to the crack, I watched Cora and Pacheco. Why was I such a coward that I couldn't rush into the bedroom and kill them both? I kept thinking of all those comedies I'd either seen or read where cuckolded husbands peeked from behind doors at their erring wives. The thought of being a comic figure was terrible to me.

Pacheco had a beard at that time and he stood in front of the mirror in his shirtsleeves combing the beard with a small ivory comb. My wife sat on the edge of the bed. She was naked and sat almost primly with her hands in her lap. They were talking about me. It seems ridiculous. There she was, naked and pawed over after a night of giving herself to another man, and she was saying that she didn't want to see him anymore because she wanted to be faithful to her husband. I nearly laughed.

Pacheco didn't turn but continued to comb his beard. He asked her if they couldn't keep meeting in some secret manner during the two or three months he had to be in the capital. He offered to rent a room. Perhaps they could meet once a week or every other week. Again she refused, saying that she wanted to make her life with me. She had a high voice, clear and rather childlike. It had been one of the things which had attracted me to her.

Pacheco spoke calmly but a trifle mockingly. He expressed some surprise at her wish not to see him anymore. But what about sex? he asked. Did she really plan to content herself with my lovemaking? Wasn't that a trifle like cold mutton? She smiled, then looked away. Maybe I would improve, she said. After all, he had taught her many things which perhaps she could teach me. But wouldn't I be suspicious? Pacheco inquired. No, she said, I had no suspicion. I would do whatever she asked. Pacheco laughed and said I must be the perfect husband.

That was enough. I crept out of the closet, then I went downstairs, located my car, and drove back to the city. My rage increased with every hour and I greatly regretted not confronting the two of them. When my wife returned that evening she too was angry. How dare I leave her to be driven home by friends, didn't I realize she felt humiliated? Without saying a word, I struck her in the face. She fell and I began to kick her, while she tried to curl herself up. Every time she attempted to get to her feet, I struck her again until I was exhausted. She didn't cry but lay curled in a sort of knot. "So I'm a terrible lover," I told her, "so you think I might improve."

She didn't cry; I was the one who cried. Then I ordered her from the house. She had friends she could stay with or she could go back to Pacheco. I didn't care. She left that night. Several times after that she tried to see me. She said she wanted to talk. But of course I refused. A month or so later she took her things and I stripped the house of all sign of her. After a while I heard she had gone to Europe, but to me she was dead. Indeed, I was already telling people she was dead.

Is what I am saying true? Yes, those bare facts are accurate, although presumably there are parts I forget. What is not mentioned is the pain I felt, the constant grief. You see, I had loved her. Pacheco had returned to the south and I believe that if I had seen him I would have killed him. How odd to think it must have been the previous spring that he had met Antonia Puccini. Then, inexorably, the years passed and my anger seemed to diminish. Several times I received letters from my wife but I refused to read them. I met other women. I made another life for myself. Pacheco mentioned a son. Naturally years ago I'd heard she had borne a child but I never believed it was mine.

I heard a noise behind me and turned and saw Dalakis making his clumsy way toward me through the bathroom. Raising a finger to my lips, I warned him to be quiet. He bumped into a chair, then caught it before it fell. How oafish he was. I motioned to him to crouch down and he lowered himself to his knees, making little groaning noises all the while.

"I wanted to see how you were," he said, crawling to the balcony.

My impulse was to push him away, even strike him, but Dalakis was probably the most harmless person of my acquaintance and my anger only made me feel worse.

"Leave me alone, Carl," I said, "I'll come downstairs in a moment."

"They've broken into a house," said Dalakis, no longer paying attention to me but looking down at the soldiers, who were still shouting and throwing things into the fire. "How could they do that? Look, they're drunk."

"We're probably safe enough," I said. "Colonel Carrera will look out for us."

"Yes, but what about those people over there?" Dalakis raised himself so his head just poked above the balustrade.

"Maybe no one was home," I suggested. Dalakis spoke loudly but I didn't think his voice could be heard over the shouting in the street.

"But why are they doing it? Don't they realize that they are government soldiers? How can they behave so badly?"

There was nothing to say to that. Most soldiers come from the poorer classes and the ones stationed in the city were usually country boys who viewed the general citizenry with suspicion. Pieces of furniture were still being thrown from the windows of the house down the street and the fire continued to burn merrily. I glanced at Dalakis. The light from the fire shone on his face. He looked shocked, indignant, and close to tears.

"Make sure you stay down," I told him. "Don't let them see you."

Dalakis turned, heaved himself around, and sat down with his back to the balustrade. I knew he had decided his main duty was to talk to me, that the city could wait, and I dreaded his words.

He spoke in a rush. "I came to tell you I'd always known your wife wasn't dead, but that I didn't care. I understand completely why you did what you did."

"What do you mean?" I wanted neither Dalakis's sympathy nor his understanding.

"Your wife had written to my wife. I knew she had gone to

Europe and that both our wives had had affairs with Pacheco. I knew that we suffered from the same condition."

"No," I said, moving away a little. Dalakis's big shoes kept touching my legs and it irritated me. "Your wife left you and mine I drove from the house."

"You drove her away?" asked Dalakis, surprised.

"I wanted nothing to do with her."

"But didn't you love her? I mean, many women were involved with Pacheco. He never stayed with them. You could have gotten her back again."

Dalakis's tone of voice was pathetic.

"Are you serious?" I asked. "She was lucky I didn't kill her. Why should I stay with her after something like that? We'd been married six months and their affair had been going on for some time. You think I should have taken her back into my bed? I'm only sorry I didn't do her more damage than I did."

Dalakis puffed out his cheeks, then exhaled slowly. He didn't look at me but stared into the dark bathroom. "We're very different," he said. "Even though Pacheco's affair with my wife had nothing to do with her leaving me, I would have forgiven her anything. She had slept with Pacheco and maybe other men as well, yet given the choice between being with her or not being with her, well, there was nothing I wouldn't have done to stay with her. I suppose you think that's weak of me. But when I think of those years without her, years that I've yearned for her, then I think my humiliation would have meant nothing. In a way, I am like Malgiolio. He chose humiliation and receives a regular dose of it. I would have chosen humiliation but was turned down. I even went to my wife after she had left me. I told her I didn't care what she'd done and that if she returned to me I would let her have all the men she wanted. But she didn't want men, or rather she was in love and wanted only one man. So what could I do?"

Dalakis's story was ugly to me. No matter how much I had loved my wife or still loved my wife, I have never regretted driving her from my house. Dalakis sat without looking at me, his legs stuck out in front of him and his great shoes resting on the bathroom floor. I could think of nothing kind to say to him, nothing that wouldn't mock his weakness. Behind me I heard the approach of a loud motor and I turned to look.

A military truck with soldiers hanging off its sides was making its way down the street to my right. Pausing by the fire, it blared its horn at the men in the street and then edged forward again. The truck was painted a camouflage green and its back was open. Soldiers were pointing to something inside and some were laughing. Captain Quatrone was hanging onto the back and he too had a big grin on his face. The truck passed under the balcony roaring its engine, then came to a stop by the dead horse, unable to pass between the carcass and a jeep parked on the other side. The driver again blared the horn as if expecting the horse to get up and trot off. I continued to watch, wondering what they would do. Quatrone shouted something and the soldiers jumped off the truck, ran to the horse, and began pulling it toward our side of the street—about three men on each foot and one pulling the tail. The horse moved slightly. The men shouted at each other and continued to pull, cursing and yelling. I wouldn't know whether to call it a scene horrible in its comedy or comic in its horror. All of a sudden Dalakis leaned over the balustrade and pointed down at the back of the truck.

"It's Schwab!" he said.

Looking, I saw that he was right. Schwab lay in the back of the truck, lay on his side with his knees bent and feet apart. His chin was thrust up. His elbows were also bent with one arm before him and one behind. He appeared to be running, as if he had been shot while running and the bullet had frozen him. It was obvious he was dead. Blood smeared his blue tunic and surrounded him in a dark puddle. His large blond face wore an expression of intense astonishment.

"What happened to him?" asked Dalakis, still leaning over the balustrade.

How irritating of Dalakis that he should think I would know. "He's dead," I said. "He was shot." At that moment, the soldiers succeeded in dragging the horse into the gutter and the truck surged forward. Quatrone cheered them on, waving a pistol over his head, and Schwab disappeared from view.

"But why?" Dalakis persisted. "Why should they hurt him?"

"My dear Carl, how can you expect me know that?"

"It must have been that captain, that Quatrone fellow."

Dalakis continued to lean over the balustrade until, unfortunately, he was spotted by the soldiers. Several began shouting and one pointed a rifle. Dalakis didn't notice but kept staring after the departing truck. I grabbed his belt and pulled so sharply that he toppled back into the bathroom like a sack of potatoes and his head bumped against the floor. At that very instant, there was a burst of gunfire and bullets smashed against the wall above the doorway, sending down a little shower of cement and debris. In truth, I think the soldiers were only trying to frighten us and in that they succeeded. Both of us scurried back into the dark bathroom and I slammed the door. We crouched together on the tiles with our backs against the tub and our hearts beating frantically. Well, I can't swear to Dalakis's heart, but mine felt ready to burst from my chest.

"Schwab's dead," Dalakis persisted.

Although I expected no thanks for saving Dalakis's life, I at least would have liked the action recognized. As for Schwab, I too was shocked. Two hours earlier, he had been large, boisterous, and full of life; now he was so many pounds of dead flesh. Even so, I had few tears to expend upon him. Hadn't I often been the victim of his bullying and mockery? And I found myself thinking that now one more person who knew about my wife was gone. And Kress too, most likely. Death had taken them both.

"Why should they have killed him?" Dalakis repeated. "It must have been Quatrone."

"Maybe it was, maybe it wasn't," I said, becoming angry. "Why do you keep asking me? Don't you know you were almost shot as well?"

"But Schwab . . ."

"Yes, yes, he's dead. Was he a great friend of yours? You never liked him and you know it." I could hardly see Dalakis in the dark, just a great bulky shape.

"I loved him. I've known him all my life."

But I didn't have the energy to discuss the intricacies of loving and liking. The trouble with sentimental people is they are always searching for opportunities to exercise their sentimentality. Standing up, I said, "We'd better get back downstairs."

Dalakis got to his feet and followed me down the hall to the stairs. "This is a terrible night. Schwab was right; our world will be irreversibly changed. Now both he and Kress are gone. How small our group is getting."

We made our way down the stairs between the candles, which were leaving puddles of white wax on the red carpet. There were only seven soldiers in the downstairs hall and five were lying on stretchers. The other two were playing some game with dice on the marble bench under the tapestry. They looked up at us as we walked to the library, and one, just to frighten us, made a growling noise deep in his throat. Several medics stood by the open front door looking out at the street.

Dalakis hurried into the library in front of me. Pacheco was sitting on the couch and Malgiolio was pouring himself another brandy. They didn't appear to be talking.

"Schwab is dead," said Dalakis breathlessly. "We saw his body in the back of a truck."

Both appeared startled. "You're not serious," said Malgiolio, and then touched his hair as if Dalakis's announcement might have somehow disturbed his design of thinning black strands. Pacheco looked at me as if to ask if it were really true and I nodded.

"It was Schwab, all right," said Dalakis, walking to the mantel. "He was lying in his own blood. They must have shot him."

"Who would have shot him?" demanded Malgiolio. "Schwab's too powerful, too clever. Besides, he had an armored car. I'm sure you're mistaken."

"We're not mistaken," I said, sitting down in the armchair near Pacheco. "Captain Quatrone was riding on the back. Carl has decided that he was responsible for the whole thing."

"But he may have been," said Dalakis. "And did you see those soldiers looting that house across the street? They've even started a bonfire."

"A labor leader lives there," said Pacheco, "one of the opposition." He didn't seem concerned. Really, he seemed more concerned about the death of Schwab. Perhaps he had loved him too, just like Dalakis. And Malgiolio as well. Perhaps I was the only one to remain unmoved.

Dalakis had begun pacing back and forth in front of the fireplace. "That's no reason to destroy his home."

"Most likely they were ordered to destroy the house. We're quite safe here, if you're worried."

"We were just shot at up on the balcony," I said. Glancing at Malgiolio, I saw him become rigid. Small teeth, small hands, even his eyes are small. If you dropped two blue marbles into a bowl of porridge, just before they sank from sight they would look like Malgiolio's eyes.

Pacheco took the pack of Gauloises from his shirt pocket, discovered it was empty, and crumpled it up. "You have to stay out of sight. Soldiers on the street drinking and shooting off their weapons, what do you expect?" From the side pocket of his gray suitcoat he took a fresh pack and began to open it. The cellophane made a little crinkling noise.

"But Schwab is dead," repeated Dalakis. "Why should they kill him?"

Pacheco looked impatient. "It's as Carrera said, Schwab had many enemies. Have you no sense of the world you live in? Glance around you, Carl, everything is upside down. Why are you surprised by any of this? Can't you see the flames?" I wasn't sure whether Pacheco was referring to the bonfire out in the street or if he was speaking metaphorically, but as if to illustrate his remark, he lit his cigarette, drew on it until his cheeks appeared hollow, then blew a great cloud of smoke in Dalakis's direction. The harsh smell nauseated me.

Dalakis stopped pacing and seemed to consider Pacheco's words. Then, throwing himself down at the other end of the couch, he pushed both hands back through his unruly hair, looked at Pacheco, and laughed, rather desperately I thought. Malgiolio continued to stand by the liquor cabinet, as if that were where he felt safest in a threatened world.

"The city is being shaken up," continued Pacheco. "It may be foolish but it's also deadly. However, none of this is connected to you. You're not involved. You're like strangers in your own country. That being so, what can we do but continue our evening?" Then, turning to me, he reached out and tapped my arm. "I hope you don't mind, Batterby," he said, "but I have another question or two about your wife."

The brazenness of his words surprised me, especially since

I had been wondering whether to feel insulted by his other remarks. Certainly I cared about what was happening in the city. On the other hand, there was nothing I wanted to tell him about my private life. "And I have a question for you," I countered. "Did you succeed in getting Señora Puccini to love you?"

"My question was first," said Pacheco.

"Yes, but I can refuse to answer." I got up and walked to the liquor cabinet, where I poured myself some mineral water. Malgiolio stepped back to give me room, while continuing to stare at me, but I didn't allow him to catch my eye.

"If I tell you what you want to know," said Pacheco, addressing my back, "will you do the same for me?"

"Whatever you wish."

"Then what was your question again?"

I returned to my seat. "How you fared with Antonia Puccini." I was lying, of course. I had no wish to tell him anything.

Pacheco faced the fireplace and stretched his legs out in front of him. Again he made a little cage with the fingers of both hands and placed it over his mouth and nose. Speaking through it, he said, "You want the details, don't you, all the ugliness. . . ."

He began to say more, then stopped and ground out his cigarette in the ashtray. His wounded cheek appeared wet and glistened in the candlelight. "I have already discussed Señora Puccini's sexuality," he said at last. "Think of us as if we were divided into many selves and among those selves there is the conscious self or ego who imagines himself to be the captain of his little ship, and there is a sexual self which sometimes seems like the entire ocean. I can remember women I've had sex with while all the time my mind is saying, this is a bad idea, she is too young or too crazy or too encumbered. Yet my sexual self pushes aside all reasoning and simply devours.

Señora Puccini also has that divided nature. I could approach her any time of the night or day. I could touch her breasts or stroke her cunt. I could walk up behind her when she was at the kitchen sink and press myself against her and then take her, right there, half up on the counter among the potato peelings and red meat. And mostly she too was swept away. There was no love in it, not even affection, just animal pleasure. The way a male cat sinks his teeth into the back of the neck of the female and just hangs on, so too I would take my pleasure in surprising her in different parts of the house, no matter what she was doing. At night I would sometimes come to her after having been with other women and still wearing their smell. And once when I had several men here for dinner I made her strip before them. I made her lean against this very mantel while I took her from behind as my guests watched and cheered me on.

"After all that you may find it difficult to believe that I loved her. But not only did I desire her, I also wanted to break through her barrier of reserve and coldness. You know the Aesop fable about the sun and wind wagering who could most easily make the traveler remove his heavy coat? The wind blew and blew and the man hugged his coat to him. The sun smiled and shone; the man grew hot and the coat slipped from his shoulders. I was that wind and I buffeted and blew and shook her from one part of the house to the other. I would catch her on the stairs and strip her clothes from her. I would find her making the beds and again I would take her. I would find her in the garden and I would push her down in the dirt and drag up her skirt. And she too would be carried away. She would bite and suck at me and fondle me and scratch and nuzzle and pretend to try to escape. She would grunt and moan like any pig, then scream out or sink her teeth into her lip. She would yank at my hair or slap me or try to drive her knee

220

into my groin as I would evade her or drag her back by her hair or slap her face. I would pull away from her and tease her and not give myself to her until she would beg and crawl after me and I would sit astride her back and dig my heels into her ribs until she threw me over onto the floor and grabbed my prick and scratched it with her nails. And one time she took a knife and scratched the words 'fuck me' into her belly and I laughed and left her here for a week and when I returned I made her crawl around my feet, for you see she would do all that I told her to do."

"Would she kiss you?" asked Dalakis, not looking at Pacheco.

"Only if I ordered her to do it. She would only do as I commanded. Nothing was offered or given freely. I would say, do this, and she would do it. And of course once we had begun our lovemaking and the passion was upon her, then she would do many things. But she would never kiss me freely and she would never initiate. Even when I knew she wanted me, she would never make the first gesture. And even when she kissed me, I knew she hated it. Sometimes weeks would go by, perhaps even a month while I occupied myself with other women, but she would never speak or make a motion even though I knew she desired me. Then I would take her again or be cruel or humiliate her or make her crawl but nothing seemed to surprise her or take her unawares, nothing broke through the reserve. Like Aesop's wind, the harder I blew, the more tightly she hugged herself to herself. And after we were done with our lovemaking, she would be as cold as ever."

"And there were no restrictions," asked Malgiolio, "there was nothing you couldn't do?" He had taken one of Pacheco's expensive cigars and was in the process of snipping off its tip.

"She wouldn't bear my children," said Pacheco, "and she wouldn't let me touch her in the room of Roberto Collura. I could interrupt her and make her come out, but I couldn't touch her inside the room. She reads to him several hours a day. I would stand in the hall and listen to her voice either reading or just talking. I would listen and think how kind she sounded, how solicitous. Could she do this for him, could she do that for him? She would have the servant boy fill a hot tin tub and then she would bathe this Roberto Collura. I would stand in the doorway and watch as she stroked and washed and petted him. You can guess how I hated him. Yet what could I do? She would only be mine for as long as he was alive and so I worked to patch and repair all his little ailments and kept him breathing and relatively healthy. Then I would stand in the hall and listen to her reading him Balzac or Tolstoy or Hugo, huge books that would take her weeks to get through. I would stand out there until I could tolerate no more and I would snap my fingers and make her come to me and take her right there on the rough carpet while she covered her mouth to keep from moaning or crying out, and after I was done she would wash herself and then go back into his room and pick up the book and continue reading."

"And he never had any idea?" I asked. One of the candles on the mantel began to sputter and Pacheco stood up to put it out, pinching the wick with two fingers.

"How should I know or why should I care?" he said. "I hate him and I keep him alive. We never speak. My only concern is her, and I have been obsessed by her for twenty years. But always she would do her work and go about the house as if I did not exist. I could have my way with her and perhaps arouse her and make her passionate but afterward she would return to acting like this dead thing, except with him, Roberto Collura, or with the cook, who was her friend."

"Twenty years?" asked Dalakis. "All that time?"

"Does it seem so long to you?" said Pacheco. "In memory

it feels like nothing. She was beautiful when she came to my house and I find her beautiful now. Changed, of course, but still beautiful. We lived in the south for eleven more years, then moved here. I had many other women and often I would bring them to the house to see if I could make her jealous. I would make love to them right in front of her. I'd order her to stand at the foot of the bed and watch as I pawed over some woman I'd found on the street, then I'd see Antonia staring with that blank dead face as if she were staring at a wall. When I was done, I'd send her away. You think this has gone on for a long time? Believe me, it seems like nothing. And still I have never broken through that dead face except in those moments of passion. And Collura is weak. He's often sick. I'm surprised he has lasted this long. In a few years or even months, he'll get some germ and develop flu, then pneumonia. It's bound to be soon. He'll die and she'll leave me. She has been my whole life and I have never wanted her a bit less than I wanted her that first time. You know, she was a virgin. She hadn't even given herself to that fool upstairs. So you see, I have had everything and at the same time I've had nothing."

"Perhaps that is your punishment," said Dalakis with his back turned. He had gotten up from the couch and stood near the door as if not wanting to be too close to Pacheco.

"Punishment? For what?" Pacheco stood by the mantel with his hands in his pockets, jingling his keys. His suitcoat was unbuttoned and I noticed that his dark gray tie was held in place by a silver clip in the shape of a running fox. "This is your little song, Carl, a world made up of punishment and reward, virtue and vice. Twenty years ago I went to a summer concert and a young woman came with her aunt and her fiancé. They happened to sit a little behind me and my hand happened to brush the young woman's ankle. And from that time on she has been like a bright light in my brain, a light which pushed me out, drove me to the very corners of myself, which obliterated my ego with desire for her until I had to fuck her just to save my life and find myself again, just to think my own thoughts, to recover myself, to be quiet by myself, to have some peace. Look at it as murder. She killed me. She filled my mind with her own image and drove me out. I had to possess her in order to resurrect myself again. I had to defeat her in order to save my own life."

"And did you really defeat her?" I asked.

Pacheco looked at me. Have I said how the blueness of his eyes reminded me of those Alaskan sled dogs one sometimes sees? Not their pale color so much as their lack of feeling. Or perhaps they could be called scientific eyes, as if I were a smidgin of tissue under a microscope.

"No, Batterby, you've had my answers. I've tried to give you an idea of my last twenty years but do you have any sense of the pain? You think I wouldn't have wanted a wife and family, a more conventional life? My life has been a rush, a great race. For you this is just a bit of gossip, something to think about in terms of that perennial book you talk about writing. How can you understand my pain if you have no heart of your own?"

"So you think I have no heart?" I asked.

"Why did you desert your wife?"

"Because she was your mistress."

"But that was over. She told you it was over and apparently you chose not to believe her."

I had no wish to tell Pacheco that I had driven her out because she had preferred him as a lover. As for the passage of time meaning little, he was right about that, for although I'd seen him with my wife just twenty years ago, I hated him at this moment as I had hated him then. The room felt hot and airless, even though the door was partly open. I imagined Señora Puccini standing behind it, listening, listening.

"Do you know you have a son?" asked Pacheco.

"That's a lie. Yes, I knew she bore a son but he's no son of mine. Claim him as your own bastard."

Pacheco looked away as if pretending to be bored with me. "He's not mine. The dates are wrong. I was in the south. He's yours and you probably know he's yours. He's a man now, do you realize that? I even saw him. He looks like you. The same square face and sandy hair. He even has your stoop, as if weak backs ran in your family. You don't think I want a son? You don't think I'd claim him if I could? What will you do when you see him, for surely he'll hunt you out? He wants to know you, wants to know why you deserted him. What will you tell him?"

"I'll tell him his mother's a whore."

"Then he won't believe you. You see, she has remarried, has other children. She's lived with the same man happily for fifteen years. He's a pharmacist, did you know that? He wears glasses. He's bald. He's almost painfully thin, so thin that his elbows stick out like little blades. Yet they're very much in love. They touch and caress each other. They spend all their time together. You could have had that, Batterby. She wanted to make her life with you. She broke off with me, wanted no more of me. And instead of accepting her and forgiving her, you drove her away. You could have had children and a family. You could have had all that I've wanted for myself but you drove her away."

"Stop it!" I shouted. Standing up, I walked to the wall and stood facing a shelf of books, hardly seeing them. Although not a violent man, sometimes I think myself capable of violence.

I heard the door open behind me. Señora Puccini entered the library. She didn't look at us but walked directly to Pacheco. "The colonel wants you to see one of his officers," she said. "He believes the man is dying."

Her voice was flat and monotonic. Stepping quickly toward her, Pacheco grabbed her arm and turned her so she faced us as he kept her pinned against him. She didn't struggle but remained passive in his arms. It was impossible not to stare at her. High cheekbones, a straight nose, and a beautiful mouth with full lips and perfect teeth, she had a large chin for a woman, almost masculine and square. Her gray eyes were set wide apart. All of us were standing. "This was what I wanted," he said. "This was what I wanted for my wife, the mother of my children."

He took her chin and lifted it, squeezing her cheeks. She kept her eyes on the rug.

"But she didn't want you," said Dalakis, retreating toward me, "and instead of listening to her, you ruined her life. What did you ever get from her?"

Pacheco grabbed the fabric of her skirt and yanked it up, exposing her white underwear. He pressed his hand against her groin. Even though he was mauling her, Señora Puccini's expression remained blank. "This is what I got," said Pacheco, "and I'll take it again and again. Do you wish to see it?"

"Leave her alone!" shouted Malgiolio, suddenly. "Leave her alone or I swear I'll strike you." He raised a fist and took a step toward Pacheco and the housekeeper.

Startled, Pacheco looked back, then burst out laughing. "So our little immoralist has scruples after all." He left Señora Puccini standing by the fireplace and took several steps toward Malgiolio, who, surprisingly, stood his ground. The photograph of the young Antonia Puccini over the older one's shoulder made it seem that both women were in the room together.

"Then strike me if you wish," said Pacheco. "Do you have the blood for it? You see where judgment gets us? We live as we can and try to do as little harm as we can, but the harm comes all the same. Even if we spent the day in a prison cell the harm would come."

"Can I go now?" asked the housekeeper. She stood watching us as if nothing violent had happened. I found myself wondering if she were entirely sane.

Pacheco brushed a hand across his face as if wiping something from it. Then he turned, turning his back to us. He appeared to look at Señora Puccini for about ten seconds and I wished I could see his expression. "Yes," he said, "tell the colonel I'll be with him directly."

I watched her pass through the door. It seemed certain she was no longer carrying the pistol. The way Pacheco had grabbed her and swept up her skirt seemed to show that her pockets were empty. Pacheco glanced back at us with a kind of scorn, then followed Señora Puccini out of the room.

I looked at my two companions. I'm sure we all felt embarrassed in each other's presence. The evening had told us too much about ourselves without forgiving or absolving us. Here we'd been looking forward to our little reunion and now we felt too uncomfortable to speak to each other. For even though we could condemn Pacheco, were we much better? And even though Pacheco had taken what he wanted, hadn't he also been punished for it? I had no wish to discuss my wife, yet I found myself wondering about her son and whether I had sacrificed our lives to some principle more connected to pride than virtue. All this had been buried deep within me and I owed Pacheco the gratitude of unloosing it. But was I the father? I had been sure it was Pacheco. But was that true or was it only what I wished to be true? To believe the boy was mine made all my actions doubly foolish. And so perhaps I refused to think the boy was mine just because I didn't want the responsibility of rejecting my own son.

I swear none of this was conscious. I swear I hadn't thought of my wife and her son for years. I had convinced myself she was dead and that the son didn't exist. Does that seem psychotic? Rather it had become an easy habit. In fact, I hardly ever analyze the actions of people around me. I watch them and find them curious, but I never wonder why they do one thing rather than another. Does that make sense? For me Pacheco had always been a romantic figure, someone mysterious and dashing, a character out of Dumas. And of course I had envied him all those women. But look at him, creeping around his own house, trying for twenty years to coax a smile out of his housekeeper. Wouldn't it be better to pity him? Yet he had corrupted the woman whom I had married and with whom I was passionately in love. He had wrecked my life, hurt Dalakis, and ruined the poor girl who had become his housekeeper. And the man in the upstairs bedroom, Roberto Collura, what of him?

Really, it seems I become as much a character as the others at Pacheco's dinner. I describe what they do, yet I don't know why they do it. I describe what I do but I hardly have any sense of my own motivation. Perhaps that is why I was never successful as a writer—I had no sense of myself, almost refused to be conscious of myself, since to be conscious would make my failures too obvious and, worse, make me responsible for my failures. Better not to think of it or I'd wind up feeling guilty for the killing in the streets.

Dalakis had gone into the hall. Malgiolio was lighting another of his colored cigarettes. What a foolish affectation! I felt extremely claustrophobic, partly because of the curfew, partly because of my own thoughts, which kept pressing against my brain with their questions and accusations. I hurried out of the library and into the hall. Pacheco and Dalakis were with some soldiers under the tapestry of the rutting centaurs. How ironic that tapestry seemed now. I quickly crossed the hall and climbed the stairs. My first thought was to go onto the balcony off the bathroom, then I decided it would be safer on the roof. We could still hear shouting and gunshots from the street and it seemed dangerous to expose myself. My mind felt confused. Instead of thinking, I seemed to be pushing my thoughts away, to be keeping my mind intentionally blank. Of course deep within my brain my thoughts were in a turmoil but they were, in a manner of speaking, too distant to reach. Taking a candle from the stairs, I hurried along the hall and up to the third floor. I moved quietly, almost stealthily, as if afraid someone might hear me. The hot wax dripped onto my hand and I had to hold my other hand before the flame to keep it from being blown out. The dark shadow of my hand was thrown forward onto the walls and floor, preceding me like a troubled spirit.

When I reached the ladder to the roof, I grabbed the rope which pulled the whole contraption down from the ceiling, then I paused. To my right was the door to Roberto Collura's room. Had I come to the third floor not to climb to the roof, but to see him instead? I imagined him thin and emaciated, having lain on that bed ever since Pacheco had moved to this house nine years earlier. I walked to his door and put my hand on the knob. The door was unlocked. With much trepidation, I pushed it open.

At first I thought Collura was asleep, he lay so still. But then of course he couldn't move; he was paralyzed. It was an odd sensation to know I had complete power over him. Most of the candles had been taken away but there was still one on the nightstand by his bed and another on the dresser against the wall. Avoiding the mobiles and other paraphernalia which hung from the ceiling, I walked to the bed and looked down. To my shock I saw that Collura was staring up at me. He had a face like a monkey, very thin and lined, and his eyes seemed gray or light blue, like the color of water. Covered only with a sheet, his body resembled a stick. For some reason, I remembered Pacheco's description of Collura riding on horseback, galloping across the fields. We looked into each other's eyes and I tried to imagine his thoughts.

"Can you speak?" I asked. Collura made no response. "Can you blink your eyes?" Collura didn't blink. "Can you hear me?" Still he did not respond, although I was certain he heard me. Indeed, his eyes followed me whenever I changed position. Perhaps he's crazy, I thought. Certainly, if I'd been paralyzed for twenty years, I'd be absolutely mad. I turned to look around the room—the pictures, toys, books, mobiles, mirrors all shimmered in the light of the two candles. The bird cages were covered. The fish hung stationary in their tank. The stuffed mongoose and cobra remained locked in their deathly embrace. I walked to the bookshelf. There were complete sets of Dumas, Hugo, Blasco Ibáñez, H. G. Wells. If he could be read to, then he wasn't deaf. I went to the dresser and opened the top drawer. There were t-shirts and hospital gowns. In the next drawer were towels, in the next were sheets. Even with my back to Roberto Collura, I knew he was watching me. I wondered if Señora Puccini had sex with him, if there was anything she could do to arouse him. I looked through a desk which was full of letters from friends in the south. I glanced at one which appeared to be from an old teacher. It was dated three years previously and began, "It was good to receive your letter." The teacher suggested books that Collura might like—Turgenev, Jane Austen—and went on to say, "Yes, I agree about Lawrence, there is a supreme silliness to the emotional lives of his characters. You remember in *Women in Love* where what's-his-name holds his horse right at the track as the train roars by?"

I returned the letter to the desk and walked back to the bed. "Presumably you can talk," I said. "Will you talk to me?"

I'm not sure what I wanted, but I think I desired to know more about Pacheco and Señora Puccini from another point of view. I stared down at Collura and he stared back at me. Occasionally he would blink but otherwise his face was expressionless. I found myself growing angry at him. In retrospect that seems foolish but I had so joined my own story to that of Pacheco's that Collura's silence seemed to deprive me willfully of knowledge about myself. To him of course I was an absolute stranger but he had seen me earlier with Pacheco, and presumably Señora Puccini had mentioned we were dinner guests and even old friends. But then if he thought I was a friend of Pacheco's, perhaps that was reason enough to be silent.

"Can you talk to me?" I asked. "Can you tell me about Pacheco? You think I'm his friend? Believe me, he ruined me as much as he ruined you."

I was hardly responsible for myself. Despairing of the young man who Pacheco claimed was my son and still grieving for my wife, unbalanced by all the talk of the evening, the violence in the city, and the very turmoil of our lives, I seemed to act not by design but by impulse.

"Do you know about Pacheco and Antonia Puccini?" I asked. "Do you know they are lovers?" Collura continued to look at me. You have seen how monkeys can have a wise expression, or at least an expression that suggests wisdom? Collura's face suggested that. So, although he made no response, I knew he knew what I was talking about. He even seemed to pity me for being so upset and foolish. It made me angry with him.

"You know he fucks her all over the house?" I said. My voice had become high, almost squeaky. I couldn't control it. "He fucks her in the hallway, right outside your door. He fucks her and she loves it and wants him to do it again, while you are stuck here helpless and impotent. Doesn't that make you want to kill him?"

But then I caught myself. What was I saying, why was I torturing a helpless human being? His face was still blank and again I wondered if he could hear. But no, of course he could hear. I suddenly felt ashamed and backed away from the bed. Again his eyes followed me. Covering his feet at the bottom of the bed was a folded blanket. I lifted it. Collura's feet were white and bony yet looked very soft. White useless things. How had he gotten this way? Was it possible that his crash on the motorcycle had been an accident? I again covered his feet. I began to be afraid that Señora Puccini would enter the room and find me. How could I explain myself? When I entered, I had blown out my candle. Now I lit it again from the candle on the bedstand. My candle was red and about a foot long. As I paused to look down again at Roberto Collura, I saw that hot wax from my candle was dripping onto his arm. He blinked but made no other response. I jumped back, then tried to brush the wax away, but it was stuck fast to his skin. Frightened, I turned and left the room.

I hurried along the hall, thinking there must be another staircase, one leading to the back of the house. Everything was silent. I no longer had any desire to climb to the roof and had decided to go to the patio for my breath of fresh air. The back stairs were wooden and uncarpeted. My feet made a clattering noise as I ran down them.

The stairs brought me to a hallway on the far side of the patio from the dining room. I hurried along it to the kitchen, which was dark except for a single candle on the long oak table. My mouth felt parched, so I went to the sink and turned the tap. Then I froze in horror. Blood was gushing from the faucet. I stumbled back, raising my candle. Of course it wasn't blood but rust which, by candlelight, had confused me. In any case, I had no wish to drink it. Closing the tap, I went to the refrigerator, where I found a bottle of mineral water. When I had drunk my fill, I began to look around the kitchen, opening drawers, glancing into cupboards. After a moment, however,

I heard the sound of sobbing coming from outside the door. Quietly, I crossed the kitchen to see who it could be. It was the cook's grandson. He was out on the patio hunched over in a chair next to the picnic table on which his dead grandmother lay surrounded by about twenty candles.

She wore a dark red dress that fell around her in thick folds and she looked quite beautiful. Her hands were joined across her chest. On her feet were a pair of silver slippers. Her round face was so smooth and unlined that she looked like a young girl taking a brief rest before leaving for a summer dance. I walked to the table and stood by her head. Her grandson glanced up at me, then went back to his sobbing, sitting with his elbows on his knees and his face buried in his hands. Madame Letendre's long white hair had been fixed into a braid which was wound around the top of her head. Crowning it was a little wreath of white flowers. On her face was even a bit of makeup, rouge and powder, a little lipstick. Looking at her, I couldn't help but remember how Schwab had gorged himself as she had lain dying in the hall. Now Schwab was dead as well.

"Did you dress her?" I asked the boy.

"It was the Señora," he said, the words squeezing between his sobs.

I realized of course that on such an evening as this I was only seeing one side of Señora Puccini. Yet looking at the flowers in the old woman's hair, seeing how carefully the dead woman had been made beautiful was like seeing a picture of another Señora Puccini. It showed her gentleness, her deep affection. Perhaps kindness was her most obvious quality, and how could we be expected to see it, or why should she show it to us, we who were Pacheco's guests and ostensible friends?

I stood by the old woman's shoulder. The candles surrounded her: three at the head and feet, six on each side. The candle nearest to me on my right was dripping wax on the red folds of her skirt and I reached forward to push the skirt out of the way. As I moved the red cloth, my hand touched something solid next to the old woman's thigh. At first I jerked back my hand, then I touched it again. I had no doubt what it was. Reaching under the cloth, I drew out the pistol I had seen in the hand of Señora Puccini. It would have been hard to mistake it, what with its polished chrome and pearl grips. It was a .32 caliber Llama and along the frame and slide was fancy scroll-work suggestive of foliage. I held the gun in my hand. It felt light and cool. Most likely the housekeeper had hidden it on the body of the cook after Captain Quatrone had told his men to search us for weapons. I assumed it was Pacheco's pistol, since only he would possess something that so combined the decorative and the useful.

As I stood by the cook's body, I heard a footstep on the tiles behind me. Turning, I saw Señora Puccini standing a few feet away. She looked at the pistol and I felt as if I had been caught stealing something.

"Wax was dripping onto her skirt," I said rather clumsily. "I moved the skirt and found this."

"I put it there," said Señora Puccini. She stared at me without nervousness or curiosity. She was just my height and her eyes were flat and passive.

"I guessed as much," I said. "I decided you thought the soldiers might find it." Even as I spoke, I wondered why I was helping her form an answer. But she seemed indifferent to what I thought. She looked past me at the body of the cook. After a moment, I put the pistol on a small table.

"You know," I said, "I've noticed the door slightly open as Pacheco's been describing his history with you and I realize you must have heard some of what he's been saying. Of course it's none of my business but I'm sorry for your life with him."

She didn't answer but moved forward so she was standing

by Madame Letendre's head. Very gently she straightened the wreath of flowers around the dead woman's brow. Again the idea of touching that dead flesh was abhorrent to me.

"Is what Pacheco is saying true?" I asked.

Somewhat impatiently Señora Puccini raised her head and stared at me with her dark eyes. I thought she was about to speak, but she remained silent.

"Presumably you don't object to his talking about it," I said. "Why do you think he's telling us?"

What was especially disconcerting about her stare was that not only didn't she blink but she kept shifting her gaze back and forth from one of my eyes to the other.

"He wants to make you respond to him, doesn't he?" I asked. "That's his passion, isn't it? To make you react. And you choose not to. But what are your feelings? Do you like making love to him?"

Once more she honored me with her cold smile. Why did I feel she was patronizing me? I moved back so I stood by the cook's feet and we stared at each other over the dark red dress. The cook's grandson had gone into the kitchen and stood in the doorway observing us. Señora Puccini started to turn away and I stepped forward and touched her arm.

"Don't you want revenge?" I asked.

She wore a white apron over her black dress and as she turned to look at me she reached behind her with both hands to unfasten the cord. Removing the apron, she dropped it on the small table, covering the pistol.

"Ask him about his son," she said.

"His son?"

"Ask him."

She stood very straight and again I was struck not only by her beauty but by her ability to resist. "Tell me about Roberto Collura," I said. "Can he speak?"

In retrospect, I wonder if I cared, but not only did I want

235

to keep her talking, I was also seeking something that might soften the expression on her face. And I found it with my question, because her face changed and she seemed to grieve.

"I don't know," she said. "He could until recently. He's very sick, not only in his body but also in his mind."

"Does he know about you and Pacheco?"

But I was asking too much; she refused to answer. I also believed she could look directly into my heart and was repelled by what she found there. Yes, that is foolish, but I felt irritated with what I imagined to be her dismissal of me and it was that irritation which prompted my next question.

"One last thing," I asked her, "why did you let the cook leave the house?"

She stepped back and her face grew cold again. I thought she might glance down at the cook, that I might see some guilty expression, but she kept her eyes on mine. Then she turned away, walked toward the back stairs, and I guessed she was going up to see Roberto Collura. It seemed so pathetic. I thought of the splashes of red wax on his arm and I knew she would realize they had come from my candle. Neither of us had glanced at or made any motion toward the pistol hidden by her apron. After she had disappeared, I recrossed the patio toward the great hall, feeling satisfied that she had at least granted me a few words. As I passed the bougainvillaea I saw the leaves quivering, quivering as if shaken by an invisible hand. Constantly in my mind was the image of Señora Puccini. I imagined ordering her to lie down on the floor as Pacheco must have done, telling her to remove her underwear. I imagined seeing her naked and desirous. Although part of me was horrified at this intrusion, this violation of another human being, another part wished I could make such a command myself, not to any woman but to this one. What had she meant about Pacheco's son? As I passed through the door into the hall, I thought of her lips. How full they were. One could almost feel their softness. How much Pacheco must want them and how fitting that he should be denied.

When I entered the library I had the impression that my friends had been talking about me. Pacheco and Dalakis were sitting on the leather couch. Malgiolio was standing by the mantel. I imagined Malgiolio and Dalakis, especially Malgiolio, telling our various acquaintances how I had persisted in my foolish lie about my wife, how she was living in Europe and had a son which I refused to believe was my own. But perhaps after this trouble, this violence in the streets, all would be different. Perhaps Malgiolio was right about there being new opportunities. Perhaps we would have new lives, clean slates to get dirty again. At least Schwab wouldn't return to mock me. Still, I hated the fact that these men had been talking about me and now felt they had to remain silent.

"What have you been up to now, Batterby?" asked Malgiolio, and he looked at Pacheco and winked. They were all smoking cigars, even Dalakis. The air was blue with smoke. It was now past one in the morning.

"I was in the kitchen," I said. "I've been talking to Señora Puccini."

"And what did she tell you?" asked Pacheco.

I poured myself some mineral water, then added just the smallest drop of Scotch whiskey. "She suggested I ask you about your son," I said.

Pacheco didn't respond right away. Certainly I had their attention. Malgiolio blew a small cloud of smoke toward the ceiling. Dalakis coughed, then pushed his glasses back up his nose.

"What about my son?" asked Pacheco.

But I wasn't ready to say more. I moved forward until I could feel a breeze from the overhead fan. My clothes against my skin felt clammy with sweat.

"You know, Pacheco," I said at last, "you've been telling us this long story and I'm not sure why. I can't believe it's for our amusement. But Señora Puccini has heard some of it and I believe you want her to hear it. Why do you humiliate her? I asked her if she didn't want revenge and she said to ask you about your son. Now I'm asking you."

Nobody made a noise. The shouting in the street came to us as an angry muttering. Relighting his cigar, Pacheco leaned back on the couch and crossed his legs. "It's not what you could truly call a son," he said. "It was a male fetus. She told me I was the father and I suppose I must have been."

"Did she miscarry?" asked Dalakis, ready as always with his sympathy.

"No, I performed an abortion. She lay on the kitchen table and I ripped my son out of her. It was, as Batterby says, her revenge. I had humiliated her in some way in front of some guests. At first she hid from me the fact she was pregnant. Then she pretended she would have the baby. But you recall our agreement, that she would never bear my children? At last she demanded an abortion. She didn't want Collura to know she was pregnant. I refused. She was more than four months along and . . . well, I wanted a child. She took sleeping pills and the cook found her unconscious. Then she tried to perform the abortion on herself by taking some sort of poison. I watched her. I even tied her up. As you may have imagined, she has a tremendous will. I knew that if she refused to have the child, there was no way to make her. I tried to persuade her. I offered her all sorts of things. She said she would only accept if I allowed her to move away with Collura with sufficient money to take care of him. But no matter how much I wanted the child, I wanted her more. So I performed the abortion."

"How long ago was this?" I asked.

"It was right after we moved to this house. She was thirty. As I say, I did it on the kitchen table. We were alone at the time. I had to induce delivery. She wanted something for the pain but I refused. After all, I wanted it to hurt her so she wouldn't forget. But once she realized I wasn't going to give her anything, she didn't make a sound. I knew I was hurting her dreadfully but she didn't make a sound. When it was over, I stood with my son in my hands. He was just five months, a perfectly formed male."

"Was he alive?" asked Dalakis.

"He was at first but there was no way to save him. He lay in my hands breathing very rapidly. I looked at her. She had a kind of smile. I realized I had made her evil in some way. Not only had I ruined her, I had made her evil."

"And all you had wanted," I said, lifting her picture from the mantel, "was to make her love you."

"Don't mock me, Batterby."

"How long did the child live?" asked Dalakis. He stood up and threw his cigar into the fireplace almost in agitation. We three stood in a semicircle around Pacheco. He didn't look at us.

"Nearly an hour. He was very strong. Of course, I could have given him an injection but I couldn't bring myself to do it. I brought him in here. It was winter and cold and there was a fire in the fireplace. I laid him on this very table on several towels. Then I watched him. He moved a little but made no sound. I just watched him. He was in no pain. I mean, he was my son. Every so often I reached out to touch the sole of his foot. It was so tiny. Then after a while he died. I buried him in the garden, planted a flowering shrub over his body. Antonia remained in bed for several days, then returned to her duties as housekeeper. She felt successful in her revenge, but it didn't

239

stop me from trying to humiliate her. I still had my passion, but I also hated her. When she recovered I had a little party and made her wait on us naked. There were four other men, all doctors. She refused and came in fully dressed. I was so angry that I tore at her clothes. She removed the rest and did her work as if nothing were out of the ordinary. You see, we jab at each other, each trying to find the weakness of the other. It has become the major occupation of our lives."

"But you love her," said Malgiolio, almost tenderly.

"That has become irrelevant. She fills my mind. It's like having a pail under a leak in the ceiling. The pail fills, then has to be emptied. When I take her or abuse her or have my way with her, that's like emptying the pail. It's only by having my way with her, by making love to her, that I can retrieve myself from the limbo of sexual obsession. Then I have a few days as the pail fills again."

"You ruined not only her life, but your own," I said.

"But I did it by choice," said Pacheco, looking up at me. "There was, as they say, a ruling passion. There may have been a point when I could have turned aside, but I chose not to. Maybe it was that day I walked beside her on the street, when I reached out and touched her breast. However, by the time that I climbed through her window several weeks later, by then I had given up any choice. But you, Batterby, you ruined your life for no reason at all, for reasons of vanity and pride. I watched my son die, watched him pant and gasp himself to death right here in this room. You had a perfectly good son and you threw him away. You know, your wife loved you. Even though we'd had our little affair she still loved you. But you couldn't stand the fact that we'd been together."

"It continued after we were married," I said. I hated him for dragging the discussion back to my failed marriage, but I kept my face from showing my feelings.

"So what? It had begun long before you ever met her. We were just saying goodbye, a little poke in the dark. It meant nothing."

"But she was my wife," I said. Dalakis and Malgiolio still stood on either side of me. I didn't see how Pacheco could sit so calmly with the three of us standing over him.

"You're a sentimentalist," said Pacheco. "You see this as betrayal and desertion. You flail at the world with your little moral standard. I'm not trying to justify myself. I'm not interested in doing so. Your wife and I had our time together, then it was over. She loved you and wanted to make her life with you. You drove her away. She told you she was pregnant and you ignored her. She told you about the birth of your son, she came to your house, she showed you the baby, she begged your forgiveness, and you drove her away."

"It was your son," I said.

Pacheco reached out one of his small black shoes and poked me in the shin. He was smiling. "No, you see I had a blood test done. It was your son. If it had been mine, I would have found it a cause for great celebration. But it wasn't mine. So you pushed her away and began to put out the story that she was dead. Soon you were saying she'd actually died on your honeymoon. Do you know how your friends pitied you for this nonsense, for such a ridiculous fabrication? And all this time your wife was still waiting for your forgiveness. How foolish of her. At last she gave up and a few years later she met this skinny fellow with whom she's lived faithfully for fifteen years. And she bore him three children. But her oldest is yours. Even his name is yours, Nicolas Batterby. Perhaps he will come back here some day. Your embarrassment should be amusing to watch. Perhaps he will ask why you deserted him and you can tell him it was for reasons of vanity and pride."

I was too angry to answer. From his seat on the couch,

Pacheco stared up at me with what appeared to be a pleasant smile. But I could feel his mockery and disdain. Dalakis seemed to be studying his hands, rubbing them together and staring at his palms. Malgiolio was pouring himself more brandy. The candles flickered from a draft and I glanced at the door, which was open a few inches. It occurred to me that even these words were meant for Señora Puccini, as if all his words, all he ever said, was part of their great conversation.

It took me a moment to compose myself, but then I was able to speak calmly, even ironically. I wanted to hurt him and I believed I knew how to do it. "I'm glad my story offers you such amusement. I drove my wife away because she betrayed me. You call that no more than vanity and pride? Certainly, you exhibit an entirely different set of values. Well, let's look at those values. What have you done to Antonia Puccini? And that poor wreck of a man that you keep upstairs, what did you do to him? You forget, Daniel, we've known you for forty years and I think you're leaving out part of the story."

"What do you mean?" asked Pacheco. He still wore a little smile, as if to show that nothing I could say would disturb him.

"When you were so caught up in your infatuation, I can't believe you would have waited and done nothing. Then, fortunately for you, this young man had his motorcycle accident. You knew his schedule. You knew when he was making his trips south, late at night on an empty road." I stopped, almost frightened of saying so much.

All three of them stared at me, then Dalakis angrily grabbed my arm. "Are you suggesting that Pacheco caused the accident?"

"You don't think him capable?" I asked, shaking Dalakis loose. Pacheco still had his little smile. Malgiolio was looking at me almost with admiration, as if, for the first time in my life, I'd impressed him.

"Look at the strength of his obsession," I continued. "He'd

broken into her house. He'd fought with Collura and would have killed him if Antonia Puccini hadn't stopped him. You think he couldn't have run down Collura on a dark road? How simple to drive up from behind, pull out to pass, then make a little jerk to the side, and there goes the motorcycle plummeting off the road at seventy miles an hour. He probably wanted Collura dead but it worked out better like this. It gave him something to bargain with. You think he didn't do it? Ask him."

Pacheco had turned and was tapping the ash of his cigar into a brass ashtray. Then he looked back at me with that same awful smile, made even more awful by his torn cheek. "Very clever, Batterby. You should try writing thrillers." Pacheco stood up and took a step toward me. I moved back to the mantel.

"Yes, I ran him down," Pacheco continued. "He stood in my way. We both wanted the same thing and he was going to get it. As you say, I knew when he made his trips from the capital. It was a simple plan but it took weeks before I could do it. Several times I went out and just watched him come roaring by. Another night I followed him all the way to Antonia's house, completely unable to act. That happened two or three times. I would follow him and curse myself for being a coward. The date of their marriage was approaching. It seemed I had either to rid the world of Roberto Collura or rid it of myself. So I went out again, I went a long way, more than a hundred miles from the city. When he came roaring by, I went after him. Still, I couldn't bring myself to do it. I remember watching his red taillight, the one light on the road. I followed him for nearly an hour, cursing and shouting at myself. I had an old Peugeot, what I thought of as a doctor's car, but strong and fast. He was doing a solid seventy-five. There was no other traffic.

"At last I slammed my foot to the floor and came up behind

him, then pulled out into the left lane. I stayed beside him, a little behind him for several minutes. He turned his head but couldn't see much, just my bright lights. Still, I couldn't do it. I decided to give it up. I pressed down on the gas, meaning to pass him and go home. I hadn't thought he might be frightened. It was early fall, my windows were open, and my car was full of the sound of his motorcycle. When I drew up beside him, he turned. Either he recognized my car or he saw me. He was terrified. He screamed my name, Pacheco! He tried to accelerate. When I heard him shout my name something changed inside me. I felt no more hesitation. I gave the wheel a quick yank to the right, clipping his rear fender and sending him off the road. In my rearview mirror, I could see his motorcycle flipping over and over. Touching his fender had made only a slight click, just a little bump that didn't even leave a mark. I heard him scream, then this flying headlight in my mirror, then darkness. I drove back to the city and went to bed. Of course I couldn't sleep. I stared up at the ceiling and saw his face as I had seen it when he screamed my name, then that crazy headlight jerking and leaping across the landscape.

"Naturally I was astonished when they brought him in. A truck driver had found him. I felt fear and knew I should kill him but I couldn't bring myself to do it. When he came out of his coma, he had no memory of the accident. I stayed close to him, often going into his room to check on his condition. When he first saw me, his expression didn't change—blank suffering, monotonous despair. I think if he'd remembered anything I would have put him away for good. . . ."

As Pacheco had been talking, I'd been watching the door. It was open just a crack, perhaps an inch. At first there was just a shadow behind it, but as Pacheco neared the end of his story I saw part of a face pressed to the opening. Of course it was the housekeeper's face but it was a moment before I recognized it, so distorted did it seem. Mostly I saw an eye. It seemed swollen, as if it were open too wide. There was too much white. Then it disappeared.

Dalakis was very upset. He refused to look at any of us and paced up and down in front of the fireplace. "But that was attempted murder. You should be in jail."

"I was never caught," said Pacheco. He glanced at the door and I realized that he'd known someone was there all along. "As a matter of fact, this is the first time I've ever admitted it. Of course, Batterby with his superior intelligence managed to guess correctly and since he did, then I had to tell you the rest of the story."

Dalakis appeared more and more distraught and his big hands were pressed to his face as if he were trying to keep his head from breaking apart. Like others in the group, he had always seen Pacheco as a hero. He still couldn't look at him but stared off in the direction of the liquor cabinet, where Malgiolio was gazing down at the rug with his arms crossed, looking rather like a statue, I thought.

"You nearly killed her fiancé, then you blackmail her," said Dalakis. "How can you justify that?"

"I don't try to. You remember in *Crime and Punishment* when Raskolnikov argues that some people have the right to kill? I think his theory had something to do with Napoleon. Of course, that's all foolishness. But there are certain courses of action, certain passions, which one follows no matter what. That is not to justify them, it is simply how the road went. From the moment I touched Antonia's ankle, the destruction of her fiancé was inevitable. Perhaps it was even inevitable that I would someday be describing it to three middle-aged men with Antonia listening outside the door. That is not to justify or apologize or condemn. It is just to describe. Clearly, it was wrong, but that wrongness doesn't affect its inevitability. Clearly, I shouldn't have done it, but that admission doesn't affect the fact I did it. I couldn't help doing it; that was the road I was traveling. That is not to say I'm not responsible. I am completely responsible. I wanted a woman and I ruined another human being in order to have her. Actually I ruined three human beings, myself included. But, Carl, knowing all this, I would still do it again, and tonight I will take her body with just as much pleasure as ever."

Pacheco stubbed out his cigar and took another Gauloise from his shirt pocket, lighting it from the candle on the mantel. Then he walked to the liquor cabinet and poured himself a small brandy. Again I was struck by the precision of his movements, that no gesture was wasted. From the street we could still hear shouting and occasional gunshots.

"If you're such a fatalist," asked Malgiolio, stepping back out of his way, "then how can you condemn me?"

"Because your relationships are based on self-hatred and a desire to humiliate yourself." Pacheco paused and swirled the brandy around in the glass, warming it. I had the sense he was tired of this talk, that he wanted us gone.

"You don't love this woman or even desire her," Pacheco continued. "She is just the tool of your punishment. That trivializes your affair to the point of ridiculousness."

"And yours is a high passion?" asked Malgiolio mockingly.

"There's nothing high about it. It's simply the hunger of one human being for another. Your relationship is basically with yourself. I had a passion and I pursued it. Batterby had a passion but he grew afraid and ran from it. Dalakis had a passion and he let it defeat him. He never fought for it. He surrendered as soon as the conflict was raised. But you, Malgiolio, your passion was with yourself and it has dwindled down to letting some fat woman piss on your head."

246

Malgiolio took a quick step toward Pacheco, who reached out his hand and pressed one finger against Malgiolio's chest, stopping him.

"This is the second time tonight you've wanted to strike me," said Pacheco. "Perhaps it is good for you. In any case, I'm not judging you, I'm describing. If I tell a patient he has cancer, that is not to judge him. You have a kind of emotional cancer."

"And what do you have?" I asked.

"Me?" said Pacheco. "Oh, I'm one of the damned: one of those fools who value something more than their own souls."

"Isn't that excessively romantic?" I asked, thinking how often that charge had been leveled at me.

"Of course, but unfortunately it's also true."

"What about her?" asked Malgiolio, still angry. "Aren't you afraid of her revenge, even that she might kill you?"

Pacheco returned to the couch, sat down, and loosened his tie. His cheek where Quatrone had hit him was still bright red and looked like raw meat. Looking at it was like looking at something inside of him. Not his soul perhaps, or psyche or id, but rather the creature he was when he was alone by himself.

"She might want to kill me but she won't," said Pacheco. "Several times during our early years together she'd come into my room at night after she thought I was asleep. I'd hear her muttering to herself. Once I saw the glint of a knife. She'd prowl around the room but she couldn't bring herself to stab me. Another time when I had humiliated her in some awful way, I forget what, I gave her a loaded rifle. She pointed it at me and I'm even sure she wanted to shoot, but she couldn't. We've played out that little scene several times."

"Why couldn't she shoot?" I asked.

"Perhaps she is not capable of hurting another human being. Or it may have been because it would have given me the pleasure of seeing her react to my prodding. Or maybe she knew that Collura would again wind up in a charity ward. Or maybe it was just to spite me. I asked her, of course, but of course she wouldn't say."

I heard some noise out in the hall and the door opened. It was Colonel Carrera who entered briskly, then stopped when he saw the seriousness of our faces. He made a little bow. "I'm sorry to bother you again, but I've heard some definite news about your friend Kress."

We all knew by his expression that Kress was dead, and so his words felt anticlimactic.

"He was shot, I'm afraid. I thought you'd want to know."

Although it was a terrible shock, I also found myself thinking that at least Kress wouldn't hear of our discussion tonight. "What happened?" I asked.

"He was killed when his regiment tried to link up with the mutinous air force regiments. We don't have the particulars but there appears to be some talk of putting his body on display as a warning."

And then I began to feel sorry for Kress and remember him as he had been at twelve years old—thin and blue-eyed with severe blond bangs cut at an angle across his forehead, a demon at soccer, a terror with girls, a coward with his teachers.

"Schwab's dead too," said Dalakis. "We saw his body." Then he began to weep. He did it entirely without shame and dragged his great gray handkerchief out of his pocket and wiped it across his eyes. Malgiolio too appeared upset.

"I know about that," said Carrera, still standing in the doorway, "but I don't know how it happened. There's a story that he was carrying gold. When Quatrone found him, he was alone in his armored car and there was no gold to be seen."

"So his own men killed him?" I asked.

"Possibly. There is no certainty in these things."

Dalakis pressed Carrera about what was happening in the

city but he knew little more than he'd known earlier. Radio communication was difficult. There was still fighting and a lot of sniping. Several of the poor neighborhoods had been turned into rebel fortresses and apparently there was a battle going on in the park downtown and around the post office as well. Yet Carrera assured us that there was no danger, the government was still in control, and within a week everything would be back as it had been.

I wondered if he were so naive as to believe that, but I felt too upset to argue. Not because of Kress or the fighting, but because I could feel thoughts surging deep in my brain which I couldn't reach. I kept imagining Antonia Puccini's startled white eye in the crack of the door. What would such an admission mean to her? What would she do? And I suppose I was thinking of my own wife and son and Pacheco's accusations. But it was still betrayal. She had betrayed me and Pacheco had betrayed me too.

I stepped out to the hall. Seven or eight soldiers lay on a row of pallets against the far wall while medics moved between them. About ten more were standing around. One was eating an orange, another appeared to be writing a letter. There was noise and moaning and people shouting at each other. Now and then the door would open and I could see soldiers in the street. The candles sputtered and there were shadows everywhere. Again I was looked at suspiciously as if I might suddenly pull out a gun.

Quickly I crossed the hall to the dining room. The table was as we had left it with the huge cake and empty wine glasses. I had neglected to bring a candle and I took one from one of the candelabra. Need I say that I also took the smallest piece of cake? I could hardly help myself. When I reached out for it, I accidentally bumped the small white-coated figure that stood for Pacheco and it fell from one layer down to the next, landing on its back in the red frosting. As I looked at the small figure, it occurred to me that perhaps Pacheco had lied about running Roberto Collura off the road. He had known that Antonia Puccini was listening. Considering his wish to shock her, he could easily have made up the story. Perhaps he had actually gone out and watched Collura go by, but as for knocking him off the road, really, we had no proof. Perhaps that is even why he'd been smiling, because I'd forced him into an admission that otherwise he would have had to volunteer. If I hadn't accused him, he would have had to make up the lie himself. Unwittingly, I had helped him. As I thought that, my eyes again settled on the vase with the scenes from *A Midsummer Night's Dream*. Perhaps the figure with the donkey's head was nobody but myself.

I crossed the hall to the patio and walked back toward the kitchen. There was no sign of Señora Puccini. The candles surrounding the old woman had been extinguished. Her grandson was curled up on the floor and appeared to be asleep. I looked for the pistol but it was gone. I moved the old woman's skirt, feeling under the folds of fabric, but it wasn't there. Lighting several of the other candles, I quickly searched through the patio and kitchen. The birds, seeing the light, began to twitter in their cages. The pistol was nowhere to be found and I could only suppose that Señora Puccini had taken it.

I hurried back across the patio. From the front door, I heard someone talking loudly. Entering the hall, I saw Captain Quatrone standing by the door with about a half dozen soldiers. They were as wary as crows and moved their automatic rifles back and forth across the room, even pointing the weapons at their own comrades. One soldier knocked over one of the standing buckets of red flowers and it fell to the floor with a crash, scattering the flowers and spilling the water. Quatrone was arguing with Carrera as Pacheco stood nearby. Dalakis and Malgiolio watched from the door of the library. You know that expression: the air felt charged? Even the soldiers were aware of it and looked uneasily at each other as if we stood on the brink of something calamitous.

"The shots came from this house," Quatrone was saying. "They were fired from an upstairs window."

"But that's impossible," said Carrera. "This is Pacheco's house. We're using it as a hospital. There're only our own men here."

"I still should search it," said Quatrone. "How do we know who's upstairs?" As before, there was a certain tension to Quatrone—both high-pitched and electric—and he seemed to bite off his words as if he didn't want them to rest too long in his mouth.

"Was anyone hurt?" asked Pacheco.

Quatrone didn't immediately acknowledge Pacheco's question and when he spoke it was to Carrera. "That's not the point. Two shots were fired. One struck a jeep. Someone could have been hit."

"Was it rifle fire?"

"No, a pistol."

Although there is no way to prove it, I was certain that Pacheco knew the shots had come from this house and was pleased by it, as evidence of something he had been waiting for. I realized he had known all along about Señora Puccini's pistol and I had the sense he had orchestrated the entire evening with her in mind, that he had meant to tell the story of his life with her whether he had three guests or fifteen, ending with the confession—whether true or false, who knew?—that he had run poor Roberto Collura off the road. And he was still trying to make her respond. The chance that she had fired the pistol into the street pleased him as proof that she had put aside her passivity. But at what point did it occur to me that there was still another alternative: that Pacheco also wanted her as the instrument of his punishment? Suddenly I wanted to take him aside and ask about Collura. Had he really run him off the road or had he said that only because he'd known that Señora Puccini was listening? But there was no way to get to him.

Carrera and Quatrone were still arguing. "You will not search the house," said Carrera. "If there were shots fired, then we will discover who did it, but I don't intend to let you and your men rampage through here doing whatever violence you care to commit."

Quatrone kept his eyes lowered but was clearly furious. Carrera, on the other hand, appeared completely calm, a sort of disdainful, superior calm. Really he was one of us. Although he didn't belong to our group, he easily could have. He was polished, urbane, and wealthy, while Quatrone belonged to another class altogether—he being one of those energetic and angry young men who join the army as a private and bully and fight their way up through the ranks. He reminded me of a bull terrier, those ferocious little dogs that sink in their teeth and refuse to let go. Just as Malgiolio saw in these troubles a chance for advancement, so, presumably, did Quatrone.

By this time I had joined Dalakis and Malgiolio by the library door—we three guests, we old schoolboys. Both appeared frightened and I suppose I did as well. Dalakis had been looking around the hall, which shone in the light of a hundred candles. Then he glanced toward the stairs and his whole body grew rigid.

I turned and there was Señora Puccini just beginning to descend the left-hand side of the staircase. She had changed out of her black dress into a blue one—a long, light blue dress with a white collar. There was something shocking about it. I had thought of her as middle-aged; yet this was the dress of a young woman. Her hair was loose, also like a young woman's, and there were flowers in it, red flowers. All this was shadowy because of the candles, and as she descended we could only see her in profile. Her arms hung at her sides and the balustrade kept us from seeing her hands. She held herself as straight as a board and never once turned her head, but something was wrong with the way she looked. There was some madness in it.

We stared at her and even the soldiers grew silent. Glancing toward Pacheco, I saw that he appeared extremely alert. He took a few steps toward the stairs. Then Señora Puccini made the turn at the corner of the bracket and as she came around to face us I saw there was blood on the front of her blue dress. She wore a necklace of flowers and the blood seemed mixed with it.

"She's done something to herself," said Dalakis. But despite the blood, she seemed unhurt and walked without weakness or hesitation. It was only later that we discovered the blood was not her own.

As she descended the lower bracket of the staircase, the soldiers across the room, who could see all of her, began to whisper and point. There must have been over thirty men in the hall and we all stared at her. Quatrone had moved away from the door and stood with his six men in front of one of the marble busts.

Pacheco walked to the bottom of the staircase, next to the small pond and fountain. The statue of the naked girl rose directly behind him. Balancing on one leg with one arm raised, she appeared to be half dancing, half falling. The fountain itself had stopped when the electricity had gone off. When Señora Puccini reached the bottom of the staircase and turned again to face us, I saw that the entire front of her dress was splashed and spotted with blood, even though there was no sign of a wound. In her right hand, which she held to her side, was the small pistol that I had seen in the kitchen.

Pacheco held out his hand but she drew back, evading him, then walked around him toward the soldiers and the rest of us. How can I describe her face? It had a joyous quality, as if she had just stopped laughing. Yet there was such a contrast between youth and age, the flowers and the pistol, the blood and the dress, the beauty and the horror that, believe me, the soldiers found it extremely alarming, and even I, who knew her story, stepped back into the doorway of the library. Then she turned again to face Pacheco. From where I stood, I could see both their faces, his full front with that awful bruise where Quatrone had struck him, hers in profile. The candlelight on the shiny chrome of the pistol danced like a live thing.

Pacheco still seemed triumphant. He had prided himself on being able to anticipate all her actions and now here was something different. Yet that very difference gave him pleasure. Again I had the sense that he had made the evening as a painter might make a canvas. Even when she raised the pistol and pointed it at him, his response was to smile.

"You won't shoot me," he said. His back was to the stairs. I hardly knew where he found the confidence to speak so certainly.

She kept pointing the gun at him but her hand was trembling and her face began to look strained as if she were attempting to lift a great weight. Had he chosen, Pacheco could have knocked the gun from her hand, she was that close. I wanted her to speak, to charge him for ruining her life and the life of Roberto Collura, to judge and condemn him, to shout out his crime so that Carrera and Quatrone and the soldiers would hear her accusation. Certainly if there had been a trial Pacheco would have been found guilty. After all, lives had been destroyed.

Instead, she lowered the pistol to her side so the barrel pointed at the floor. Slowly her face began to change again. She started to smile and once more her face took on that joyous quality. She looked happy and youthful. She looked like a girl greeting her lover. Stepping forward, she raised her face, lifting her mouth to be kissed. For the first time Pacheco looked uncertain, but then he too started to smile, partly with relief, but also with love and pleasure, as if the two were a young couple who had been separated and were now together again and reconciled. And he stepped forward to accept her kiss and to embrace her.

But almost as their lips touched she reached back the hand with the pistol so that it pointed toward the soldiers and Quatrone, and she pulled the trigger. Even for a small gun, the noise was immense in that enclosed marble space. The bullet struck the floor and ricocheted back among Quatrone's men. Then she fired again and again. Three shots in rapid succession. And Pacheco, instead of grabbing the gun, put one arm around her waist and continued to kiss her. But perhaps he knew he had no time, that everything was over, because as rapidly as Señora Puccini fired the pistol, so did the soldiers respond. One of the young men with Quatrone opened fire with his automatic rifle, then a second and a third. I saw the bullets strike Pacheco. They picked him up and hurled him back into the small pool so that a wave of water splashed out onto the marble floor. Señora Puccini collapsed upon the stairs. We were deafened by the rattle of gunfire.

Carrera ran forward. "Stop firing!" he shouted. "Put down your weapons!"

Only a few seconds had passed but the damage was done. I ran forward with the others, pushing the soldiers out of the way. Reaching the fountain, I knelt down on the wet floor. Pacheco was dead. The bullets had struck him in the chest.

He lay on his back in the water with his arms outstretched. His eyes were open. I had expected his face to show anger or fear or pain. Instead, he looked as if he were listening to a noise far away, as if someone in the distance had just called his name. I found myself angrily wondering what right he had to look so peaceful. His blood had dyed the water, as if the pool were full of blood, the blood of many people. The goldfish swam through it as calmly as before.

Señora Puccini had also been hit several times, but she was still alive. With her last strength she was attempting to crawl up the stairs, pushing herself up, dragging herself to the next step, collapsing, then pushing herself up again—one step, two, five, seven. No one attempted to help her. She had dropped the pistol and Quatrone was holding it. We watched Señora Puccini, her light blue dress drenched with blood, the chain of red flowers breaking and scattering around her. But then after a dozen steps she could go no farther. Raising herself up on her arms, she lifted her head so the skin of her neck was stretched tight. She opened her mouth as if to call out, but then she clamped her jaw shut, rolled to her left, and tumbled back down the stairs, head over heels, dead as she fell, rolling half into the pond so that her head and shoulders were in the water and her legs were still on the floor. Her long skirt was pulled up to her thighs and I found myself staring at her bare legs. Then I reached forward and pulled it down. Her arm was flung backward and lay across Pacheco's chest. Her eyes were shut. Did her face look peaceful? It looked black and secretive. Whatever her last feelings, they had disappeared within her. We stood in a semicircle around the pond and looked down at them. Even Quatrone looked amazed and stricken.

That really was the finish of our evening. The soldiers who had done the shooting certainly couldn't be blamed. We tried to tell Carrera what had been going on, why Señora Puccini had done what she had done, but it remained a mystery to him. He'd heard that Pacheco had a bad reputation with women and this was a final example of it. As for Quatrone, he didn't even try to understand. Crazy people doing crazy things, was how he explained it. Dalakis tried to tell him the story but he didn't want to listen. Not that we were coherent. After all, Pacheco had been our dear friend, and our grief, as well as our horror at the manner of his death, of both their deaths, rendered us, if not speechless, then at least inarticulate.

Upstairs we found Roberto Collura also dead. Señora Puccini had shot him; the blood on her dress had been his. I imagined her listening to Pacheco's confession about how he had tried to kill Collura by running him off the road. I imagined her hurrying back to the kitchen and getting the pistol. But then she must have picked the flowers and changed into that blue dress. I couldn't understand that. Why had she dressed herself like a young woman? I imagined her entering Collura's room in her blue dress with the necklace of flowers and more flowers in her hair. What did he think, what did she say? She had been wearing lipstick and although I blush to admit it, I looked closely at Collura's mouth, his lips, his cheeks and forehead, for a trace of that lipstick as if she might have kissed him goodbye. But there was nothing. All I know is that she changed her clothes and entered his room. I don't even know if he was awake. Yet considering how his blood had covered her dress, I imagined that she had lain down on top of him, giving him one last embrace before putting a bullet in his heart. Then she had fired her pistol into the street from the upstairs balcony. And why did she do that? Again, there is no answer. Perhaps to make the soldiers fire back or to frighten them. Had she already formed her plan to make the soldiers shoot them both? Had she already decided to present Pacheco with that last kiss, the one freely given?

The single good thing that came out of all this, if that night can be said to have had anything good, is that Colonel Carrera offered to escort the three of us—we old boys—back to our homes. Of course we accepted, having no wish to sleep at Pacheco's. I wanted to be by myself, far away from these friends of my childhood. Better to hide our grief in the privacy of our own homes.

I was also just as glad to get away from Malgiolio, who had begun to act in a way which was an embarrassment to Dalakis and myself. Inexplicably, he had begun to laugh. Clasping his arms to his fat belly and doubling over, he had begun to explode with loud hoots. He didn't say anything and I felt that even he was embarrassed because once he realized that he couldn't stop, he went into the library and shut the door. But out in the hall, I continued to hear him. It was a high unattractive laugh, almost effeminate, and I could see that the soldiers thought badly of him. I found myself thinking again of his promise as a poet. What a sordid end he had come to.

Dalakis wept openly, mopping his eyes and uttering great sobs. He also kept asking where Señora Puccini had obtained the pistol. Of course I didn't speak or admit my knowledge, since I thought it would be misunderstood. Actually, I felt certain that Pacheco had given her the weapon some time in the past. In any case, as I came to realize, Pacheco too had known that Señora Puccini had had the pistol. Therefore I couldn't be judged for not telling him. He, after all, had orchestrated the evening. I was only part of the stricken audience. It occurred to me that he had even placed the picture of the young Señora Puccini on the mantel just for this occasion, just so we would see it and comment upon it. I tried to ask the cook's grandson if this were indeed the case but his extreme grief made him unable to give me a coherent answer. As for calling her "Señora," that too was an example of Pacheco's constant pressure: the pretense that she was a married woman.

Before leaving, I went back into the dining room. There were the remains of the cake with its sixteen small figures meant to represent us sixteen old boys, now thirteen with Kress, Schwab, and Pacheco dead. And others dead as well for all I knew on this difficult night. I found the little figure that was meant to be Pacheco—a man in a white coat with a stethoscope around his neck—and I took it away with me. How grateful I have felt to be able to take the chaos of that evening and order it into a history, to make it digestible. Proud and self-assured, as if my friend were with me still, that small figure has stood attentively to the left of my typewriter in these months following the dinner party as I have composed my history and the city has put itself back together. There have been changes, of course. The old man who sold vegetables from his cart has disappeared and familiar faces are no longer in the news. There is talk of treachery and treason. Still, we have begun to reknit our lives, to make them as they had been before. I have resumed my old habits, my charitable work, and my neighbors continue to think of me as a middle-aged widower who keeps to himself.

As for that night and the violence in the streets, it remains something of a mystery, an upheaval brought about by a profound dissatisfaction, even unhappiness. Unfortunately, as I have indicated before, I have little interest in politics and so most of the details of that night are vague to me. But still we move forward, the pages are daily ripped from the calendars. Happily, the next dinner is almost upon us. This time the host will be Julio Hernandez, the priest. Does it seem so odd that already I am looking forward to seeing my old friends once again?

But my last act at Pacheco's was to lift the carving knife and cut another piece of that divine cake. Taking one of the

blue linen napkins, I wrapped the cake within it and slipped
it into my jacket pocket so that I could better enjoy it within
the solitude of my own home. Then I took another slice, meaning only to touch a few crumbs to my lips, but that proved
impossible and I ate the whole piece from my hand as the pink
crumbs and bits of strawberry cascaded down my jacket and
shirt front, just pushing it into my mouth, eating more like
Malgiolio or Schwab than in my normal manner. Even though
the sugar was like poison to me, I couldn't help myself. That
cake was so good, so sweet.

READ MORE IN PENGUIN

In every corner of the world, on every subject under the sun, Penguin represents quality and variety – the very best in publishing today.

For complete information about books available from Penguin – including Puffins, Penguin Classics and Arkana – and how to order them, write to us at the appropriate address below. Please note that for copyright reasons the selection of books varies from country to country.

In the United Kingdom: Please write to *Dept. EP, Penguin Books Ltd, Bath Road, Harmondsworth, West Drayton, Middlesex UB7 0DA*

In the United States: Please write to *Consumer Sales, Penguin USA, P.O. Box 999, Dept. 17109, Bergenfield, New Jersey 07621-0120.* VISA and MasterCard holders call 1-800-253-6476 to order Penguin titles

In Canada: Please write to *Penguin Books Canada Ltd, 10 Alcorn Avenue, Suite 300, Toronto, Ontario M4V 3B2*

In Australia: Please write to *Penguin Books Australia Ltd, P.O. Box 257, Ringwood, Victoria 3134*

In New Zealand: Please write to *Penguin Books (NZ) Ltd, Private Bag 102902, North Shore Mail Centre, Auckland 10*

In India: Please write to *Penguin Books India Pvt Ltd, 706 Eros Apartments, 56 Nehru Place, New Delhi 110 019*

In the Netherlands: Please write to *Penguin Books Netherlands bv, Postbus 3507, NL-1001 AH Amsterdam*

In Germany: Please write to *Penguin Books Deutschland GmbH, Metzlerstrasse 26, 60594 Frankfurt am Main*

In Spain: Please write to *Penguin Books S. A., Bravo Murillo 19, 1° B, 28015 Madrid*

In Italy: Please write to *Penguin Italia s.r.l., Via Felice Casati 20, I–20124 Milano*

In France: Please write to *Penguin France S. A., 17 rue Lejeune, F–31000 Toulouse*

In Japan: Please write to *Penguin Books Japan, Ishikiribashi Building, 2–5–4, Suido, Bunkyo-ku, Tokyo 112*

In Greece: Please write to *Penguin Hellas Ltd, Dimocritou 3, GR–106 71 Athens*

In South Africa: Please write to *Longman Penguin Southern Africa (Pty) Ltd, Private Bag X08, Bertsham 2013*

READ MORE IN PENGUIN

A CHOICE OF FICTION

Felicia's Journey William Trevor
Winner of the 1994 Whitbread Book of the Year Award

Vividly and with heart-aching insight William Trevor traces the desperate plight of a young Irish girl scouring the post-industrial Midlands for her lover. Unable to find Johnny, she is, instead, found by Mr Hilditch, pudgy canteen manager, collecter and befriender of homeless young girls.

The Eye in the Door Pat Barker

'Barker weaves fact and fiction to spellbinding effect, conjuring up the vastness of the First World War through its chilling impact on the minds of the men who endured it ... a startlingly original work of fiction ... it extends the boundaries not only of the anti-war novel, but of fiction generally' – *Sunday Telegraph*

The Heart of It Barry Hines

Cal Rickards, a successful scriptwriter, is forced to return to the Yorkshire mining town of his youth when his father, a leading voice in the 1980s miners' strike, suddenly becomes ill. Gradually, as Cal delves into his family's past and faces unsettling memories, he comes to reassess his own future.

Dr Haggard's Disease Patrick McGrath

'The reader is compellingly drawn into Dr Haggard's life as it begins to unfold through episodic flashbacks ... It is a beautiful story, impressively told, with a restraint and a grasp of technicality that command belief, and a lyricism that gives the description of the love affair the sort of epic quality rarely found these days' – *The Times*

A Place I've Never Been David Leavitt

'Wise, witty and cunningly fuelled by narrative ... another high calibre collection by an unnervingly mature young writer' – *Sunday Times*. 'Leavitt can make a world at a stroke and people it with convincing characters ... humane, touching and beautifully written' – *Observer*